A Killing at the Creek

Also by Nancy Allen

The Code of the Hills

A Killing at the Creek

AN OZARKS MYSTERY

NANCY ALLEN

WITNESS
IMPULSE

An Imprint of HarperCollinsPublishers

This book is a work of fiction. The characters, incidents, and dialogue are drawn from the author's imagination and are not to be construed as real. Any resemblance to actual events or persons, living or dead, is entirely coincidental.

A KILLING AT THE CREEK. Copyright © 2015 by Nancy Allen. All rights reserved under International and Pan-American Copyright Conventions. By payment of the required fees, you have been granted the nonexclusive, nontransferable right to access and read the text of this e-book on screen. No part of this text may be reproduced, transmitted, decompiled, reverse-engineered, or stored in or introduced into any information storage and retrieval system, in any form or by any means, whether electronic or mechanical, now known or hereafter invented, without the express written permission of HarperCollins e-books.

HB 08.16.2022
Epub Edition FEBRUARY 2015 ISBN: 9780062325969
Print Edition ISBN: 9780062325976

For my favorite storytellers:
Janice, Carol, Susie and John

My son, if sinners entice thee, consent thou
   not.
My son, walk not thou in the way with them;
   refrain thy foot from their path: For their
   feet run to evil, and make haste to shed
   blood.

PROVERBS 1:10, 15–16

Chapter 1

THE BLOODY YELLOW school bus wound through the hills of the Missouri Ozarks in the early dawn of a June morning. The blood inside the bus pooled under the driver's feet, trickled in the aisle, drained out the back exit, and ran over the rear bumper.

The young man at the wheel kept his eyes on the road as he maneuvered the vehicle up and down twisting roads shrouded by oak and sycamore trees, looking for the turnoff that would lead him back to the Interstate.

The road flattened out as he approached the Oklahoma state line. Shortly after crossing into Oklahoma, he spotted a McDonald's, built atop and over the highway, spanning all four lanes of I-44. He took the exit and drove into the parking lot.

He could have parked at a distance from the other vehicles, but didn't bother, pulling the bus into the open spot nearest the door. Reaching into a duffel bag, he pulled out a handful of money and shoved it in his jeans pocket.

His shoes tacky from the mess in the bus, he made prints on the pavement as he walked to the entrance. He paused to wipe his feet on a black nylon mat. A flight of stairs led up to a bathroom; he made that his first stop. The boy took care to wash his hands, rubbing them vigorously with the pink liquid soap, watching the rust-colored water circle the drain. The mirror in the bathroom showed that his dark brown hair needed shampoo, and his eyes were red-rimmed, with dark circles from the long night.

He kept a neutral expression as he left the toilet. Passing an ice cream stand, he paused to examine the contents in the refrigerator case. A white-haired woman in a hairnet, armed with a metal scoop, let him look at the buckets of ice cream in the case for a minute before asking, "You want something?" The boy stalked away without looking at her, toward the McDonald's counter to order. Though there were no customers ahead of him, he had to wait while two uniformed cashiers held a whispered conversation, two young girls laughing. One girl, a short blonde in heavy makeup, with four studs in one ear and two in an eyebrow, finally noticed him standing there. She leaned on the counter and said, "Can I take your order?"

"Big Mac. Large fry, medium Dr Pepper."

"Want to try the Mac Wrap?"

He shook his head. "I want what I ordered."

Something about him made the girl take a half step back. She spun around and pushed a button to pour his Dr Pepper. Her friend, a pretty Cherokee girl with long black hair, looked behind the boy and said, "Hey, big shot, you're tracking mud in here. Don't you know they make us mop that up?"

He didn't respond. He dug in his pocket and pulled out a wad of money, mostly ones, and counted out the exact change for his order.

"For here?" the blond girl asked him, in a more respectful tone. He nodded. She hastily set his food on a tray.

He took the tray to the video arcade, and ate his food in a leisurely fashion. Pumping quarters into the machines, he held the sandwich while he played with one hand. He lingered for half an hour, nursing his drink.

When he departed, a fry cook was walking out into the parking lot at the same time.

"Hey, man," the fry cook said to him, "can I have a light?"

"Sorry."

"Come on, man. I can see it in your pocket."

The pocket of the boy's white T-shirt clearly revealed a pack of Camel cigarettes and a Bic lighter.

"Fuck off."

The cook bristled and grabbed the young man by the arm, but he ripped his arm away and turned with such ferocity that the cook backed off. Stepping backward, raising the palms of both hands, the fry cook said, "No problem, dude. Forget about it."

The young man jumped behind the wheel of the bus and threw it into reverse; before he drove off, he rolled down the driver's window and thrust his arm out, extending the middle finger of his left hand.

"Eat shit!" the cook yelled in response.

The young driver's arm disappeared inside the bus. He grappled under the seat, then brandished a blood-stained item in his hand for the cook to see.

It was a bloody knife.

The cook took one look and ran like hell back toward McDonald's as the school bus took off for the highway.

Chapter 2

ALL IN THE world Elsie Arnold wanted was a murder case.

She was late for the Monday morning staff meeting at the McCown County Prosecutor's Office, but she didn't feel a bit guilty about it. She'd burned the midnight oil all weekend in preparation for a Monday afternoon preliminary hearing for a manslaughter case. She was as ready as she'd ever be, but the heel of her shoe had ripped the hem out of her skirt when she was getting dressed, costing precious minutes on the hunt for scotch tape. When she couldn't find it she substituted safety pins, jamming them through the fabric, cursing all the while.

The manslaughter assignment was a major breakthrough for Elsie's career: her first death case. It was a major step, a badge of honor. But a vehicular homicide was not a murder.

All I want, thought Elsie, as she trod the worn marble

steps in the interior of the old stone courthouse, *all I want is a goddamned murder.*

Elsie certainly didn't wish any harm to befall her fellow citizens of McCown County, Missouri. She appreciated the quiet community nestled in the Ozark hills; she had chosen to return to her hometown after law school, back to the hills where she was born and raised. It was not the big city, like St. Louis or Kansas City or Little Rock, where murder cases were a common tragedy. Even with the middling crime rate, Elsie had a fine record as assistant county prosecutor; but she hadn't handled a murder case, and was conscious of the hole in her experience.

She bypassed the front door of the office, displaying the name of her boss, Prosecuting Attorney Madeleine Thompson, in bold letters, and slipped in the back way. The meeting was under way; she could see the attorneys clustered on the sofa in the boss's private office. Elsie squared her shoulders and entered the meeting with what she hoped was a confident air.

All eyes were on her. The new chief assistant, Chuck Harris, flashed an electric smile her way. He struck her as a wolf in pin-striped clothing.

"'A diller, a dollar, a ten o'clock scholar,'" he said.

"The hell you say," Elsie retorted. "It's barely past eight."

"Eight-fifteen," said her boss. Madeleine double-checked the time on her Rolex watch, regarding Elsie with an ill-humored expression.

Elsie and Madeleine were not on the best of terms these days. Madeleine viewed her position as a political stepping stone, having been appointed, not elected, by the prior governor as a political favor to her wealthy husband, the local John Deere distributor. Her entitled attitude constantly irked Elsie, who was passionately dedicated to her job in law enforcement.

"Don't even start with me," Elsie said, approaching the sofa where her friend Breeon sat hip to hip with three other attorneys. There was no vacant seat in the crowded office, so she dropped her purse and the big accordion file she'd been carrying and leaned against the door frame. "I lived here this weekend. Should've had a cot and a hot plate in my office, I logged in so many hours."

Her comment was met with silence. Elsie began to backpedal; she didn't want to sound like a complainer, not when she had finally been assigned a death case.

"Of course, I didn't mind being here, because I'm ready for the prelim. 'Ready for my close-up, Mr. DeMille.' Do you think the TV stations will cover it?"

Madeleine looked at Chuck, her chief assistant, and back at Elsie. "We need to bring you up-to-date, Elsie. There's been a change of direction."

Elsie eyed her warily, like a dog guarding a bone. "What do you mean?"

"The defendant is waiving preliminary. He's going to plead."

Elsie took an involuntary step forward. "Nobody told me!" Her chest clutched as she felt her case slip away.

Chuck said, "We just worked it out, Elsie. His defense attorney only okayed it late last night." His tone was con-ciliatory, with a hint of condescension.

"Why were you talking to him without me? This is my case," Elsie said hotly.

"It's my case," Madeleine said shortly. "I'm the county official, the one appointed by the governor. They're all my cases. We've had this conversation before, I think."

"Well, hell," Elsie muttered. "Guess I'll tell the judge there's a plea."

"Don't bother," Madeleine said. "Chuck will do it. He'll appear on the waiver and take up the plea."

Elsie felt her blood boiling.

She tried not to resent Chuck's position as chief assistant, but it was tough. When the spot opened up recently, both Elsie and her friend Breeon Johnson had made a bid for it; either of the two women seemed a likely choice, from their stellar trial records. Madeleine overlooked both of them and brought Chuck Harris in from the Jackson County office in Kansas City, Missouri. Predictably, Chuck's father was a big shot in Republican politics. Since that disappointment, Elsie knew that Breeon was considering leaving the office and moving back to St. Louis, but Elsie would remain in McCown County. The Ozarks was her home.

Madeleine continued, "Chuck worked out the plea bargain; he got the deal." The ring of her cell phone interrupted the exchange. As she answered, Chuck turned to Elsie; he had the good grace to look a little abashed.

"Hey, Elsie, sorry about your lost weekend. But you know, all the good work you did was important. The defendant knew we were ready. That's why I was able to get this plea bargain."

Madeleine waved a manicured hand at them in irritation; moving the phone away from her mouth, she
snapped, "Can't hear over you."

The office fell silent. Madeleine grimaced with dis-
taste as she listened to the voice on the other end of the
phone. "Who found it?" she asked.

She listened silently for several moments while her
staff watched. "No," she said into the phone, "I can't get
out there, Shelby. I'll just send someone else."

Shelby Choate was the county sheriff. *Something's up,*
thought Elsie.

"Did you call anyone from the Barton City Police Department?" Madeleine asked. Elsie could hear the crackle
of the reply all the way across the room. "I know, Shelby; I
know it's outside the city. You all can still work together."

Madeleine spun slowly back and forth in her chair
while the lawyers watched and waited.

"Don't worry, I will; I'll get someone out there to take
a look. I'll send my new first assistant. I don't know if you
all have met yet; his name is Chuck Harris."

Chuck Harris's chin jerked up. *No,* he mouthed,
waving his hand to catch Madeleine's attention. *Not me.*

She ended the call and sat up straight in her chair,
looking the picture of professionalism; a snowy white
collar and cuffs peeked out from her smartly fitted jacket.
To Elsie's eye, her boss's garb was a costume, designed to
look like a character from *Law & Order.*

The head of a safety pin scraped Elsie's thigh. She
shifted to escape the sting.

"Someone outside the city limits stumbled onto a

dead body dumped under a bridge in the county. Sheriff Choate wants someone from the office to take a look at the scene. I told him you'd go on out, Chuck."

"I've got the manslaughter appearance." Harris rose from his chair and made for the door.

"Not until one o'clock. You've got all morning."

Elsie seized the chance. "I'll go."

Chuck turned back to face the boss. "I'm wearing my good suit," he exclaimed. "They'll have me tracking through cow pies."

"I don't mind. I'll go. I'm free."

"I'm sending you, Chuck," Madeleine said, without a glance in Elsie's direction. "You've only been in the office for a couple of weeks. You need to make contact with the sheriff, work with the law enforcement personnel."

She stood, making a neat stack of her notes to signal the end of the meeting. "Meanwhile, I've got a meeting with the head of the statewide Republican party this morning, so I am"—firmly shutting a desk drawer—"all. Tied. Up."

She flashed an artificial smile to no one in particular and dismissed the staff, saying, "Let's get to work."

Elsie followed behind Harris as he headed for his office and flung his door open wide.

"I'm serious about coming along. I'll help out. You can bounce your ideas off of me." When he rolled his eyes, she said tersely, "Hey. You owe me. You took my manslaughter right out from under my nose. Now, you take me to see this dead guy."

Harris considered, frowning as he looked at her.

"Okay," he said. "Let's go."

Chapter 3

THE JUNE SUN was already hot at 9:00 A.M. when they pulled up to the scene. It was in a lonely spot, a dry creek bed under a one-lane bridge on a farm road that didn't see much traffic.

Chuck Harris and Elsie exited his car and walked over to the deputy who stood nearby. Joe Franks, a short, wiry man in his fifties, had been with the Sheriff's Department for over a decade, even prior to the election of the current county sheriff. He smoked a cigarette as he jotted notes on an incident report form.

"Who's this dude?" Harris asked Elsie before they reached the deputy. Harris hadn't been in Barton long enough to know the deputy by sight.

"Joe Franks," she whispered.

"Hey, Joe," Harris greeted him, clapping him on the shoulder like a long-lost pal, "what you got here?"

"Body down in the creek bed. Dead as a doornail. Throat cut."

Harris let out a low whistle. "No shit."

Franks eyed Elsie with interest. "Why'd they send you out here, hon? You're gonna run your hose."

"Not wearing any," Elsie replied shortly, containing a flash of irritation. Often it seemed that southwest Missouri was still mired in the past century, when law enforcement was strictly a boys' club.

A tall, solidly built plainclothes detective sporting aviator sunglasses ducked under the crime scene tape and approached them. Chuck Harris waved in greeting.

"Hey, Ashlock! Did Madeleine manage to hustle you out here? She said she hoped the Barton PD would keep an eye on the county sheriff's office—JK, Joe."

Bob Ashlock was the chief of detectives at the Barton City Police Department, and Elsie's current flame. In fact, the two of them had spent some quality time together at her apartment less than twenty-four hours prior, engaging in the kind of activities that put them in a happy place . . . but at the moment, Bob looked grim.

Chuck addressed him again: "What did you see down there? How long has the body been there, you think?"

"The coroner says a couple of days, maybe more. Franks, you better get down there and collect what you need before the doctor fucks up the crime scene." He glanced at Elsie and said, "Pardon my French, Elsie."

Elsie winked at him and brushed the apology aside with a wave of her hand, as Harris exclaimed, "Hell, Ashlock, don't worry about Elsie. Have you been around her? She swears like a sailor!"

Ashlock turned on him with a look that would make a sensible man quail. "Yep. A whole lot."

Harris turned to gaze down through the bushes at the trickle of the dry creek. "What do you make of the dead guy?"

"There's no dead guy down there."

"Say what?"

"Nope. Victim is female."

"No shit!"

Elsie's brow wrinkled as she tried to recall whether the news had reported an abduction in the area. "Do you think she's a local, Ash? Because I don't remember anything about a woman going missing lately."

Ashlock shook his head. "Identity won't be a mystery in this case; she's got a license, a chauffeur's ID in her pocket. Michigan license says her name is Glenda Fielder. I'm going to call the information in to Patsy at the department, so she can cross-check it on the database."

"Did the ID have a picture?" Elsie asked.

Ashlock nodded.

"Well, does it look like her?"

He squinted at the sun, as if trying to blot out an image. "Not anymore."

Chuck followed Ashlock as he turned and walked to his car, peppering him with conversation as Ashlock leaned against the car door and pulled out his cell phone to dial the police station.

Elsie wandered past the shoulder of the road, to the area roped off with crime scene tape. Drawn by a morbid curiosity, she paused at the tape, which bore the familiar order, DO NOT CROSS. With a sense of bravado, she thought, *I'm part of the investigation. I'll go wherever I want.*

Elsie ducked under the tape and walked briskly down the rocky grade to the creek, where several officers were milling around. A sign identified the spot as Muddy Creek, though currently, with rain scarce at this time of year, it had dried up to a feeble trickle of water.

The smell struck Elsie as a warning, but it was too late; she stumbled so close to the creek bed, where the dead woman lay, that she could reach out and touch her, if she dared. She flinched from the grotesque sight: the woman's body was swollen, her face bloated beyond recognition. Elsie focused involuntarily on the corpse's sightless eyes and the gaping slash under her chin, extending from ear to ear.

She tried not to scream, but a shriek burst out before she could stifle it. Blindly, Elsie backpedaled until she fell on her backside; she turned over and scrambled on her hands and knees to bring herself to a standing position and run for the road, away from the creek and the horrible sight.

Bile rose in her throat and she was afraid she would vomit, horrifying as that would be: she'd spent the past four years demonstrating to this very group of cops that she was tough as nails. As she ran up the shoulder of the road, she could see Ashlock and Chuck Harris in her peripheral vision, but she didn't stop; she headed for a tree and braced herself against it, trying desperately not to be sick.

A calm voice came up behind her. "You all right, sweetheart?"

Elsie shook her head, unable to speak, because she was crying, and talking would make it worse.

Ashlock put a supporting arm around her and walked her a short way into a wooded stretch, away from the road.

"You've never seen a dead body like that, have you?"

She shook her head again.

He talked on, in a soothing tone, "If you need to, just let it come on up. No one can see."

Elsie tried, bending over a knee-high patch of Queen Anne's lace, but nothing happened. She wiped tears from her cheeks with both hands. "I'm so embarrassed."

He pulled her into his arms and rubbed her back. "Now, that's silly. First time anyone sees a sight like that, it makes them sick. It's a shock, a terrible thing to witness. Every cop I ever knew lost their lunch at their first murder scene."

Elsie felt better, if only marginally. She sniffled; she needed a Kleenex in the worst way.

"But I feel so unprofessional."

"Baby, this isn't your profession. You're a lawyer, not a cop. I'm supposed to be out here in the weeds with the dead body. You're supposed to be in the courtroom, putting the defendant away."

He stroked loose tendrils of blond hair away from her face. "Am I right?"

She reflected a moment. Actually, he was right. She nodded.

"You ready?"

She sighed. "Yeah, we better go back," she said with regret. She wished she could linger, leaning against Bob

Ashlock in the shade of the old hedge apple tree. But they both had work to do.

They walked side by side through the high weeds and up to the spot where the police cars were parked on the shoulder of the road. Chuck Harris hopped off the hood of his car.

"Where'd everybody go? Did I miss something?"

Ashlock looked to Elsie, but she just shrugged nonchalantly, unwilling to confess her skittishness to Chuck Harris.

Harris looked from one to the other, suspicious. "What?"

"I needed to use the restroom. Ashlock was showing me where they are," she said casually.

Skeptical, Chuck said, "There's no bathrooms out there."

Elsie smiled at Ashlock. "City boy," she scoffed.

"Well," Chuck said, digging for his keys, "I've got to get out of this heat. Bob, can we meet somewhere? We should go over the information, so I can fill Madeleine in this afternoon."

"Okay. It's about time for a lunch break."

Lunch, Elsie thought, a cold sweat breaking out on her upper lip. Her stomach twisted.

"Where should we go?"

Ashlock considered for a moment. "The Wagon Wheel isn't too far. And we'll be hitting it before noon, so we should be able to get right in."

"Okay. Come on, Elsie," Chuck said, double-clicking the unlock button on his key chain. "You can give me directions."

Elsie looked longingly at Ashlock, wishing she could hop into his City of Barton sedan, and tell Chuck Harris to find the Wagon Wheel himself with his damned GPS.

But Ashlock shrugged and said, "I could stand to change into a fresh shirt. I'll see you there."

Elsie slid carefully into the passenger seat of Harris's car. It had been sitting in full sun on her side, and the hot vinyl nearly took the hide off her. Fiercely, she wished herself out of that hot seat, and into the company of Bob Ashlock.

"Detective Ashlock seems okay," Harris observed. "Not a dumbshit like most of these hicks from around here."

"I'm one of these 'hicks from around here,' by the way."

"Yeah, I figured. No offense, Elsie. But you've got to understand that this is a big change for me, coming down here to southwest Missouri. I'm from the Jackson County office; I was raised in Kansas City."

"Kansas City. Kansas City's a cow town, right?"

He shot her a look. "Do you ever get up to the Plaza?"

"Not lately," Elsie replied. Grudgingly, she'd be forced to admit that the Kansas City Plaza was pretty doggone fabulous. "You need to take a turn here."

"So you think Ashlock is a good man to work this murder up for us?"

"No question. The best."

"You know him pretty well?"

"Uh-hmm." Elsie nodded, thinking, *Every inch of him.*

Chapter 4

ELSIE AND CHUCK pulled into the graveled parking lot of the Wagon Wheel Café at eleven o'clock sharp. Chuck put his car into park and moved to cut the engine, but Elsie stopped him.

"Let's listen to the news on the radio," she said. "I want to hear if they picked up anything about the dead woman from the police band."

"Okay." He turned the volume up a notch.

They didn't have to wait long. The announcer's voice crackled with excitement as he said, "Breaking news on KZTO. Prosecutor Madeleine Thompson announced at the courthouse today that a body was discovered in rural McCown County just this morning."

Elsie shook her head. "She can't keep her mouth shut. She'd tell a kid there's no Santa Claus."

Chuck eyed her reproachfully. "How about a little respect here?" Elsie shushed him as Madeleine's voice came through the speaker.

"'This horrific crime is a blot on our community. We'll leave no stone unturned to find the person who committed this vile act. And I promise you: we will seek the maximum penalty under law. You have my personal guarantee that we will see justice done.'"

"You have my personal guarantee that she will get her hair done," Elsie said. "Anything more heavy-duty, not so sure."

"What's your problem?" Harris asked.

Elsie snorted, a genuine response, if not a dainty one. "You haven't worked for her as long as I have. You're still on your honeymoon."

As Chuck turned off the engine, Elsie spied Ashlock's car across the lot. "Look, Ashlock beat us here. Damn! How'd he do that?"

"Hope he got us a table," Chuck said as they walked to the doorway together. "I'm starving."

They entered the restaurant, a ranch-style house converted to a diner in the 1960s and by appearances, not thoroughly scrubbed since then. Elsie slid into a booth beside Ashlock, her hand swiping through a sticky syrup spot on the side of the table.

"I love this place," she said. "My mom never let us eat at the Wagon Wheel when we were kids, because the bathrooms were so nasty. Coming to the Wagon Wheel is still like forbidden fruit to me."

"Best breakfast in town," Ashlock said.

"And the atmosphere is delightful," Harris said dryly, taking care to set his jacket where it wouldn't brush the greasy curtain adorning the window.

"If you're particular about that sort of thing," Ashlock said.

Elsie surveyed the two men. Ashlock, powerfully built, wearing a short-sleeved poly/cotton shirt and military buzz cut, made a stark contrast to Chuck Harris in his crisp pastel cotton shirt and silk tie, with an auburn hairdo that might have required more attention than Elsie's. She remembered her mother's admonition, *Steer clear of a peacock!*

A waitress walked up, pulling a pad out of her white nylon apron pocket. "You'uns want coffee?"

"Lord, no. Too hot," said Elsie.

Chuck shook his head. Bob Ashlock turned over the crockery cup in front of him and nodded. The waitress put her pad away and walked off to find a pot. "Diet Coke, please?" Elsie begged as the waitress walked away.

"You command respect, Ashlock," Chuck said.

Ashlock stared at a nick in the Formica and chrome table, circling it with his index finger. Elsie knew that look: the wheels were turning.

He looked up, addressing Elsie. "I got word just before you came in. The deceased had a chauffeur's license on her because she was transporting a school bus from Detroit to northwest Arkansas. The bus was supposed to arrive a week ago. There's been a bulletin out, to be on the lookout for either the driver or the vehicle."

"We've got the driver. So where's the bus?" Elsie asked, as the waitress returned to pour Ashlock a steaming cup of coffee.

"How come your cops can't find a big yellow bus in the Ozarks?" asked Chuck.

Elsie took the Diet Coke gratefully, tearing the paper off the straw and taking a long pull on the cold drink. When the waitress clicked her pen, Elsie said, "You guys go ahead. I'm not so hungry this morning."

"What's up? I've seen you eat like a field hand," Chuck said.

"I'm a girl with a healthy appetite," Elsie said. Ashlock caught her eye and smiled.

"I'll have the Pioneer Special with patty sausage and hash browns. Eggs over easy," Ashlock said to the waitress.

"Biscuits and gravy or toast?"

"The biscuits, ma'am." He handed her the plastic menu.

Chuck ordered a club sandwich on whole wheat, hold the mayo. As the waitress walked off, he said, "Seriously, how the hell do you hide a school bus? It's not like it's hard to spot on the highway. What kind of fools do you have on the highway patrol down here who can't spot a runaway bus? Sounds like they couldn't find their fucking ass with both hands."

Ashlock's jaw twitched. "Watch how you talk in front of a lady."

Elsie quit sucking her straw as Harris jerked his thumb at her. "You mean Elsie? Christ, Ashlock, you obviously don't know who you're talking about. Elsie couldn't kiss her mother with that mouth."

"Shut up, Harris," Elsie said, "and watch what you say about our local police." Turning to Ashlock, she said, "Honey, I love your old-fashioned he-man side, I really do, but you can't threaten everyone who drops an f-bomb in front of me. Especially since I've been known to drop a few myself." *More than a few*, she amended silently. She reached onto the table and took Ashlock's hand, rubbing the sensitive spot between his thumb and forefinger. "You *are* kind of like Prince Valiant. Like old Vernon Wantuck told us at the jail last winter."

Chuck Harris eyed them. "So. You two have a thing going on."

A smile played on the corner of Ashlock's mouth. He squeezed Elsie's hand, and she leaned in close to him.

Ashlock's phone rang, breaking the spell. He checked the ID, and answered, "What you got, Patsy?"

Elsie and Harris watched as Ashlock took Elsie's crumpled napkin and made notes on it with a pen. Ashlock nodded as he held the cell phone, saying, "Yep. Got it. Got it. Call me back when you hear."

He disconnected. Elsie said, "So, Ash? What is it?"

"They located the bus. It's in Oklahoma."

"For sure?" Elsie asked.

"Oh yeah."

"It's definitely the one the dead woman was transporting?" Harris echoed.

"Public Schools of Rogers, Arkansas," Ashlock quoted soberly. "They've impounded it."

"Anything to tie it to the offense?" Harris asked.

"It's covered in blood."

They fell silent as the waitress walked up with plates balanced skillfully up her left arm. She set down the sandwich and the breakfast platter, topped off Ashlock's coffee, and walked away.

"Whose case is it, then," mused Harris. "Missouri or Oklahoma?"

Elsie cocked an eye at him, surprised that he didn't know the answer. "Crim Law I, dude. We've got the body. We don't know where the offense occurred, so since the body was dumped in McCown County, it's definitely our case."

Harris picked the toast off the top of his sandwich. "No mayonnaise, thank God. Who's testing the bus, then? Us or Oklahoma?"

"It's our case," Ashlock said. "Our people will do it."

"I want Missouri Highway Patrol," Harris countered.

"Our crime lab is perfectly capable of doing blood, hair, and print analysis. They do it all the time."

"I don't want some local Barney Fife screwing my case up. This is a murder investigation, not a speeding ticket."

A cloud went over Ashlock's face. Harris saw it and backed off.

The men ate in silence for a few moments while Elsie rattled the ice cubes in her empty soda glass. Ashlock squirted ketchup onto his hash browns and cut his sausage with his fork, dipping it into the egg yolk. When the tone of his cell sounded again, Ashlock answered, his fork in midair. After listening intently, he hit End. He looked at the lawyers and said, "We have a suspect in custody. Oklahoma Highway Patrol is transporting him here this afternoon."

Elsie said, "That's fast. Do you think they'll deliver him to the county jail or the city police department?"

"Neither. He's going to juvenile."

Both Elsie and Harris froze, stunned.

"He's fifteen."

"Oh shit," Elsie said.

Chapter 5

As Elsie unlocked her office door, Madeleine's voice stopped her cold.

"Where's Chuck? I want a report."

Elsie wheeled around to face her boss. "Madeleine, he went straight to court after we got back. He's got to do the appearance on the vehicular homicide case. The preliminary hearing waiver." When she saw the blank look on Madeleine's face, she added, "My case. Remember?"

"Why aren't you doing it?"

Elsie was glad she wasn't holding a gun, because if she had one, her boss would be dead.

"You wanted Chuck to do it. Remember? This morning? The meeting?"

Madeleine's face twitched with irritation. "Fine. Come along." Turning on her heel, she stalked down the hallway in her expensive shoes.

Elsie followed reluctantly. One-on-one conferences

between Elsie and Madeleine had a history of going sour.

Once inside Madeleine's office, Elsie lingered in the open doorway. The better to beat a hasty retreat, if necessary.

"What did you and Chuck find out there?" Madeleine picked up a pen, poised it to write.

"There's a corpse under a bridge about five miles outside the city limits. It's a woman. A farmer found it—her—and he called the Sheriff's Department."

"Can we identify the deceased?"

"She had an ID on her. Ashlock says she was transporting a bus from Detroit to northwest Arkansas. Somebody killed her and dumped her."

"Cause of death?"

"Cut her throat. She bled to death, medical examiner says."

Madeleine shuddered. "Did they do a good job at the scene, you think? Forensic samples? Photos?"

A vision of the bloated corpse with the gaping slash flashed into Elsie's mind; she shook her head with a jerk to dismiss the image. "As thorough as possible, considering she was out in the woods. It's not as tidy as finding a body in bed with white sheets and latex paint on the walls. But Ashlock was there, and he took charge."

"Good. I don't want it mishandled, for heaven's sake. I made a promise to the voters."

"Right."

"I told them I'll personally see to it that this terrible crime is punished."

"Yeah, I heard that." Elsie advanced a couple of inches into the office. It was time to make the pitch, she thought. "You know, Madeleine, I'd really like to be part of this case."

"I have a second chair. Chuck will assist me."

"I could be third chair. Assistant to the assistant."

Madeleine paused, refusing to meet Elsie's eye. She exhaled as if ridding herself of an unpleasant burden. "You don't have the necessary experience. Chuck has been exposed to these kinds of cases in Kansas City. You've never tried a murder."

And you haven't faced a jury in a dog's age, Elsie thought. Madeleine cherry-picked high-profile cases, either pleading them out or handing them off to her assistants when they hit a wrinkle. Elsie kept a genial tone as she replied, "If you don't let me in on a murder case, I'll never get any experience."

Madeleine ignored the remark. Dropping her pen on the notepad, she pushed her chair from the desk. "I wonder how on earth they'll ever find a suspect."

Elsie stepped into the room and dropped onto the sofa that faced Madeleine's desk; with excitement overtaking caution, she said, "But they already have, Madeleine; didn't anyone tell you?"

Madeleine answered with a blank look. "Tell me what?"

"They found the bus the dead woman was transporting. And the guy who was on it is being brought in, straight to McCown County. As we speak," Elsie concluded.

"Who is it? Who would be crazy enough to kill the bus driver, and remain in the vehicle? That doesn't make any sense."

"It's a kid. He's fifteen. They're taking him to juvie."

Madeleine was struck dumb. Elsie could swear she saw her swallow. Elsie edged off the couch, anticipating a curt dismissal and bracing herself.

But Madeleine began to nod, focusing on a crystal paperweight on her desk. "You're right," she said.

Elsie cocked her head, not certain she'd heard correctly. "What's that?"

Madeleine picked up the paperweight and hefted it in her hand. She regarded it for a moment before switching her gaze to Elsie. "You're right," she repeated, sounding assured. "You need to get your feet wet." She set the paperweight down with a careful hand, focusing her attention on its facets. "You're in. Assistant to the assistant."

Sitting back, Elsie opened her mouth to express her gratification at the decision, but Madeleine swiveled in her chair, showing Elsie her back.

"Go find Chuck Harris. I want to talk to him. *Now.*"

Elsie didn't require urging. She hit the floor running.

Chapter 6

DRIVING IN THE heat at the end of the workday, Elsie signaled a turn at the grocery; she knew without doubt that her cupboard was bare. Her refrigerator contained two cans of beer and a bottle of salad dressing. But before taking the turn, she changed her plan; ignoring the blare of an angry horn as she veered back into the traffic, she headed for her parents' house.

George and Marge Arnold lived in the old section of Barton, a short drive from the town square where the county courthouse sat. Elsie pulled her Ford Escort along the curb beside her childhood home, a sturdy brick colonial built in the 1920s. Trudging through the wall of humidity outside, she reached the side door and walked into the kitchen. Her mother stood at the counter, chopping cabbage on a cutting board.

"Hey, Mom," Elsie said as she pulled a kitchen chair from the table and sat. Seeing the flush on her mother's face, she shook her head. "You're killing yourself in here. You could get stuff for coleslaw in a bag at the store. Ready-made."

Swiping at a trickle of sweat at her hairline, Marge scoffed. "I wouldn't set that store-bought business on my table. It's full of preservatives. Who knows what all they put in there." Huffing a tired breath, she added, "I'd give you a hug, but I'm sopping wet. Let's go cool down a minute."

Elsie didn't argue; the temperature in the kitchen was stifling. She followed her mother into the living room, where a window air conditioner blasted cool air. Elsie's parents had toyed with the notion of installing central air in the old house for many years, but the trouble and expense involved in retrofitting a century-old house had caused them to decide against the update. It was a family joke that the house would be air-conditioned when the Arnolds won the Missouri lottery.

Marge pulled a pair of French doors shut, closing the living room off from the rest of the house to maintain the temperature. Settling into her recliner with a sigh of relief, she said, "All right, then. I want to hear how your manslaughter preliminary went. Walk me through the whole thing."

"Didn't happen."

Marge's brow rose. "Continued?"

Elsie shook her head. "Waived. They had a plea bargain worked out." Kicking off her shoes, she stretched out on the sofa.

"What on earth? You worked all weekend on it," Marge said, leaning forward in her chair to protest.

When Elsie shrugged, Marge settled back. "So you're happy with that? You seem all right."

"Yeah, sure; whatever." Smiling with satisfaction, Elsie rolled on her side and faced her mother.

Marge studied her. "Something's up. It's not like you to be so casual about losing hold of that case. You worked like a dog on it, hardly came up for air."

A laugh bubbled out of Elsie; she couldn't contain it. She felt like a grade school kid with a good report card to show. "I've got bigger fish to fry."

Marge gasped. "No."

"Yep."

"What? A murder case. Am I right—is that it?"

The excitement in Elsie's chest inched up another notch; telling the news was part of the thrill. "Big old case, and I'm in. Not first chair; not even second. But I'm in."

Pushing back on the arms of her recliner, Marge released the footrest.

"Is this some new crime? In Barton? The batteries on my radio are dead. I haven't listened to the news all day."

Elsie's voice dropped to a near whisper, as if she were telling a secret. "It's not in Barton; it was out in the county. A woman was found in a creek bed with her throat cut."

"Oh," Marge moaned, shaking her head. "Terrible. Good Lord."

"And they've apprehended a suspect already."

With a sober expression, Marge nodded. "That's fast."

"Yeah." With a shade of hesitation, Elsie added, "It's a juvenile."

Marge's brows drew together over her eyeglasses, giving her face a forbidding look. "A juvenile."

Elsie remained silent, waiting for her mother's assessment. It occurred to her, later than it might have, that her mother's thirty years as a middle school teacher would color her reaction to the news.

"How old?" Marge asked, after a pause.

"Fifteen."

A look of profound sadness passed over Marge's face. She closed her eyes. "Fifteen," she repeated. "A boy." It wasn't a question.

It nettled Elsie a little. Clearly, the focus of her mother's sympathies didn't rest with the woman in the creek, or Elsie's triumphant assignment. "Yes. It's a male suspect." Keeping her voice casual, she added, "A man."

Marge said, "A fifteen-year-old is not a man."

Elsie looked away. This was not how she hoped her announcement would be received.

Returning the footrest of the recliner to a seated position with a decisive clunk, Marge rose. "I'd best make up some dressing, so the slaw can chill by suppertime."

Elsie hopped off the couch. "Oh, I'm not staying."

"What? I thought for sure you'd eat with us. Your dad will be home any second."

Elsie shrugged. "Sorry." She couldn't handle the reproach in her mother's eyes, not tonight. Right now, she needed the wind in her sails. Her case depended on it.

Her mother followed her into the kitchen, pleading as Elsie retrieved her purse. "Don't run out like this. I've got a pork roast in the Crock-Pot. Your dad will be so disappointed."

"Tell him I said hi," Elsie said, waving goodbye with a brisk flip of her hand. The hurt in her mother's voice gave her a mean sense of satisfaction, but the feeling faded as she recalled that she had nothing to eat at home, and her debit card was tapped out.

Chapter 7

THE JUVENILE STOOD with his head bowed, his hands cuffed behind him. Two Oklahoma state troopers, a lieutenant and a young patrolman, stood in close proximity to the boy. The lieutenant pushed the buzzer at the McCown County Juvenile Hall, scrutinizing the teen as he waited.

"You're going to get a lot of attention, son," the lieutenant said. The boy didn't react. The young patrolman standing a pace behind them coughed, a hint of warning in the sound.

"A lot. A whole lot of attention. When they lock you in prison, you'll be Queen of the May. Everybody will want a piece of you." The lieutenant drew close to the boy's ear and whispered, "They'll line up to ream you."

The boy's head jerked up so suddenly, the trooper jumped back in surprise. The lawman laughed, embarrassed by his involuntary reaction.

Without speaking, the boy stared at the trooper through narrowed eyes.

The younger trooper said, "Let's just get him inside. After we drop him off, we can get something to eat."

The lieutenant grasped the juvenile's arm in a tight grip. "Don't forget who's in charge, kid. It's the man wearing the badge and toting the gun."

The indoor button was released and the automatic door to Juvenile Hall opened. A petite young woman with bright red hair greeted them.

The trooper's face lit up. "Well, what have we got here?"

"I'm the juvenile officer. I've been waiting for you. Is this young man Mr. Monroe?"

"Yes, ma'am."

Behind them, the younger patrolman let out a slow whistle. "Good thing you wasn't a juvenile officer when I was a kid. I'd have been in trouble all the dang time."

The woman ignored the remark. "Do you have the paperwork for the transfer?"

Before the troopers could respond, the boy spoke up. "They threatened me."

"What the hell," said the lieutenant holding the boy. He jerked the young man's arm, trying to force him to face him.

The boy kept his face trained on the woman. "They harassed me, they said I'd be raped. Gang raped. Help me."

The young woman's eyes widened. She pushed a button by the door; an alarm sounded, and footsteps could be heard running toward them.

"We'll investigate," she said. "I'll get someone from the Sheriff's Department to take your statement, Mr. Monroe. Come on in with me."

As the juvenile stepped inside the building, the young trooper standing at the rear cursed audibly, saying to his partner, "Now we'll be here all night. Why do you have to talk that crap?"

The juvenile walked into the hallway with the juvenile officer, who laid her hand on his arm. "It's okay," she said. "Everything's okay. I'm Lisa. I'm here to protect you."

LISA OPENED THE door to a small cinder-block room and stood back to let the juvenile enter.

"This is it," she said. "Not exactly the Hampton Inn. But you'll be safe here."

Monroe paused before entering, taking in the room and its battered furnishings. Stepping inside, he set a plastic bag of items atop a battered dresser.

"Hey, man, that's mine," said a boy reclining on the lower berth of a metal bunk bed.

Monroe shrugged and shoved the bag onto the floor.

Lisa spoke up. "Barry, I've brought someone to be your roommate. Tanner Monroe, this is Barry Bacon."

Monroe glanced briefly at the boy before pulling a folding chair from the wall and sitting in it. He opened his bag, rummaging through the contents.

Eyeing him, Barry's face registered awe. "You're that guy. Shit, man, you're the guy on the bus."

Lisa said, "Barry, don't mess with Tanner. He's had a long old day." Surveying the two with uncertainty, she added, "You all gonna be okay?"

Neither boy answered. Barry swung his feet to the floor, bouncing on the mattress in excitement. Tanner focused on Lisa as she turned to go.

"I'll check on you later," she said.

As her footsteps echoed down the tiled floor, Barry hopped off the bunk bed.

"They said you cut a woman's throat. Did you?"

The juvenile didn't answer.

"Did you kill her?" The boy was breathless, waiting for a response.

Monroe exhaled wearily, looking at Barry for the first time. Barry was younger than Monroe, only fourteen, but he was tall and gangly, with a bad case of acne. A patchy mustache on his upper lip drew attention to his protruding front teeth.

"Did you?" Barry persisted.

"If I killed somebody, do you think I'd tell you?"

"Oh yeah," Barry said with wonder, absorbing the response.

"I didn't kill anybody," Monroe insisted. "Shit."

Barry waved his hand at the beds. "You can have whichever bunk you want. And the dresser. I don't have nothing much in there."

Monroe stayed in the chair, impassive.

Barry said, "They put us together in here because we're badasses. Not like the rest of them, runaways and dumbshits they got at juvenile. I got busted for sale and possession. At school. Wasn't the first time, that's why they're riding me so hard."

Barry picked up a pillow from the bunk and punched it. "Man, if I was on the street, I could get you some good shit. Anything you want. Even in this shitty little town."

"That's cool."

Barry beamed, proud to receive the affirmation. He extended the flat pillow to Monroe, like an offering.

"I been using your pillow. I didn't know you was coming."

Monroe accepted it, grasping the stained white covering and tucking it behind his back in the metal chair.

After a moment, Barry picked up the other pillow, the one that remained on his bed.

"You can take my pillow, too. I don't mind."

Tanner Monroe took it without hesitation. "Yeah. I will."

Chapter 8

COURT WAS NOT yet in session at 8:30 A.M. on Tuesday morning. The first pot of coffee percolated in the courthouse coffee shop; Elsie could smell it as she marched past, exiting the courthouse through the side door to make her way to Juvenile Hall. She encountered Ashlock in the parking lot, and they fell into step, though she had to walk fast to keep up with him.

Treading along the sidewalk, Elsie felt sober. She had awakened early, struggling with the task that awaited.

"Why you looking so glum?" Ashlock asked.

She laughed, embarrassed that her feelings were so easily read. "I'm a little nervous," she confessed.

Ashlock gave her a quizzical look. "You, Elsie? Why? I can't imagine that taking a statement would ruffle your feathers. Not sure what would."

"Aw, come on, Ash. Twenty-four hours ago, I was barfing in the woods."

"Oh, that. Ancient history."

"And this morning, we're interrogating a juvenile. I haven't handled a case involving a juvenile suspect before."

"I thought you wanted this assignment. You've been waiting for a murder case."

"Yeah. I know."

"Didn't you tell me you came out and asked her for it? And for once, she gave you what you wanted?"

"I know; I wanted a murder case. It's just that I started thinking last night. I'm not sure that this is the murder case I wanted." She exhaled audibly, rubbing at her eyebrow. "He's so damned young. Is it weird, interrogating a juvenile? How do you feel about it?"

"Tell you how I feel," he grinned reassuringly. "I feel good. I feel a big confession coming on."

They walked across the lot to Juvenile Hall, converted from an old granite schoolhouse decades earlier. As they climbed the front steps together, Elsie asked, "Did you talk to the Oklahoma guys? Who brought the juvenile in?"

"Yes, ma'am," Ashlock said. "Had a little conflict, I hear. They said he's a snake. Said the kid was cold as ice."

Elsie clutched his arm, dismayed. "Oh Lord, Ash, they didn't question him, did they? Because if they did, we're in a terrible mess. We have to make sure he's read all of his rights, that it's done like the courts require in Missouri. Have those Okies fucked it up?"

Ashlock shook his head. "Just listen to you. They didn't take a statement, I told them not to. They didn't question the kid. Good God, honey, settle down."

Ashlock held the door for her, and Elsie took a deep breath. "I'm doing the government's job. A woman is dead," she muttered, like a mantra to equip herself for the undertaking. "Here goes nothing," she whispered to herself.

When the uniformed officer at the metal detector saw Ashlock, he waved them through, and they walked into the entryway. In the waiting area sat Chuck Harris, surrounded by crying children and anxious adults and teenagers.

He jumped up when he saw them.

"Thank God you're here. I was about to call Madeleine. I can't get anyone's attention. It's like trying to raise the dead."

Ashlock walked up to a receptionist sitting behind a glass window which bore the sign, DO NOT KNOCK ON GLASS. He rapped on the glass and slapped his badge up against it, barking, "Barton PD."

A stony faced receptionist slid the window open just a crack. "You here about the Monroe boy, aren't you?"

Oh Lord Lord Lord, he's only a boy; she called him a boy, Elsie thought.

"We've come to take his statement."

Chuck tugged at Elsie's elbow. "Did you do the research?"

"Yeah, I read up on the Missouri cases last night. How about you?"

"I'm the assistant," he said with a wink. "Research is the job of the low man."

Ashlock was still talking to the receptionist. "Before we

see Monroe, we'd appreciate talking to the chief juvenile officer first. I'd like him to give me some background."

The woman shook her head, taking a swig from a large Styrofoam Sonic cup. "Well, you're out of luck. Hank isn't here; he's at the summer teachers' meeting at Lake of the Ozarks. He's doing a seminar there, speaking about the mandated reporter law."

Ashlock's brow creased. "His assistant, then."

"He's at the meeting, too. It's pretty quiet around here today."

A shriek from one of the children waiting on the bench nearby made Elsie's ears ring. She shoved her face into the glass, next to Ashlock.

"Who's in charge today if Hank and the chief deputy are gone?" Elsie asked.

"Lisa Peters. Hank told me she'll handle it."

"Who's Lisa Peters?" Elsie muttered as the receptionist picked up the phone. She knew most of the county personnel by name or by sight, but Peters didn't ring a bell.

"She's a juvenile officer, brand-new. She'll take care of you. I'm going to let her know you're here."

The receptionist waved them in as she pushed the buzzer to the electric entryway into the juvenile office. As they walked through the doorway, Elsie whispered to Ashlock, "What do you think's going on? Should we wait and do this another time?"

Ashlock frowned, but didn't answer. She turned to Chuck and said, "The juvenile people are out of pocket, and this is their area. We're new to this, Chuck. It would be smart to hold off. Don't you think?"

"Hell no," Chuck responded.

With a shrug, Ashlock led Elsie and Chuck Harris back into the main hallway of the juvenile facility. A young woman appeared in the doorway. She looked like a schoolgirl, half a head shorter than Elsie, with a heart-shaped freckled face and carrot red hair pulled back into a ponytail.

"Hold it," the girl said in a no-nonsense tone. She blocked their procession with her slight frame.

Ashlock paused, but Elsie stuck out her hand.

"I'm Elsie Arnold, from the Prosecutor's Office," she said briskly.

"Lisa Peters, deputy juvenile officer," the woman said. Peters ignored Elsie's overture; her hands stayed at her sides. Smothering a smartass remark, Elsie withdrew her hand. The juvenile officer had a definite attitude problem, she thought.

Chuck gaped at Lisa. "Jesus, how old are you? You look like a kid out of school."

"Missouri State U, class of 2013," Peters said. "You want to come on back?"

As they followed, Elsie said in a conversational tone, "Hey Lisa, I went to summer school at Missouri State."

"A hundred years ago," Harris quipped, earning Elsie's evil eye. Her thirty-second birthday was fast approaching, and she was sensitive to old maid jokes.

"We'll have to meet down in the rec room," Lisa said, ignoring the small talk. "We don't have an office big enough to hold five people. I didn't know you all were going to dog-pile the poor kid."

"That's not our intention," Elsie began, as they followed Lisa single file down a narrow stairway.

"Whatever. Two lawyers and a detective going up against a fifteen-year-old boy. Call it what you want."

"Ashlock will be doing the interrogation; Chuck and I are just here to make sure everything goes smoothly. We don't want any legal issues. I've done all the research; I'm on top of this."

"Wow. Impressive," Lisa said in a voice that implied the opposite.

Laughing, Chuck asked, "What was your major? ROTC?"

"Social work," Lisa said, stopping at the bottom of the stairs. Pointing into the rec hall, she said, "Make yourself at home."

Elsie peered through an open doorway into the dank basement room, dimly lit by a few overhead bulbs covered in chicken wire. No windows provided natural light. A sputtering box fan moved the hot air in the room. The only furnishings were a black vinyl sofa flanked by two matching chairs.

Elsie said, "Detective Ashlock will read him his Miranda rights. I read *State v. Seibert*, so I think I'm on top of this stuff."

Lisa dropped onto the black sofa and sat cross-legged, pulling her sneakers under her on the couch. "Yeah? Well, his parents aren't here. I don't even think you can question him without a parent present. Never heard of a case where the cops tried to do such a thing."

Chuck Harris stood over the juvenile officer, frowning. He demanded, "Why didn't the juvenile office cover that? Can you get the parents here?"

The juvenile officer shook her head. "I don't know where they are."

Ashlock asked, "How about a conference call?"

"I should've said: We don't even know *who* they are. No contact info. Tanner didn't provide any family information during intake."

Elsie wiped a sheen of sweat that beaded on her forehead. It was hot as hell in juvenile detention. "Lisa, does he have a GAL?"

"A what?" asked Harris.

"A guardian ad litem. Surely the juvenile judge appointed one if he's got no parents around."

Lisa said, "The judge appointed Maureen Mason. She handles a lot of juvenile cases."

Ashlock nodded. "I know Maureen. Let's see if we can get her over here."

"Call her," Chuck barked at Lisa, with a kingly wave of his hand. "Now."

Lisa blinked, but made no other movement. "I don't take orders from you," she said matter-of-factly.

"I'm just asking you to do your job, Ms. Peters. Do I need to talk to the juvenile judge about you?"

"Talk to whoever you want. I don't give a shit what you do."

Chuck Harris gasped in mock outrage, and said, "Is that how you communicate with your superiors?"

Lisa flushed, her face as red as her hair, and jumped out of her seat. "You aren't my superior. I don't work for you."

As Chuck opened his mouth to answer, Elsie held up a restraining hand. "Chuck, for God's sake, why would we pick a fight with the juvenile office? Now look you all, I've got my phone." Elsie reached into her bag and fumbled for her cell phone. After a brief search, she found it and handed the phone to Lisa. "We can't proceed without the guardian. Come on, Lisa, call Maureen and ask her to head on over. She mostly does juvenile stuff, so with the whole juvenile staff at the Lake of the Ozarks, she ought to be free today."

Lisa pressed her lips together in a thin line. Refusing to look at Chuck, she took the phone and walked off to a corner of the basement room to make the call. Chuck got up from his chair and stretched, strolling casually in the opposite direction from Lisa.

Ashlock turned to Elsie. "Good thing I brought you along. The floor would be wet with blood without your people skills."

"Oh, I've got skills," she whispered impishly.

His jaw twitched and he winked at her.

Lisa returned with a report that the guardian would be at Juvenile Hall within a few minutes.

"See?" Elsie said, beaming at them, "this is going to work out. Ash, where do you want to set up?"

He glanced around the basement room; the only other equipment was a much-abused foosball table.

"Looks like this is it. Miss Peters, do you think we could rustle up a couple more chairs? We'll be a little too cozy, otherwise."

Lisa pointed at Chuck, where he lounged across the room. "I thought they were stepping out."

Before Chuck could respond, Elsie spoke up. "That's not a bad idea. Maybe we ought to scoot out of here. We can be nearby, if anything comes up."

"We're staying right here," Chuck said.

Elsie looked at him, disconcerted. "Seems like we ought to clear out. I think it's the best thing to do, under the circumstances."

"I want to talk to you." With a sidelong look at Lisa, Chuck added, "Privately."

As Lisa and Ashlock went to find chairs, Chuck said, sotto voce, "This is the first big case Madeleine has put me in charge of. I need to be in here; I don't want anything to go wrong."

"That's why we need to leave. We shouldn't be present at the interrogation of the defendant. What if we get called as witnesses down the road?"

"That's not what I'm worried about; I have to ensure that this investigation proceeds like Madeleine wants it to. I'm worried about a small-town cop bumbling the job."

In disbelief, Elsie shook her head. "Ashlock? You're nuts. Ashlock can handle this."

"It's not your call, third chair."

Elsie leaned in toward him, and said in a stage whisper, "You better back off. And watch how you treat that juvenile officer."

"She's hot, isn't she?" he responded conversationally. "I think I saw a picture of her in *Barely Legal* magazine."

Elsie reached over and shoved him. "That's what I mean. That shit is sexist. Stop it."

He leaned back against the cinder-block wall and surveyed her with a knowing eye.

"Mm-hmm, that's what I heard. You know, Madeleine warned me about you."

Caught off guard, Elsie stepped back. "What do you mean?"

"Madeleine told me about you when I came to work here. She said you'd think you were in charge. She told me to watch out for you bossing me around, telling me what to do. Yesterday, she said you'd want to take over this case, too."

Elsie looked at him silently, anger washing over her in a wave that brought a flush to her face.

"You should see your face," he said, but broke off when Ashlock and Lisa Peters returned, bearing two pairs of folding chairs. Chuck jumped up to offer assistance; switching to a jovial tone, he said, "I'll take those. Are we ready now?"

"When the guardian gets here," Lisa said. "Because the juvenile has to have a friend, someone who is here on his behalf."

Elsie stood, shaking off her indignation toward Chuck, and focusing on the task at hand. Pleasantly, she said to Lisa, "We're lucky to have you in charge here. Thanks for helping us out today."

Lisa didn't meet Elsie's eye. In a challenging voice, she said, "I can't believe you all are ganging up on him like this. What is the Prosecutor's Office even doing here?"

Flustered, Elsie said, "A dead woman was pulled out

of a creek bed, Lisa. We're investigating a murder, for God's sake."

"Since when does the prosecutor run the investigation? Tanner hasn't been charged, hasn't been certified. It just feels wrong to me."

This time, Elsie didn't respond. She was beginning to believe the juvenile officer had a valid point.

Chuck spoke up. "The prosecutor has a legal right to all the information regarding a juvenile suspect. It's a sensitive case; that's why Madeleine wants us to keep a close eye."

Lisa did a count with her fingers. "Three against one. Nice odds. Very subtle."

Chuck said, "Hey, you're here for him."

Lisa shook her head. "I have to tell him that I'm not here to be his advocate, or to stand in like an attorney. But I'm certainly going to ensure that he understands his rights. And to see that this big ole detective follows due process."

Ashlock unfolded one of the chairs and sat in it, smiling at the group. "'Due process' is my middle name," he assured them.

Lisa Peters produced a set of keys and said, "I'm going to get him out of his detention quarters now. If you're ready."

"Ready," Elsie said, hoping they weren't making a huge procedural error.

Seeming reluctant to proceed, Lisa asked, "Do you need me to go get some rights forms? I could go upstairs and copy the ones we use."

"The juvenile office faxed the forms to me yesterday. I've got them right here," Ashlock said, flipping open a notebook and showing her the forms.

Lisa nodded, her mouth pressed in a thin line as she left the room.

"What's her problem?" Chuck Harris asked, shaking his head.

Ashlock ignored the question. He instructed Elsie and Chuck where to sit, so that he could set up the interrogation in the most effective way possible, considering the conditions. Elsie watched as he tinkered with the tape recorder, testing it and playing it back.

Before Lisa returned, Maureen Mason arrived, a stout woman with graying hair pulled into a tight knot. "It's a lucky thing for you that I came in to look through my mail, or you never would have dragged me in for this," she said. "I figured the whole juvenile division was shut down today. Thought I'd have a little vacation day for myself. I guess there's no rest for the weary."

The door to the detention hallway swung open, and all heads turned to get a look at the juvenile.

He'd had a chance to rest and clean up, and he looked nondescript, a typical teen of moderate height, with dark brown hair in need of a haircut, and a splash of acne on his forehead. If Elsie saw him in line at the convenience store, she wouldn't look twice.

Maureen patted the spot beside her on the couch. "Come sit by me, Tanner."

Ashlock intervened, a commanding note in his voice. "Ms. Mason, I believe it would be best if Mr. Monroe sits in this folding chair right here, facing me." Ashlock placed his hand on the metal seat of the empty chair. "I've set the recorder up already, and we need to make sure he comes through loud and clear."

Maureen shrugged. "Whatever." She tried to grasp Tanner's hand as he walked by. "How are you today, Tanner?"

The boy snatched his hand away from her. Turning to Lisa, he asked, "Will you stay by me, Lisa?"

Elsie's radar went off. *Sounds like Ferris Bueller playing sick.*

But Lisa was moved. "You bet, Tanner; I'll set my chair right by you, and I'll be here the whole time." Lisa shot an inquiring glance at Maureen, but the older woman ignored her.

Ashlock walked the teen through the rights forms, first reading his Miranda rights. He and his guardian signed off on the form.

"Okay, shoot," Tanner said.

"Not quite yet," Ashlock said. Pulling out another form, he advised Tanner again of his right to remain silent and right to counsel. He then said, "The offense you're being questioned about would be a felony if committed by an adult. Do you understand?"

The boy nodded. Ashlock handed him a ballpoint pen, and he checked "Yes" on the form.

Ashlock continued, reading from the form, " 'If you are alleged, at any age, to have committed First Degree Murder, Second Degree Murder, First Degree Assault, Forcible Rape, Forcible Sodomy, First Degree Robbery,

Distribution of Drugs, or if you have committed two or more prior unrelated offenses which would be felonies if committed by an adult, a hearing will be held to determine if you should be prosecuted as an adult.'"

Ashlock paused. Monroe met his look without flinching.

"Do you understand?"

"You bet." He marked "Yes."

When Ashlock finished reading the form, he handed Tanner the pen again. Tanner took it in his right hand, but leaned over to Lisa and placed his other hand on her shoulder.

"What do you think I should do, Lisa?" he asked in a low voice.

She shook her head. "I can't advise you, Tanner. It's like that paper says, I'm your adversary, I'm not your advocate. I really wish your parents were here. But you've got a guardian, and she's a lawyer."

He sighed and cast a scornful look at the guardian. "I'm definitely not taking advice from that fat bitch," he said.

Maureen blinked, taken aback. "Mr. Monroe. You realize that the Juvenile Court appointed me to look after your interests in the absence of your parents."

The teen tipped back in his folding chair, rocking it precariously with the toe of his left foot. "I know what you're interested in. Food."

"Tanner!" Lisa said.

"She needs to go on *The Biggest Loser,*" Tanner said in an aside to the juvenile officer.

"Despite your insulting attitude," said Maureen coldly, furrowing an angry brow over her reading glasses, "I'd advise you that it's in your best interest to shut up. Don't answer any questions. In fact, it would be wise if you refrain from speaking entirely."

The boy gave the guardian a look of appraisal, then shot them all an ironic half grin.

"If Fatty thinks I should shut up, then I'm definitely talking. Abso-fucking-lutely. Ask me whatever you want."

Lisa looked anxious. "Tanner, are you sure?"

"Yeah. Bring it." He stretched his arms and folded his hands behind his head.

Lisa gestured toward Maureen. "What do you say?"

With irritation still etched in her face, she shrugged. "It's his decision."

"Okay, then," Ashlock said briskly. "Mr. Monroe, we'd like to know how you happened to be on that bus. Let's start at the beginning, with your name."

The teen provided his name, age, and date of birth, and told Ashlock that he lived in St. Louis, Missouri, with his mother.

"We need your mother's information. Why didn't you provide it at check-in?"

"Because I'm emancipated."

"At fifteen?" Ashlock asked with a dubious expression.

"Oh hell yeah."

"Do you mean there was a judicial determination? A judge declared that you were independent?"

"I don't know about judicial. But I'm totally independent." The boy held up five fingers. "I. Do. What. I. Want," he said, ticking off the words with the fingers of his right hand. "I crash at my mom's place if I feel like it. If not, I don't."

"Then your mother is still your custodian? Your parent and legal guardian?"

"Man, I don't know. I guess."

"What about your father?"

Tanner huffed a humorless breath. "Yeah, what about him?"

"What is his role in your life?"

"His role." The young man shook his head, and tossed his hair back. "You tell me. Never met him."

"Never? Does he pay support?"

"If he does, I don't know nothing about it."

"Your mother would be entitled to support."

"I don't think he's one of those support-paying types."

"What type is he, then? What information did your mother give you about your father?"

"We don't talk about him too much."

Ashlock sat, waiting for Monroe to say more. After a moment's silence, the boy said, "Seems like she said he was doing time. That was a while back."

"So you've been in your mother's sole custody all your life."

"Yeah. Except for foster care. Does that mean not in her custody? Because they never terminated."

Elsie made rapid notes as Ashlock leaned closer to Monroe. "By terminated—you're talking about her parental rights. Is that correct?"

"Yeah. They didn't do that. She always got clean. Then I'd go back."

"How many times did this happen?"

"Shit, man, who can remember? But this last time, since she left rehab, it's been all right. Now that I'm fifteen, we kind of go our own way. It works out okay. We can hang, but we both do what we want. Right now, I'm seeing the country."

"How's that?"

"Hitchhiking. Going where the road takes me."

Ashlock set his pen down and regarded the boy with a level look. "And where has it taken you?"

The boy snorted. "For a ride on that bus, I guess."

"Tell us about that. Where did you first see the bus?"

"At the Diamonds truck stop. The one outside St. Louis. I figured I could get a ride from there. And there was this woman with a school bus. She was taking it to Arkansas."

The boy paused. He said, "Can I have one of my cigarettes?"

"No," said Ashlock. "Tell us about the woman."

"Old. Ugly. Stupid." The boy rolled his eyes at Ashlock's solemn expression. "Okay, not that old. Forty? Thirty? You all look alike to me, old people, I mean. She wasn't getting by on her looks, though. Tell you that much."

"How did you get a ride with her?"

"I just asked. She said I could come along. Said I'd keep her company."

"So you wanted to go to Arkansas?"

"Hell, no. Arkansas blows. But I thought I'd get off at Springfield, maybe go to Branson, go down to the lake. Camp out."

"So what happened?"

"Everything was cool. With her and me. But she picked up another dude."

"At the Diamonds?"

"No, at a gas station down the road."

"Where?"

"I dunno. Maybe Rolla. Maybe somewhere else."

"Why did you stop again so soon? Rolla's not even two hours from the Diamonds."

"Hey, she was driving. Maybe she needed to take a piss." Turning to Lisa, he said, "When's lunch? I'm starved."

Before she could answer, Ashlock said, "Describe the gas station where she picked up the passenger."

"Gas, man. I don't know. It was dark. I was kind of dozing in one of the bus seats. Laying down."

"How did she meet up with the passenger?"

"He asked for a ride. I guess. I wasn't filming it."

Elsie shifted on the vinyl couch, trying to hide her growing impatience, as Ashlock asked him to describe the passenger.

"Seems like he was big. Real big."

"Height?"

"Dude, I don't know."

"Approximately, roughly. Compared to you."

The boy yawned. "I didn't go head to head with him, man. But he was big, I kid you not. Big and scary-looking."

"Weight, build?"

"Big. Not fat."

"Race?"

"White guy."

"Hair color?"

"Ummm. Black."

"Eye color?"

"Shit, man, I don't know. Brown."

"Distinguishing features?"

"What's that mean?"

"Tattoos, scars, marks, facial features."

Monroe rubbed the back of his neck and exhaled audibly. He screwed his eyes shut, saying, "Thinking, thinking, thinking," then fell silent.

After a pause, Ashlock prompted, "Well?"

His brown eyes popped open. "Scar on his cheek. Right there," indicating his cheekbone.

The adults all made notations on paper. Elsie shifted in her seat on the couch, unhappily conscious that she was sticking to the vinyl.

"And tats," the boy added. "Jailhouse tats."

"Where?"

"On his fingers. Couldn't make them out, though. He turned to stare at Lisa Peters. "You know what?"

"What?" she responded.

"If you were mine, I'd protect you. I wouldn't let anybody near you. No fucking way."

Chapter 9

ELSIE SHUFFLED SHEETS of paper, still warm from the copy machine, which contained Tanner Monroe's handwritten statement.

At the conclusion of his interrogation that morning, the juvenile had asked for pen and paper.

"I want to make a written statement," he told them. "In my own words."

Ashlock advised him that it wasn't necessary, they had the tape recording of his answers, and if he wanted to add anything, he was free to speak up. But the boy shook his head.

"Somebody could fuck with a tape recording," he said. "No offense, dude, but it's the truth. Erase something, add something, switch the questions up. I better put it down in handwriting, so I can be sure it's my own words."

Ashlock nodded. "Okay, then." He instructed Elsie to

hand Tanner her legal pad and pen. The adults watched in silence as the boy wrote.

Elsie observed as the boy scratched on the paper with the ballpoint pen, crossing out words and frowning in concentration; then he wrote at a rapid pace, only to pause again. Studying his face, she observed a faint sprinkling of hair on his upper lip, and the scatter of adolescent acne on his brow. Recalling her mother's words, she pondered, *Cutting a woman's throat: how could he do it?* Then she shuddered as a chilling thought followed: *Did he do it?*

Focusing on his hands as he wrote, she tried to envision them handling a knife rather than a pen. The hands were big enough; though the boy was normal height, he looked strong enough to overpower a middle-aged woman. Certainly, holding a weapon would give him the advantage. But as she stared at the hairless backs of his young hands, she wondered how he could be cold enough, at the tender age of fifteen, to take a human life. Maybe her mother was right; she generally was, Elsie knew from long experience.

Had he confessed on those written pages, her job would be much easier. But the photostatic copy in Elsie's hands contained no confession, no admission of wrongdoing. She laid the statement before her on her desk, wishing she had a clearer barometer of the events on that school bus than the scrawled paragraphs provided. Still, Elsie thought it might hold a clue, a key to reveal the true events of the murder.

With a highlighter poised in her hand, she read:

I, Tanner Dylan Monroe, swear this is the truth.

Here is what happened with the bus. The true story.

I was hitchhiking from St. Louis like I said. A woman with a school bus gave me a ride at the Diamonds but there was another dude too she picked up later.

So I was asleep in the back but there was a lot of noise. And I saw them fighting and he had her pinned. Then he had a knife and he cut her throat when he held her down. I couldn't do nothing because I was in the back.

Anyway after she was dead he took me prisoner. He made me drive and go in the middle of nowhere so we dumped the body there.

Then he made me drive and if I didn't do what he said he would kill me, too. I couldn't run or get help cuz he never let me out of his sight. He finally got off somewhere. I don't know where it was at. I drove the bus but it ran out of gas and I stayed with the bus because I didn't have money for gas and nowhere to go. The dude ran off.

That's it except to say I am innocent and I just want to go back to St. Louis. And see my mom.

This is what happen.

Underneath those words, in a cursive scrawl, he signed his name: "Tanner Dylan Monroe."

ODDI defense, Elsie had immediately thought. *Other Dude Done It*. It was easy to anticipate what the jury would want the state to provide when the defendant raised that defense; on rebuttal, the prosecution needed to show that there was no second passenger. They needed to prove to the jury that the crime was Monroe's own act, and they must prove it beyond a reasonable doubt. That was the state's burden, the prosecutor's job.

But first, Elsie must prove it to herself. She did not believe in proceeding on any case where she was unsure of the defendant's guilt, and that was especially true in this instance, where the defendant was a boy of fifteen. Regardless of orders issued by Madeleine or Chuck, she could not present a case to a jury if she didn't believe in it.

If the juvenile had committed a murder, he would have to pay; Missouri followed the trend in recent years toward certifying minors to be tried as adults for criminal acts. The state legislature had made it clear that the criminal courts would handle serious crimes committed by juveniles. But Elsie needed to be absolutely certain that the crime was his; that the evidence pointed to Tanner Monroe, and no one else.

Elsie toyed with the highlighter, thinking, *Let's see what you were up to when you were on the road, Tanner Monroe.*

She tossed the marker on her desk and said, "Oklahoma needs a visit from a big ole Missouri gal."

Chapter 10

ELSIE WALKED INTO the Baldknobbers bar shortly after five, grateful for the frosty air blasting from the window air conditioner. The bar was an old dive, the type of establishment that kept the windows covered day and night. Upon entering, she peered through the smoky haze for Ashlock, but didn't spy him. With a wave at Dixie, the longtime barmaid, she headed for a booth. As she dropped her purse on the seat, she recognized a familiar figure at the bar.

Walking up alongside Chuck Harris, she tapped him on the arm. "Happy Tuesday."

He glanced up, glum, and hunched back over his beer mug. "Right."

"What's the matter?"

"She's gonna dump it on me. I can see it coming."

"Huh?"

"That case with the kid. What a dog."

Elsie slid onto the bar stool beside him. "I understand, I've been ruminating about it myself. But maybe we're just borrowing trouble, Chuck. We're still putting the evidence together; Monroe's not even certified yet. If the case doesn't look strong enough to convict, Madeleine surely won't file."

"Of course she'll file. A dead woman in the county, and a kid in the bloody bus? She has to file. And then we'll have that piece-of-shit case."

She didn't respond. Staring blindly at the mirror behind the bar, she struggled with her own reservations.

Chuck continued, "He didn't confess. No jury will convict a fifteen-year-old of murder without a confession."

Soberly, Elsie nodded. "It would've been handy if the kid confessed. But suspects usually don't; we both know that. And his statement has holes in it." She leaned in close to him, and in a determined tone, said, "We need to follow the trail of the bus, to disprove the kid's story about the other passenger. You and me. And Ashlock."

Chuck traced the water ring his beer mug made on the wooden bar. "This really isn't your case, Elsie. Madeleine told me that in no uncertain terms. You're just the water boy; the case is assigned to me and Madeleine. Which actually means it's all on me."

Elsie sat back on the bar stool, fighting a surge of resentment. Madeleine was already creating obstacles. If Elsie was to have a meaningful role in the case, she would have to make it happen.

"Let me go to Oklahoma," she urged. "I'm good with witnesses; I can establish rapport, start piecing the puzzle together. I'll be a lot of help."

"How? How do you prove a negative? How do you show that the 'mystery man' never existed?"

Overlooking their conflict earlier in the day, Elsie put an arm around his shoulder and gave him a squeeze. "That's what we've got to figure out. We'll do it. And if we can't disprove the mystery man, well, it's important to find that out, too. We'll put our heads together. With Ashlock."

"Do you know what she said to me this afternoon?"

Lord, no telling, Elsie thought, but she kept her voice even. "Madeleine? No, what did she say?"

"She said, if the evidence points to the kid, she's filing murder in the first degree. In the *first*."

Elsie was taken aback. "You mean, she's made her mind up, even before we see what kind of evidence of pre-deliberation they'll find?"

"Yeah. She told me that with a bloody school bus and a woman victim and a slit throat, deliberation should be assumed. The jury won't be caught up on details."

"Premeditation isn't a detail."

"You think I don't know that?"

Elsie stared down at the scarred wooden bar without seeing it. "Maybe she's right. The weapon, the method of killing her; it would have to be intentional, require fore-thought. Anyway, we can always include the option of second degree murder in the jury instructions, if it comes to that."

Chuck groaned softly into his beer mug. "Here it comes. I'll be holding the bag, with an overcharged murder case against a fifteen-year-old kid."

"Lucky for him he's fifteen," Elsie said.

"Huh?"

"If he was sixteen on the date of the crime, and he was convicted of first degree murder, he could get the death penalty. Since he's fifteen, they'll just lock him up and throw away the key. Life imprisonment without eligibility for parole."

"I know that," Chuck said, snappish. "Don't lecture me. Sometimes you act like you're the Oracle at Delphi."

The side door of the bar opened and a flash of daylight blinded Elsie. She shielded her eyes with her hand and made out the outline of Detective Ashlock. "Ash!" she called, with a wave.

As he walked over, she saw he wasn't smiling. He approached the bar, asking Elsie pointedly, "Aren't we sitting at a table?"

"Sure. Got one." With a final pat, Elsie said to Chuck, "Talk to you later."

Walking to the booth, she felt Ashlock's hand pressed possessively at the small of her back. When she scooted into the booth, though, he sat across from her.

"Is something the matter?" she asked.

"Why do you say that?" Looking around, he signaled Dixie to come to the table.

"You were a little rude to the new chief assistant. Didn't say hello."

"I guess that's because I don't like him too much."

Elsie examined him as Dixie came up to take their order. "You're jealous."

"You want a beer, honeybun?" Dixie asked her.

"Corona for me," Elsie said.

Ashlock smiled at Dixie. "Coke."

Leaning back in the booth, Elsie observed that Ashlock offered up a smile for Dixie, but had not yet spared one for her. A little nettled, she said, "You're no fun."

"You're surely shining a spotlight on all my bad qualities this evening. Rude. No fun. Jealous."

She slipped her foot out of her shoe and propped it upon his thigh, under the table across from her.

"You've got nothing to be jealous of, Ash."

When he didn't answer, she slipped her toes under his leg and nudged him.

"Hey," she said.

As her foot inched its way to his crotch, he grabbed her ankle and cracked a smile.

"You're incorrigible," he said.

"Since when do you need to worry about being the focus of my attention? You know I'm hooked."

He didn't reply, but his eyes crinkled at the corners. With a devilish expression, she leaned across the table and said in a stage whisper, "Let's play the game where you're taking me to the home for wayward girls."

When he responded with a laugh, she smiled, glad to see him restored to good humor. Dixie bustled up, setting their drinks in front of them. Picking up her beer bottle, Elsie tilted it toward Ashlock.

"First swallow?" she offered, but he shook his head. Elsie took a long drink from the neck of the cold bottle.

"My mom called today," she said. "She and Dad want to know if we're coming over for dinner on my birthday. It's two weeks away, but she's already wanting to set the table and plan the menu."

He squeezed her foot under the table with a warm hand. "What do you want?"

"Well, I hate to disappoint Marge and George. They're chomping at the bit. But I'd really like to go out, just you and me. There's a new steakhouse in Monett. People are talking it up."

"Sounds good. We'll check it out."

Elsie watched as Ashlock toyed with his glass, turning it in a circle with his fingers. "Hey," she said. "What's up?"

He let out a tired breath. "Just got off the phone with the next of kin. Glenda Fielder's niece."

"You mean the deceased didn't have any closer relations? Just a niece?"

"That's right. Never married, parents long gone, one brother who passed in a car wreck a couple of years back. The niece wasn't a bad source, though. They were pretty close, considering."

"What did she say?"

"For one thing, she said her aunt was bitching about the employer: the transport company had been leaning on the workers to speed up delivery time. She had to drive through the night to make her deadlines. That's why she picked up hitchhikers; it helped her to stay awake."

"Okay, that makes some sense anyway," Elsie said. "I

couldn't figure out why on earth she'd pick up a hitch-hiker. It's a hell of a gamble."

Peering over Ashlock's shoulder, she saw Chuck leave his bar stool and head toward the men's room. "Finally. He's in the bathroom; I can tell you the buzz."

"What buzz?"

Leaning across the table, she spoke in a hushed voice. "Bree got the goods on our new chief assistant."

"How's that?"

"She's got a friend, an old law school buddy, who works in the Jackson County office. Bree was on the phone with him last night, and the guy asked what we thought about Chuck."

"And?"

"He told Bree that Chuck was in hot water in Kansas City. He was nailing one of the secretaries. The girl thought it was a big romance; and when she figured out it was just recreational on his part, she threatened to file a Title VII complaint with the EEOC for sexual harassment."

Ashlock was nonplussed. "This story doesn't surprise me, for some reason."

"Chuck's dad is some big-time lawyer up there; we already knew that. And he had political ambitions for Chuck. So he called Madeleine, and they agreed that Chuck would come down here and work until the dust settled in Jackson County."

"How does he know Madeleine?"

"Politics, maybe? They're both Republicans. Or maybe it's the money magnet." She picked up her beer bottle and took another swallow. "In my experience, rich people always seem to find each other. Like bees to honey."

"Yeah?"

"Yeah. Like flies on shit."

When Chuck emerged from the restroom, Elsie changed the subject. "School's out," she said. "The elementary across from my apartment is quiet as the tomb. So I was wondering: When are the kids coming?"

Ashlock had three children from a prior marriage. They lived in the Bootheel of Missouri with their mother, but Ashlock did everything in his power to exercise his visitation schedule: every other weekend, a handful of holidays, and a portion of the summer. Though Elsie and Ashlock had been keeping company since the winter months, she had yet to meet them.

When he didn't answer immediately, she asked again: "When will you get them?"

His face became neutral. "I'll pick them up in July. They'll be here a month."

"That's great. Can't wait. I'm looking forward to seeing them while they're here."

He nodded, but his face was noncommittal. Elsie persisted.

"There's great stuff to do here in the summer. We can go to Silver Dollar City; I love the roller coasters, all the wild rides. I've been there a million times; we won't even need a map." She took a quick swallow of beer, and added, "And the Ozark Empire Fair will start the end of July; we'll take them to that. Marvelous carny stuff: the food, the games, the old-fashioned carnival rides. It's a hoot."

"We'll see," he said.

Elsie knew she'd been shut down. Hurt, she glanced around the bar, ready to change the subject. She saw Chuck Harris order another drink; he was still sitting alone.

"I think the chief assistant is a little blue," Elsie whispered, her eyes on Harris's back. "He's flipped out about the murder case."

Ashlock flashed a look of impatience. "What's he got to flip out about? We're still putting it together."

"He says it's going to be a weak case, a loser. And Madeleine is going to dump it on him."

"He's a punk. A spoiled kid. If the Juvenile Court certifies Monroe to stand trial as an adult, I bet Harris never touches that case. Watch out, sweetheart."

At his word of warning, Elsie focused on Ashlock, her brows drawn together.

He said, "When the going gets tough, your boss Madeleine and her number one man are going to scatter like chickens."

"Hmmm." She leaned forward. "So how do you think the murder case looks?"

He reached for her bottle and took a quick swig. "Ain't no telling. Not till I get to Oklahoma."

Chapter 11

ON WEDNESDAY, ELSIE took time to bolt down lunch at the downtown Dairy Queen, and sped back to work in the punishing heat of her car, air-conditioning vents blasting. The heat in southwest Missouri was reaching record highs, though it was not yet July. Her phone buzzed as she neared a stoplight; she rummaged in her purse and checked the text. It was from Ashlock, inquiring about lunch.

She nearly missed the green light, replying to the text: *Sorry! Too late!* A horn blared behind her and she felt a moment's remorse for texting while driving. It was a bad practice, she knew.

"I'll never do it again," she swore.

After a few blocks, the phone hummed again. Snatching it up, she read, *See U 2nite?* She texted back *Yes!* and pushed Send before she realized she had broken her vow.

"Busted a resolution. Again." She sat up straight as she

pulled into the courthouse lot, tugging her damp blouse from the vinyl seat back. Addressing herself in the rearview mirror with a jaunty expression, she added, "Aw, well."

She took the elevator instead of the stairs in a vain attempt to cool down. Entering the reception area shortly before one, she passed the receptionist, Stacie, a cute local girl who made an attractive first impression for people entering the Prosecutor's Office. Stacie looked the part but had minimal interest in the clerical particulars of her position.

Poking a fork into a Tupperware container, Stacie said to Elsie, "You're in Division 2."

"I most certainly am not," Elsie said.

"You are. There's a change of venue hearing in there, and you're doing it."

"I don't even have a case with a change of venue motion pending."

"No, but Chuck does. He handed the hearing off to you." Stacie looked up from her lunch, twirling her fork in pasta salad. "Ask him if you don't believe me."

"I'll fucking ask him right this fucking minute," Elsie muttered, heading down the hallway to the chief assistant's office. As she drew near, she saw Chuck slip out the door with his jacket on his arm.

"Where do you think you're going?" she asked.

"I'm going to lunch, Wicked Witch. That's what you sound like at the moment."

He hooked his jacket over his shoulder and moved to continue down the hallway, but Elsie blocked him.

"Why aren't you heading to Judge Callaway's court to handle your change of venue?"

"Because you're such a good lawyer, I have complete confidence in your ability to handle it." He flashed a brilliant smile. Elsie noted that he seemed fully recovered from the fit of pique he'd suffered at the Baldknobbers the night before. Her momentary sympathy for him dissolved accordingly.

"You're trying to butter me up, but I'm immune," she warned.

"How could you be immune to hearing what a really great lawyer you are?" In a plaintive tone, he added, "Please do this for me, Elsie, okay? I'm dead on my feet. I was in there all morning on a motion for new trial, and I am wore slick."

Elsie frowned. She knew why Chuck was pushing his hearing onto her. Judge Callaway was notorious for his prejudice against air-conditioning. Even on the hottest days of summer, he insisted on keeping the windows open and the air-conditioning off. The Division 2 courtroom was stifling from early June through mid-September. Longer, if there was an Indian summer.

"I'll get faint in there," she complained.

"What about me? I have to wear a tie and jacket."

Elsie shook her head, unmoved. "It's your case."

"I wrote notes for it, everything you need to know, from A to Z. It'll be a breeze," he said, reaching out and massaging her shoulder. "Please?"

"How's the bailiff today?"

Emil Elmquist, the Division 2 bailiff, had the same

contempt for deodorant that his boss had for temperature control. In the summer, Emil's body odor was legendary.

"Not so fresh, I must confess. Grab the counsel table at the far end of the courtroom."

"Oh Lord," she groaned.

"Tell you what," Chuck said, backing away from her. "If you do me this little favor, I'll talk Madeleine into taking you along with me tomorrow."

"Along where?"

"To Oklahoma."

Elsie's interest perked up. "You're going tomorrow? I think I'm free."

"Okay, then. Ashlock is scheduled to collect evidence off the bus at the Tulsa Highway Patrol headquarters. Plus, he's tracking the kid's trail, and Madeleine's sending me along."

Why didn't Ashlock tell me about Tulsa? Elsie wondered, a little injured; but maybe he would have filled her in on the plan at lunch, had she been able to meet him.

Chuck said, "I've got to tag along, because I'm supposed to make sure the case is airtight in case she files. Because it's tough to convince a jury to lock a juvenile up for life." He pretended to wipe away tears. "Boo hoo."

Elsie followed as Chuck attempted to get away.

"What time are you going?"

"First thing in the morning. Is it a deal? You'll get to see the bus. All *bloody.*"

With the back of her hand, Elsie wiped sweat from her forehead. She would have liked to shut down Chuck's off-putting wisecracks, but she stifled the impulse; she needed to ingratiate herself with him, so she could see what the Oklahoma evidence revealed. And she needed to prove to herself that the juvenile was a murderer, before she could prove it to a jury. "Okay. Deal."

"Great, thanks," Chuck said, dashing through the door before she could change her mind.

Elsie followed, walked around the courthouse rotunda, and hurried into Judge Callaway's courtroom, eager to seize the far counsel table. The bailiff was reading the newspaper as she entered. When he saw her, he folded the pages.

"You doing the change of venue?" he asked.

"Boy oh boy, Emil. I won the prize."

"You got witnesses in the hallway."

"Thanks, Emil. I'll go out there in a minute."

Elsie flipped the file open and scanned the contents. The defendant was charged with methamphetamine production. The case had received some play in the news, because the meth lab was discovered when it set fire to a local hotel room. Still, the coverage was far from extraordinary. The file contained copies of articles from the local paper, reporting defendant's arrest and preliminary hearing. Both articles ran photos alongside the text. One showed the smoking interior of defendant's hotel room. The other photo depicted defendant and his attorney entering the courthouse. Elsie didn't think either story could be branded as sensational.

Walking to the courtroom door, she poked her head out. "Any witnesses for *State v. Maggard*?" she called.

Several people raised their hands. One man rose from the bench, protesting that the subpoena didn't make sense; he didn't even know anyone named Maggard.

Elsie approached him, extending her hand. "Let me see your subpoena," she said. She scanned it, nodding. "You've been summoned for a change of venue hearing. The defendant claims he can't get a fair trial in McCown County." She smiled, turning to include the citizens nearby. "I don't mean to be mysterious, but with a change of venue motion, we don't need to consult before you testify. The less we talk, the better."

Elsie gave a brief overview of the basic mechanics of a change of venue hearing. Sometimes, when there was a great deal of pretrial publicity, the defendant asked the court to order that the case be tried in a county where the community had not heard so much about the facts of the case, to ensure an impartial jury.

After Elsie provided a thumbnail sketch of the hearing procedures, she walked back to the courtroom door. With a hand on the knob, she said, "I really appreciate you all coming today. It shouldn't take long."

"I want to get back to work as quick as I can," said the man who'd spoken up earlier. "This still don't make much sense to me, why I'd have to miss work for some guy I don't know nothing about."

Elsie gave him a conciliatory nod. "Appreciate it," she said again. Then she returned to the courtroom, leaving the witnesses on the benches outside.

As she rummaged for a pen and legal pad at her counsel table, the defense attorney, Billy Yocum, ambled into court with his client in tow. His genial expression disappeared when he saw Elsie.

"Where's Mr. Harris?" he asked.

"I'm filling in. How's it going, Billy?"

Elsie and the elderly attorney had gone around a time or two. Billy Yocum was old school, a master litigator who learned the trade from his time in the Prosecutor's Office, decades earlier. Yocum had more tricks up his sleeve than a riverboat gambler.

"Well, I don't know. Seems like Mr. Harris should handle the hearing if he's assigned to the case."

"Billy, you're just going to have to get over it. I'm all you've got."

She slid back in the wooden chair, determined not to let Yocum rile her. Yocum was famous for turning tables on the prosecution, making it appear that the defense wore the white hat and the prosecution was the bad guy, rather than the other way around.

He had countless tactics that infuriated her. At jury trials, after wrangling an evidentiary point before the judge at the bench—and outside of the jury's hearing—Yocum would invariably claim victory for the jurors' benefit. Whether the judge ruled in Elsie's favor, or in Yocum's, the old attorney would swing back toward the bench on the way to the counsel table with a jubilant: "Thank you, your honor! The defense appreciates your excellent ruling on that issue."

The first time it occurred, Elsie just stared at him with her mouth open, like she was catching flies; Yocum had managed to make himself look like a victor on an evidentiary point he had, in fact, lost to Elsie.

Now that she was educated to the trick, she had become adept at beating him to the punch, chiming in with her own words of appreciation on behalf of the state, and punctuating the statement with an expressive wink to the jury. She had developed an array of nonverbal cues in her years as a trial lawyer and prided herself on her ability to connect on an unspoken level with the jurors. No one in the Ozarks could match her on that score—with the possible exception of Billy Yocum.

The bailiff emerged from the judge's chambers and asked whether the parties were ready.

"All set," said Elsie.

"Yes, sir," said Yocum. "Tell Judge Callaway we can start any time."

The bailiff disappeared and Yocum's client, a disheveled young man, said, "Does he stink?"

"Hush," Yocum replied.

The judge emerged from chambers. Elsie stood as the bailiff cried, "All rise!" After Judge Callaway took his seat, he invited the parties to do the same.

Opening the file, Judge Callaway said, "What you got here, gentlemen?"

Elsie frowned.

The judge caught his gaffe and corrected himself, while Emil snickered in his bailiff's chair.

"I apologize, Ms. Arnold. I was expecting Mr. Harris. You all ready?"

Billy Yocum rose slowly from his chair and drawled,

"As a courtesy, I'd be glad to give the state the chance to go first."

Elsie jumped up, her blood pressure shooting up in response to Yocum's suggestion. "Your honor, this is defendant's motion. We didn't ask for a change of venue. If defendant doesn't have any evidence in support of his motion, he should say so, and we can free up the court's time."

Yocum turned to her, laughing. "Judge, tell the prosecutor to settle down. It's too hot to get riled up over nothing. My witnesses are right outside; I'll be glad to call them. I guess Miss Arnold's not particularly concerned about inconveniencing the witnesses for the state." As an aside, he said to Elsie, "Those benches out there are mighty hard."

Elsie gave him a sour look. Billy Yocum always knew how to get her goat.

The judge said, "Call your witness, Billy."

Yocum called a Mrs. Cooper to the stand, a pleasant-looking middle-aged woman, wearing church clothes. Under examination, she told the court that she had read about the case in the newspaper and seen it on TV, and she'd already made up her mind about defendant's guilt. Because of the news coverage, she couldn't be impartial. The man could not get a fair trial in McCown County, she added.

"No further questions," Yocum said, favoring the woman with a courtly nod.

Elsie stood. Advancing toward the witness stand, she asked, "Ma'am, are you acquainted with the defendant?"

"Never met him."

"How about his attorney, Mr. Yocum?"

"No."

Elsie paused, puzzled. Yocum would not call a witness to the stand for a change of venue hearing unless she was certain to be in his pocket.

"You don't know Mr. Yocum from church? Rotary? From a civic organization?"

"No," the woman said, as Yocum objected: "Asked and answered."

"Sustained," the judge murmured, eyes closed. He looked ready for a nap.

Elsie studied the witness for a moment. Oozing respectability, the woman was clearly a law-abiding citizen. She could not be connected to the meth business, or the defendant sitting next to Billy Yocum.

"Where do you work?"

"I'm a homemaker."

Elsie smiled. *Gotcha*, she thought.

"Are you acquainted with Mr. Yocum's wife? Peggy?"

The woman flushed. Glancing at the defense attorney, she said, "Yes."

"How do you know Mrs. Yocum?"

"We're in PEO together."

"Ah," said Elsie, nodding sagely, "that's a sorority, right?"

Pursing her lips, the woman answered, "It is a philanthropic educational organization."

Elsie knew better. And she knew she couldn't ask what "PEO" stood for; it was a closely guarded secret of the society. The old gal could tell Elsie, but then she'd have to kill her.

"Did Mrs. Yocum ask you to appear today?"

"Yes." She shifted in the chair, as if the seat had become uncomfortable; she knew the cat was out of the bag.

"What did Mrs. Yocum say or do?"

"Well. It seems like she showed me the newspaper article, and asked me to read it. We talked about the case a little bit. We agreed he couldn't get a fair trial here."

"Where did this conversation take place?"

"At the PEO meeting. During luncheon."

Elsie glanced out into the hallway. Two other women waited on the bench that the present witness had vacated. They looked like her clones, from their lacquered silver hair, right down to their pantyhose.

"Are you acquainted with any other witnesses who will appear today on defendant's behalf?"

"Objection! Calls for speculation!"

"Overruled," said the judge, with a meaning look at Yocum.

The witness hesitated. "Yes."

"Are they outside?"

"Uh-huh."

"What are their names?"

The witness provided the names of two women.

"How do you know them?"

"PEO."

Elsie leaned against the jury box, smiling at the witness. "So essentially, Mrs. Yocum came to PEO with newspaper clippings, and drummed up three witnesses for her husband's hearing."

The woman opened her mouth to respond, but shut it as Yocum shouted, "Objection! How dare you?"

The judge said, "Sustained."

Yocum waved a dramatic arm in Elsie's direction. "She has attacked the integrity of my wife. My *wife*, for God's sake."

"Settle down, Billy." The judge no longer looked sleepy.

"I demand that the prosecutor be censured."

Elsie rolled her eyes.

The judge said, "You got any witnesses other than the PEO ladies, Billy?"

"Your honor, my witnesses are of the highest character."

The judge nodded. "That's true. But if the remaining testimony is going to be a repetition of the current witness, how about if I take judicial notice that you had three witnesses to testify to that effect." He twirled his gavel. "That suit everybody?"

"Yes, your honor," Elsie piped up.

Yocum didn't answer immediately. He made a show of consulting with his client. After they huddled together for a long moment, the attorney said, "As a courtesy to those fine ladies outside, for their comfort and convenience, we will accept the judge's generous proposal."

The judge dismissed the witness, and she departed in haste.

Judge Callaway pointed his gavel at Elsie. "Any witnesses on behalf of the state?" he asked.

Elsie stood, pulling the damp skirt off the back of her thighs. She wondered what temperature the courtroom would register. The back of her blouse was soaked; she could feel it.

The judge, cloaked in a voluminous black robe, looked comfortable, cool as a cucumber, she thought. His high forehead bore no beads of sweat, his shirt collar was dry. Maybe it helps that he's bald, she decided. Or maybe he's made of ice. The defense attorneys found that pleas for mercy on their client's behalf almost always fell on deaf ears in Callaway's court. The nickname they coined for him was "Maxaway," because he often imposed the maximum penalty and rarely granted probation.

"The state has seven witnesses outside, Judge," she said.

Lazily, he stretched and leaned back in his chair. "Well, let's hear what one or two of them have to say."

Got it, Elsie thought. The judge didn't want any overkill.

She called three witnesses. Two of them had never heard of the defendant or his charge. They told the court they could be impartial, if called as jurors for the case. The third witness thought he'd seen something about it on television. He remembered a fire at a hotel. Under questioning, he assured the court that he could put the news coverage out of his mind, and decide the case on the evidence alone.

By the time her third witness stepped down, the heat made huge sweat rings under Elsie's arms, and her hair was damp with perspiration. She asked the judge whether she might put on further evidence: he shook his head.

"I have to wrap this up," he said. "We have a court en banc meeting at three. Defendant's motion for change of venue is overruled. Court is adjourned."

After the judge departed, Elsie turned to the defense attorney. "Always a pleasure, Billy."

His tone was hostile as he said, "I won't forget that remark about my wife." Without waiting for a response, he turned to his client.

Flush with the satisfaction of her victory, Elsie said to his back, "I figured you were going to call her next. Or your mother, maybe. Is your mother out there in the hall?"

He wheeled back, outraged. "My mother passed away when I was a boy. Have some respect."

"Oh. Sorry." Elsie blushed, but her face was already red with heat.

I never know when to shut up, she thought, as Yocum stormed out with his client.

Chapter 12

INSIDE THE HOT cinder-block room, Tanner Monroe sat on the top bunk of the metal bunk bed, swinging his bare feet over the side, jabbing at his middle finger with a ball-point pen.

He looked up. "Don't move," he said.

In the corner facing the wall, Barry Bacon crouched with his arms wrapped around his knees. "My legs are cramping up, man," he said.

"That's too fucking bad," Tanner said, adjusting his position on the narrow mattress. "I gave you two chances."

Barry breathed heavily. His skinny fingers snaked around his calf, and he rubbed the offending muscle.

"Stop it."

Barry wailed in reply. "This is killing me, man. This is bullshit."

"I warned you, asshat. Yesterday and this morning."

Barry didn't reply. He rolled over on his back, stretching out his legs. He turned his face, twisted into a grimace of pain.

Tanner laughed. "Look at you. Pussy."

A rap at the door interrupted Barry's response. Tanner whispered, "Sit up," as a key rattled in the lock.

Lisa Peters's head popped through the open door. "You guys ready for lunch?"

When she looked at Barry huddled on the floor, a puzzled expression replaced the smile she had worn. "Barry? What are you doing?" With a laugh, she added, "That floor's pretty dirty."

He began to gasp in distress. Lisa hurried to him and knelt at his side. "Barry! Are you sick?"

"I picked my nose!"

"Shut up," Tanner said.

"What?" asked Lisa, looking from one boy to the other.

"He said I had to crouch down here like a dog. Because I picked my fucking nose. Jesus," the boy wailed, as he began to cry.

"What's going on here? Tanner?" She turned on the bunk bed and glared at Tanner, her body tensed like a boxer's.

"Oh man, Lisa," Tanner said, hopping down from the top bunk. "It's a sick habit, it'll lose him friends. I was trying to help. Like behavior mod."

"He ain't helping me," Barry cried.

"Oh, dude." Tanner grasped Barry's arm and pulled him to a stand. "I learned it in psych class. Last year. It's like, when you want to quit something, you got to reinforce it. Helps you remember not to do it."

"Tanner, it's not your place," Lisa said, as Barry twisted his arm away from Tanner's hold.

"He made me crawl on the floor like a dog," Barry cried.

Tanner slipped both hands into the pocket of his jeans. "Shit, girls will never come near you if you can't lose your nasty habits. You'll be jerking off your whole life."

"Quit it," Barry said.

"Stop," Lisa ordered. Pointing at the folding chair under the window, she said, "Tanner, give us some space."

Tanner sauntered over to the chair and sat. Crossing an ankle over one knee, he watched them with an innocent face. Lisa gave Barry's shoulder a squeeze. "Do you need anything? An Advil? It's lunchtime. Do you want some private time before you go down to the cafeteria?"

Barry shook his head. His nose was running, and he swiped at it with the back of his hand.

"Dude. Barry," Tanner said in an encouraging voice. "Let's get some damned food. You and me need to hit it before those fucks get their germs all over everything."

Barry nodded, mute.

Tanner rose from the folding chair, approaching Barry with a grin, slapping him on the back. "Let's move. Don't want anybody to sit in our spot." To Lisa, Tanner said, "Me and Barry sit on the end. Near the food line. We always sit there, across from each other."

When Barry didn't respond, Tanner put an arm

around his shoulders and gave him a little shake. "Ain't that right, man?"

Barry bobbed his head, slowly. "Yeah. We got a special spot."

"Come on," Tanner said, walking through the door, but Lisa restrained him with a hand on his arm.

"We're going to have to talk about this. This isn't over. You know I won't tolerate bullying. I won't put up with it."

Tanner Monroe flashed a smile at her, displaying a set of white teeth that were perfectly straight, except for one eyetooth that protruded through the gum like a fang. "Talk with you, Lisa? Hell yeah. Anytime."

Chapter 13

ELSIE BUCKLED HERSELF into the front seat of Ashlock's car. She'd awakened twice the night before, tossing in her bed with nervous anxiety about the challenges of their mission in Tulsa. But now that they were embarking, she found herself in high spirits. She nearly hooted as she said, "I feel like a kid skipping school. Oh my God. Leaving the courthouse on a Wednesday morning, and hitting the road to Tulsa. This is cool."

"Can you turn up the air conditioner any higher?" Chuck said from the backseat.

Ashlock shook his head. "This is as good as it gets."

In misery, Chuck lolled his head on his neck. "Are you a masochist? Get it fixed."

Ashlock adjusted his sunglasses with his right hand. "Car doesn't belong to me. This old sedan is the property of the City of Barton, Missouri. Got to make do with what we've got."

"I don't even care," said Elsie, rolling the window

down on the passenger side and letting the hot wind blow through her hair. "I'm on a road trip to Tulsa. Ash honey, pull into the Sonic so I can get me a big old Diet Coke. I love their crushed ice."

Ashlock did as she asked, and once Elsie had her Coke in hand, they hit the Interstate and headed west.

They drove in silence for several minutes. Once outside the city limits, Elsie watched the countryside fly past. The roadside was blanketed with Queen Anne's lace, dotted with clumps of black-eyed Susans. Colorful roadside tents, striped green and white, red and yellow, stood empty, awaiting delivery of their seasonal fireworks inventory.

"Hey, Ash," Elsie asked, as they zoomed past a bright red and white tent, "why can't they sell fireworks all year round? Is it state or local?"

He smiled. "Look at the lawyer, asking for legal advice. I know we've got a city ordinance banning them in Barton. There's county and state regulation—federal, too. Gunpowder. Serious business." He winked at her behind the sunglasses. "So who's running the show at the office, with you and Harris out of pocket?"

Elsie snickered. "You won't believe this. Madeleine has to cover one of the courts this morning, since we're on the road. She's in Associate Division 1. Handling traffic tickets." Elsie threw back her head and howled.

"Why is that so funny?" Chuck asked.

"Let's just say it's unprecedented."

Elsie read Ashlock's case reports as they drove. When the road flattened out and they made their way across the Oklahoma state line, Elsie asked Ashlock, "What's the plan?"

"We'll check out the bus. It's impounded at the Oklahoma Highway Patrol facility in Tulsa. Then we'll head over to the casino where the boy left the bus. I've set up an appointment to talk to the guy in charge."

"What does he know?"

"He's supposed to line up people who had contact with the kid."

Leaning forward, Chuck asked Ashlock, "What if they hold out on us? What if the manager doesn't line up any witnesses?"

Ashlock made eye contact with him in the rearview mirror. "Then I'll hunt them down, I reckon."

A McDonald's appeared, stretching across and over the highway.

"Pull over at this McDonald's, baby," Elsie said. "I gotta pee."

"We're not that far from Tulsa," Harris complained. "Can't you wait?"

But Ashlock was already in the exit lane. Elsie said, "If I could wait, I wouldn't have asked."

To the silence in the backseat, she added, "Aspartame irritates the bladder."

Ashlock shook his head. "Honey, why do you drink all that diet stuff, then?"

Elsie sighed. "Because I love it."

They exited the vehicle and trod upstairs to the restaurant, which looked over the highway. Elsie detoured into the women's room, while Chuck checked out the Cherokee Indian souvenirs.

When Elsie emerged from the women's room, she saw

Ashlock engaged in conversation with a woman at the ice cream booth. Elsie sidled up to him.

"Never saw him before," the woman was saying.

"Take a good look at the photo," Ashlock urged, holding it where the woman could see it clearly. "It would have been recently, just a few days ago, that the boy might have passed through."

"No," the woman said, steadfastly refusing to look at the mug shot. "I can't remember every face I see."

Ashlock gave Elsie a sidelong glance, and as they turned to go, she whispered, "What's up?"

"Just a shot. It makes sense that he would've stopped here. But I can't get anyone to confirm it."

"Your ice cream buddy wasn't being very helpful."

"No ma'am, she was not."

"Maybe you should love her up a little." She squeezed his arm. "Works on me."

A chuckle escaped from Ashlock as they surveyed the McDonald's counter, where a short blond girl stood alone. "Maybe you'd rather work your magic on that little cutie at the counter."

"Tried it. No luck." But he gave the girl a penetrating look. "Knows more than she's saying, I think."

Chuck walked up, breakfast burrito in hand. "This isn't bad."

He proffered the bag in his hand as they turned to leave, adding, "It came with a hash brown. Anybody want it?"

"Yeah," Elsie said, reaching into the bag. Before taking a bite, she said, "Yum. You sure you don't want it?"

Chuck shook his head. "Deep-fried. Processed."

Elsie split the patty in half and handed a piece to Ashlock, who ate it in a single bite. "Thanks," he said.

When they returned to the vehicle, Elsie leaned back in the seat, drowsy from the morning heat. She dozed the rest of the way to Tulsa, awakening when Ashlock pulled up to the Oklahoma State Highway Patrol building. A state trooper escorted them to the facility where the bus was impounded.

The bus loomed before them, its bright yellow paint still glistening and new, the black letters stating PUBLIC SCHOOLS OF ROGERS ARKANSAS standing out in bold relief. Ashlock pulled out a camera and began to snap photographs of the exterior.

Soberly, Elsie stared at the rust-colored stains on the bumper, forcibly reminded of the woman in the creek bed. She took an involuntary step back from the bloody bus. Was it the juvenile? she pondered. Did he spill this blood? Or was someone else responsible: the mystery man with the jailhouse tattoos?

Ashlock stood by his bag of equipment, snapping on latex gloves. "Elsie?"

She looked up at him. "What?"

"If you all want to go into the vehicle, you'll need to wear some protective gear."

Elsie and Chuck followed Ashlock to the doorway of the bus. When it opened, Elsie was assaulted by the sight of dried blood, saturating the mats, discoloring the floor, and giving off a coppery smell. Elsie recoiled, backing away.

"I don't need to go on it," she said.

Chuck stood behind her. "Me neither, man. You're the doctor."

Ashlock nodded. As he ascended the steps into the interior of the bus, he said over his shoulder, "This is going to take a while."

"We'll wait," Elsie said.

Chuck took a look around. "There's nothing for us to do here. I'll hitch us a ride to the casino." He stuck his head into the doorway of the bus and called to Ashlock, "We're going on to the casino. We'll poke around, wait for you there."

Elsie followed Chuck out of the enormous garage, tension easing with every step that took her further from the bloody bus. As she beat a retreat, she reproached herself for being gutless, escaping the hard reality of the crime with Chuck, while leaving Ashlock to do the dirty work. She'd seen plenty of blood and corpses in the evidence she'd handled at trial, but looking at evidentiary photos was vastly different from confronting the real thing. For the first time in years, she entertained a moment of self-doubt; maybe Madeleine was right, maybe she wasn't ready to prosecute a murder case.

Numbly, she followed Chuck to the reception area of the patrol headquarters. She remained in a funk, barely listening as Chuck used his big city schmooze to charm a female trooper into giving them a ride to the Jackpot Casino, outside the city limits of Tulsa.

From the front seat of the patrol vehicle, he turned to Elsie with a mischievous grin. "We're going to have a little fun. Okay?"

Chapter 14

A FRIGID BLAST of air-conditioning struck Elsie as she and Chuck entered the Jackpot Casino.

Coming in from the midday sun of a cloudless Oklahoma summer sky, she was temporarily blinded by the darkness inside the casino. As her eyes adjusted, they took in glittering colored lights from rows of slot machines.

Though it was only noon, the Jackpot was doing a brisk business. The musical play of the machines rang in Elsie's ears. She waved her hand through a cloud of smoke emanating from players nearby.

"I guess they have a smoking section," she said to Chuck.

He barked a short laugh. "This is an Indian casino, sweetheart. The whole place is a smoking section. The American Indian introduced us to the tobacco leaf."

Elsie followed Chuck as he threaded his way past

gaming tables and through jangling machines occupied by gray-haired women, some with walkers and oxygen tanks in tow. When he walked up to the bar and slid onto a stool, she followed suit.

"I'll have a Boston Lager," he told the bartender.

Elsie gasped. "You can't have a drink."

"Watch me."

"But we're working."

"I'm taking a lunch break."

He paid for the beer and slipped a twenty-dollar bill from his wallet.

"We're way outside the McCown County line, pal," he said to Elsie. "I'm going to play some slots. If you see Ashlock before I do, come look for me. I'll be out on the floor."

With that, he walked off, leaving Elsie alone on a bar stool.

She would've followed, but he clearly didn't seek her company. She wasn't sure what she should do. Twirling on the stool, she sniffed the air of the casino. It wasn't so bad. Pretty smoky, but combined with a nice air freshener smell. She'd been in worse places.

The bartender approached. "Can I get you something, ma'am?" He was a good-looking young man with jet black hair.

Elsie sighed, propping her elbow on the bar. "I could use a soda, I guess."

"Soda's free. On the house," he said, filling a plastic cup with ice. "Coke or Diet Coke?"

"Give me a real one," Elsie said. "Maybe I'll live a

little." She was morose; maybe a shot of corn syrup would lift her spirits. *Goddamned case*, she thought. *The suspect's a kid, and I'm odd man out on the prosecution team, but it doesn't matter—because I'm afraid of the sight of blood. I'm a total loser.*

As the bartender set down the Coke, he pointed out a customer service area. "See that over there? If you go register with them, they'll give you free play."

"What do you mean?"

"Sign up for your Jackpot account, and they'll give you a ten-dollar credit. You can play on the house."

Elsie blinked. "No kidding?" She looked over at the customer service booth. She had nothing else to do, and no one to talk to. Chuck was immersed in a game of Flaming Sevens. And she was not too happy, being left alone with her private reflections.

"Thanks for the tip," she said, and put fifty cents by her napkin. Wandering over to the customer service window, she obtained a J card in her name, with a ten-dollar credit.

She had to put money in the machine to initiate the credit account. Checking her purse, she saw that all she had was a five-dollar-bill. She counted on Ashlock to pick up her lunch tab. With a shrug, she pulled out the lonely bill and slipped it into the machine. After carefully viewing the buttons, she made a twenty-cent bet.

Which she lost.

"This is no fun," she muttered, but she pushed the button again, nonetheless. This time, her twenty-cent bet earned her six cents.

She laughed ruefully. "Why does anyone play these games?" Looking around at her fellow inhabitants of the dark casino, she shook her head, feeling a little superior. Glad she was playing on the casino's dime, she doubled her bet and pushed the button again.

Nothing. A waitress in a black rayon miniskirt sauntered by, calling, "Beverages. Cocktails. Beverages."

Elsie saw that she was bearing a tray of icy colas.

"Are those free?"

The woman nodded. Elsie took one from the tray. She would have tipped the woman, but every penny she had was locked up in the Triple Diamonds slot machine. She gulped a mouthful of Coke and hit the button again.

The machine lit up. Happy music played. Fireworks and flying coins appeared on the computer screen.

"What the fuck," Elsie pondered, clutching her plastic cup.

"Look there," said a man sitting nearby, pointing at her game screen. "You won one hundred and seventy dollars."

"No," Elsie said.

"Yes, ma'am."

"No way," she countered, but she studied the screen; the numbers confirmed her neighbor's words. The words BIG WINNER danced before her eyes.

"Oh my gosh," she said, registering the thrill. "Oh my goodness gracious sakes." She turned to her new friend at the nearby machine. "What do I do now?"

He said, "Do whatever you want. You can keep playing, or you can push that button to print out your ticket. Then you can play with the ticket or cash it in."

She gave the cash-out button a jolly tap with her index finger. "I'm cashing it in," she said jubilantly. "I want to hold that money in my hand."

Elsie ran up to the cashier's window, where they paid out the money. She shut it up in her purse and walked up to Chuck.

"I won. Can you believe it?"

"Well, sit down here and rub some luck off on me. I can't win shit."

She sat down at the machine next to him, smiling expansively as the cocktail waitress approached them. It was the same woman who provided Elsie her soda earlier, a trim woman in her early forties with frosted highlights in her lacquered hair.

"Can I get you guys something?"

Chuck looked up at her, morose. "I'll take a bottled water."

"You want another Coke, honey?" the woman asked Elsie.

"No, I think I'll have something else. Bring me a gin and tonic." She turned back to the slot machine, slipped a twenty-dollar bill into it, and watched it light up.

Chapter 15

WHEN ASHLOCK ARRIVED after two, Elsie jumped from her red vinyl casino chair and flung herself on him.

"I'm winning," she cried. "Look, I'm up thirty bucks. Isn't that cool? I'll buy your lunch."

He held her at arm's length, scrutinizing her. "How much have you had to drink?"

Her hundred-watt smile faltered. "I had a victory drink. Or two."

"Two times what?" Ashlock swung on Chuck Harris, who was standing nearby. "What the hell are you two doing?"

Chuck shook his head. "I'm just killing time, playing some penny slots. But I think your girlfriend's on a toot."

Elsie gasped with outrage. "You liar! You ordered the first beer."

Chuck picked up his jacket, neatly draped over the vinyl back of a red chair, and put it on. "I had a beer—

about two hours ago," he said, buttoning the top button of his coat.

Elsie blinked with surprise. Could so much time have actually passed? She said, "That could not have been two hours ago. It feels like it's been thirty minutes. Maybe twenty." Sneaking a glance at the half-full plastic tumbler nearby, she tried to calculate whether it was her second or third, but her recall was a shade fuzzy. The Jackpot poured a strong cocktail.

Ashlock shook his head, disapproval lining his face. "You smell like gin. I can't believe this." He turned to go, with Chuck Harris at his heels.

"Where are you guys going?" she cried.

"I'm going to talk with the manager, see what witnesses he drummed up."

Elsie punched a button on the slot machine. "Let me cash out. I'll come with you."

Chuck turned back to her. With reproach, he said, "You can't take a statement, not in the shape you're in. Why don't you just stay here and sober up?"

Elsie watched them as they walked away and ducked into the customer service booth. She dropped back onto her red chair, deflated.

This is all Chuck's fault, she tried to tell herself, but she couldn't truly believe it. She knew it was her own fault; she'd thrown her professional obligations out the window. Though she would like to blame her slipup on the tensions regarding the case, or her reaction to the bloody bus, she knew either was a shabby excuse.

Gambling was stupid, a vice she could ill afford;

and she could hardly believe she had trifled with it. The gin helped. *Guess that's why they're so obliging with the drinks*, she thought, shamefaced.

Sighing, she read the voucher she held in her hand. How had she managed to turn one hundred and seventy dollars into thirty-seven dollars? "Easy come, easy go," she said aloud.

The friendly cocktail waitress walked by again, stopping when she saw Elsie.

"You want another G&T, hon?"

"No, don't think so," Elsie said with an embarrassed laugh. "Hey, is there a snack bar in here?"

"Sure thing, right behind the Wheel of Fortune. Buffet is on the other wall."

Elsie cashed in her ticket and headed to the snack bar with her fistful of small bills. Sitting with a hot dog and chips, she ruminated over her bad behavior. She'd messed up, big-time, she knew.

Chuck might tattle on her to Madeleine, which would further complicate Elsie's relationship with her boss. But he couldn't do so without incriminating himself, she reasoned. At any rate, Elsie and Madeleine never enjoyed mutual admiration. If Elsie could whistle "The Missouri Waltz" while tap dancing and drinking a glass of water, Madeleine would still fail to be impressed.

But aside from the specter of Madeleine's displeasure, she knew for a fact that Ashlock was mad at her; that stung. She valued Ashlock's good opinion almost as much as his affection, and as she moped over her hot dog, she feared she had threatened both.

"Your luck run out, hon?"

Startled, Elsie looked up to see who had spoken. Her cocktail friend stood at the snack bar, eating a soft pretzel.

"Give me a little cup of Velveeta, Earl," the woman told the man at the counter.

"No," Elsie said, in reply to her question. "I mean, I made some money on the slots."

"Then why are you looking blue?"

"I'm in the doghouse." Elsie made a face. "Drinking on the job."

The waitress laughed, walking up to Elsie's table in her high-heeled shoes, and taking a seat beside her. "Oh my. It feels good to get off my feet for a minute. These old shoes are killers."

"I bet."

"If the boss saw me sitting on my butt, I'd be in the doghouse with you. But he's in a closed-door meeting." She turned around to see that the door to customer service was still secured, then whispered to Elsie, "With some cops."

Elsie nodded, pulling her chair closer to the woman as her brain clicked into investigative mode. "What's up?"

The woman shrugged. "No one knows. Some big secret deal. Probably about that bloody bus."

Elsie smiled to encourage her. "Tell me about that."

The woman said, "It hasn't even hit the papers around here, but there was this kid, living in a bloody school bus parked right out there in the parking lot. At the Jackpot. Can you believe that?"

Elsie inched closer, trying to keep her expression neutral, and continued to dig. "Did you ever see the kid?"

The woman shifted in her seat. "You better believe I saw him. He hit me up on two different days, trying to get served. Nervy little shit. Didn't look a day over sixteen. Wouldn't take no for an answer."

"Was he alone?"

"Yeah. When I saw him."

Inwardly, Elsie cheered as she calculated the impact the waitress's testimony would have on the boy's "mystery kidnapper" claims. Nodding, her eyes glued to the woman, Elsie said, "What did he look like?"

"Nothing special. Not that big. Strong, though. Stronger than he looked."

"How do you know that?"

The waitress dipped a hunk of the pretzel in the bright orange cheese sauce, stirring the bread around the cup.

"Because he hit on me. Here I am, old enough to be his mother. But when I was walking to my car after my shift last week, he sure enough hit on me."

She sucked the cheese off the pretzel, leaning in to whisper in Elsie's ear. Elsie could smell Velveeta on her breath.

"Wouldn't take no for an answer."

An expression flickered over the woman's face, but disappeared so quickly, Elsie couldn't read it. Was it a look of simple annoyance? Or had Elsie seen a gleam of pride?

Chapter 16

No one spoke as the Barton police vehicle made its way back toward Missouri. Behind sunglasses, Ashlock's eyes were trained on the road. In the backseat, Chuck Harris worked the crossword from the *Tulsa World* newspaper.

Elsie held a legal pad on her lap, smoothing the top page. The gin and tonic buzz was gone, replaced by a guilty sense of accomplishment. A triumphant smile played on her mouth.

She broke the silence. "Good thing I found that cocktail waitress. She's the only witness we nailed down."

Her companions maintained an unhappy reticence.

She continued, "It's not your fault that the Jackpot manager wouldn't cooperate. Looks like he led you guys on a wild-goose chase."

No response.

Elsie was determined to wrest an acknowledgment of her coup from her companions in the vehicle. She held up the notepad containing the woman's signed statement. Tucked inside the pages, a copy of the juvenile's mug shot bore the waitress's initials, marked in blue ink.

Displaying the statement so that Ashlock could not ignore it, she said, "Do you think I missed my calling? Maybe I should've been a cop."

"Maybe you should've been a barfly," Chuck offered from the backseat.

Elsie paused, waiting in vain for Ashlock to come to her defense. When no retort came, she turned partway around in her seat to face Harris.

"The grapes. The grapes are very sour, I think."

"The grapes at the winery? Fermented grapes?" Chuck quipped.

"Damn," she said, turning back around and facing forward in the passenger seat. "Give me a fucking break. I saved the day."

Ashlock still didn't speak. Elsie fidgeted for several long moments, considering how to best break the ice. She decided to do the right thing, and admit her gaffe. Surely if she owned up to her misconduct, he would relax and be restored to good humor.

At length, she said, "Hey, Ash. Sorry about the slipup. The gin. You know I'd never want to let you down."

He spoke at last, keeping his eyes on the road. "You lucked out. But it was stupid and irresponsible."

Uncomfortable, she shifted in her seat. "I know. I said it was."

"Maybe you should stick to the courtroom."

Maybe you should stick it up your ass, she thought.

After all, everything had turned out okay. And he could hardly be totally surprised at her blunder; she had a history of looking for trouble, as Ashlock knew perfectly well. Exhaling a frustrated breath, she asked, "How long do you want me to grovel?"

"I just want you to understand."

"I do. I understand." With a rush of anger, mixed with guilt, she said, "You used to be nicer to me. You know that?"

When he didn't acknowledge her, she knew she should back off. But she turned to him and increased the volume of her voice. "You used to be nicer to me, before I was sleeping with you."

Shaking his head, he said, "Not the time or the place." Signaling a right turn, he took an exit off I–44.

"Why are you pulling off? You said no one at this Mc-Donald's could identify him, when you asked them this morning."

Ashlock parked the car near the entrance of the Mc-Donald's they had visited earlier in the day. Unbuckling his seat belt, he said, "There was a McDonald's cup in the bus. Just a hunch. I'm going in to check it out." Looking through his mirrored glasses, he said, "I won't need any assistance. You two can stay in the car."

He slammed the door shut and strode toward the entrance.

Elsie and Chuck looked at each other.

"Trouble in paradise?"

"Yeah. Afraid so," Elsie said.

"He'll get over it."

Elsie nodded in agreement, surprised at Chuck's sympathetic tone.

After a brief silence, Chuck observed, "He's kind of controlling, huh? Typical cop."

"He's not, really," Elsie said, thinking, *Is he? Didn't used to be.*

Chuck clucked his tongue. With a grimace, he said, "Typical. I've been around a lot of cops. They're not bad guys, they're just bad for women. Not very good relationship material."

Shifting in her seat, Elsie searched for a response to defend Ashlock. "I don't think you can make a blanket generalization like that. About an entire profession."

Troubled, she perused the waitress's witness statement again. It was a lucky find, because the woman established that she had encountered the juvenile on multiple occasions, and the boy was always alone. No mystery man, no kidnapper, no hulking figure with a knife at the boy's back. The waitress's testimony would contradict Tanner Monroe's claim that he was a prisoner of the "other dude" who purportedly committed the murder.

Despite the tension with Ashlock, holding the witness statement in her hands gave Elsie a sense of relief. It lessened the anxiety that had been nagging at her, when she wondered whether it was possible that Tanner Monroe was innocent of the crime. She skimmed the casino waitress's statement yet again. It did not mesh with the story provided by Monroe. And they couldn't both be telling the truth. Either Tanner Monroe was, as he claimed, the prisoner of the "other dude" who killed Glenda Fielder;

or Monroe was the "nervy little shit" that the waitress described, acting alone.

"So the other casino employees had nothing to say?" she asked Chuck.

"Got nothing. Zip."

The casino employees who met with Ashlock and Chuck in the manager's office told a different story from the waitress; they maintained, individually and collectively, that they could not identify the juvenile. Although the manager acknowledged that the bus sat in the casino lot for several days, he steadfastly refused to provide further information.

Ashlock's search of the bus had netted an important find, however. In addition to blood and hair samples on the bus, he discovered a bloody knife wedged under the driver's seat. The weapon was bagged and tagged, soon to undergo testing at the Barton Police Department.

Elsie slipped the waitress's witness statement into a file folder as she thought about the knife. The knife would tell the tale, she thought. It was surely the weapon used to cut Glenda Fielder's throat; and the forensic results would determine that with certainty. If that knife could also be tied to Tanner Monroe, through prints or other tests, she would put all her doubts to bed and shut the door on them. She would set herself to the task of convicting the boy of murder, and go after that conviction, whole hog.

While Elsie and Chuck waited for Ashlock to return from the Oklahoma McDonald's, Elsie opened the passenger side door, hoping to catch a passing afternoon breeze. Glancing in the backseat, she saw that Chuck appeared to be asleep. She dug ice from the bottom of her

Coke cup, and rubbed a melting cube along her neck. It seemed that Ashlock had been gone a long time.

She considered going in after him, but then he appeared, walking to the car with a leisurely stride. She couldn't read his face, partially hidden by the sunglasses.

He opened the car door, slid inside, and put the key in the ignition.

"Well?" she said.

He started the car and put it in gear.

"Any luck?" she asked.

He nodded. "There's a little dark-haired girl, works at the counter. She didn't positively ID the mug shot. But she said it resembled a kid who was in last week."

In the backseat, Chuck roused himself. "Good job, Ashlock. What about a second passenger? The 'other dude'?"

"She said the kid she remembers was alone. Hung around after he ate, played video games."

Elsie reached over and gave Ashlock's arm a happy squeeze. "Ash, that's great. It knocks the stuffings out of his claim. Does anybody back her up?"

"Her coworker, the blonde I talked to this morning, still claims she can't remember. The girl acts like a scared rabbit. But I got another witness, a guy who works in the kitchen."

"What did he say?" Elsie asked.

"He identified the bus. He said he was on break, smoking a cigarette in the parking lot, and noticed that school bus had blood stains down the back. Thought it was strange."

"What else does he know?"

"Nothing. Never saw the driver."

Chapter 17

IT WAS DUSK when Ashlock pulled the car into the courthouse parking lot. Chuck Harris hopped out without ceremony and raced off for the comfort of his own vehicle. Elsie and Ashlock sat in silence, watching Harris hurry away.

Elsie spoke first. "You want to get something to eat?"

Ashlock frowned, shook his head. "I should log this stuff in right now. I better get my reports written up, too, while everything is fresh. I'm heading straight over to the PD."

"Oh," said Elsie. "You still mad about the casino?"

He exhaled, taking off his glasses and rubbing his eyes. "I'm not happy about it."

Unbuckling her seat belt, she turned in her seat so that she could see his face at a better angle. "Are we going to go around and around on this?"

"I'm still disappointed in you."

"You ain't my daddy, Ash. I get this feeling that you want to punish me for what happened back there. Just stop it. Snap out of it."

"You think I can just overlook it?" He turned his head to look her in the eye. "I think what you did was unprofessional. Immature."

His words stung, but she affected a careless air. "I know. I have feet of clay. I've never deceived you about that." She leaned against the inside of the door, uncomfortably aware that the armrest dug into her back.

"I gotta be honest. You've got a lot of growing up to do."

Her heart hammered with hurt, but she tried to keep her face impassive. "Because you're so grown up."

"I'd say that's right. I am."

"While we're being so honest, here's something that has me puzzled. If you're so grown up, such an old-fashioned fucking straight arrow, why aren't you interested in forging a real relationship? That integrates all the parts of your life?"

He started to speak, but she interrupted him. "Because you obviously are delighted to fuck my brains out every chance you get. But you don't want to make a commitment. Won't let me anywhere near your kids." Her voice broke on the last sentence, but she covered it with a laugh. Mockingly, she added, "That seems pretty goddamned immature to me."

She thought she detected a flinch.

"Cops make bad husbands. Just not good marriage material," he said.

"I know you've got a divorce under your belt. Not that you've ever confided in me about it," she said. "But you were a kid then."

"And you're a kid now."

She fumbled for the door handle.

"Okay. That's it." She managed to unlatch the door and flung it wide open. "You're not looking for a relationship that's going anywhere. And you're not too crazy about me."

She struggled to get her papers and purse in one armload. With a ball of rage wedged in her chest, she added, "If I'm just going to have a fuck buddy, maybe I'll find one who's more fun."

He didn't respond. Elsie slammed the door, stalking off in search of her car. She didn't look back.

Chapter 18

THE HEAT ON July 4 was merciless. As Elsie pulled her car into the lot adjoining Juvenile Hall, she heard the newscaster announce that the temperature was nearing the record set in the legendary heat wave of 1954. His voice over the radio sounded positively jolly. Elsie assumed it was easy to exult over the blistering temperature while sitting in an air-conditioned studio.

In the juvenile facility, she gasped at the stifling atmosphere. Sitting behind the glass enclosure, a woman fanned herself with a manila file.

"Central air's on the fritz," she said.

Elsie groaned. The woman waved her inside. Elsie passed into the juvenile office, where she saw Lisa Peters sitting in front of a sputtering fan.

Lisa fixed her with a suspicious look. "What are you doing here?"

"I got holiday duty. Same as you, I guess. I'm making the rounds to see if any charges need to be filed today."

Lisa laughed. "How did you pull Fourth of July?"

"I live a charmed existence." Elsie had in fact volunteered for Fourth of July duty. A long-anticipated holiday with Ashlock at nearby Table Rock Lake was out, since their relationship hit the skids. The holiday duty had fallen to Bree, but Elsie she reasoned that, since she was stuck in town anyway, with nothing to do and no one to do it with, she should let Bree have the chance to enjoy the Fourth with her daughter, Taylor. And Elsie might make headway with the Monroe case while checking in on the juvenile office.

As a gesture of thanks, Bree had invited Elsie for dinner at her house the night before. It had started out as a pleasant evening, relaxing on Bree's back porch while she grilled burgers. But Elsie wore out her welcome when she got on a rant about Ashlock, cataloguing his flaws. When Bree's daughter moved from the supper table to the TV, Elsie amplified her whining; and when Bree let out a yawn, Elsie knew it was time to go.

She had headed home to her apartment, determined to do something productive: clean out a kitchen cabinet, or cull out the expired bottles of salad dressing from the refrigerator. But when she opened the refrigerator door, she saw a bottle of Chardonnay, three-quarters full and enticingly cold.

She drank it down. It was enough wine to fuel determination: she would have it out with Ashlock. She picked up her cell phone and called his number.

A drunk dial.

When Ashlock picked up, Elsie had tried to sound cheery. "Happy Fourth of July Eve."

A moment's silence followed, then: "Elsie?"

"Yeah, Elsie. Sorry I didn't identify myself. I didn't figure you'd forget my voice so quick."

Another pause. "What can I do for you?"

The formal tone of his voice made tears sting her eyelids; she rubbed her eyes with an angry swipe, glad he couldn't see it.

"Ash, Jesus; what the hell is going on with you? I thought we had something solid, a real connection. I can't believe that two gin and tonics could make you turn tail and run."

"It wasn't two."

"Goddamn it, it doesn't matter whether it was two or not. The issue—what I'm talking about—is, what happened to us? What happened to you?"

Ashlock cleared his throat into the receiver; she knew that quirk, it meant he was buying time before he answered. "I have a lot of affection for you. And respect. But Elsie—"

"Affection? And respect? Am I your grandmother? Your kindly old grade school teacher? It doesn't sound like you're talking to me; sounds like you're talking about someone you haven't been in the sack with."

"We've had a lot of fun. But I've got more to consider."

She pinched her lips together. This was not how she'd wanted the conversation to go.

"I have my kids to consider. I'm a father."

"You were a father last winter, weren't you? When you were so hot to hook up with me?"

With that, she had heard him sigh into the phone. "My son is going into high school. Burton, he's fourteen. He wants to be in Barton with me, full-time, and his mom is considering it."

"And why," she said, her voice sounding strangled, "why would that mean we can't see each other?"

He was silent for a long moment; Elsie knew he was choosing his words carefully. "You don't know my ex. Don't know how it is with her. Since she moved back to the Bootheel, she got religion again. If she hears about you, if one of the kids carries back stories, there will be hell to pay."

"So she's got religion. Good god, Ash, I'm a lawyer—a prosecutor. I'm not a crack whore. What's she going to hear?"

"Elsie, she's Assemblies. Assemblies of God. No drinking, no cussing. No dancing."

"Okay. I'll give up dancing."

She waited for his laugh, but no sound of mirth came through the phone.

When he spoke, she could hear it: that note of finality in his voice. His mind was made up. "Elsie, I have only the highest regard for you—"

"Fuck you," she said, and tossed the phone on the kitchen table.

By morning, she had a new resolve: true romance was not her skill set. But prosecution was something she was good at, an important job that deserved her full attention. It was time to quit thinking about Bob Ashlock. She would focus on Tanner Monroe.

At the hot office in Juvenile Hall, Elsie prepared to tangle with Lisa.

Lisa said, "I don't have anything for you over here. Things are pretty quiet, considering. Maybe they're all in a coma from the heat."

"Is the air-conditioning out all over the building?"

Lisa made a face. "Yeah. God, it's awful down there in detention. I've got to make the rounds in a minute, but I've been putting it off. I know they're going to go off on me, and there's nothing I can do."

Elsie sat in the chair Lisa had vacated. "You're scaring them straight, baby."

"Hey, this isn't funny. Those kids are going to riot if we don't cool things down." Turning to the sweltering secretary, Lisa asked, "Do you think the juvenile judge would consider some kind of break for the holiday? I thought I might try to take the kids to the city swim park."

I think the heat is getting to you; you must have lost your mind, Elsie thought.

However, she didn't need to voice her objection, because the secretary said, "You won't be able to get ahold of him today, unless somebody turns up dead."

Elsie nodded in silent agreement.

A dozen grocery store cupcakes sat upon a crowded desk, frosted with garish red and blue icing, and topped with plastic picks bearing the American flag. Lisa gestured toward it. "Don't let it be said that the judge wasn't thinking of those kids in detention on the holiday. He brought these in yesterday and said that we're to deliver a cupcake to each of our detention charges. A little Fourth of July gift from the judge."

The cupcakes were suffering from the heat. The icing was melting; drops of red and blue food coloring soaked into the pleated paper holders.

"He's all heart," Elsie offered.

"I get to play Santa," Lisa said. Gingerly, she picked up the plastic box, trying to keep the icing off her. "I'd best get going. These cupcakes aren't improving with age."

"Take them picks out first," the secretary snapped. "You don't want somebody jabbed in the eyeball."

As Lisa pulled the little flags from the cupcakes, Elsie rose. "I'll keep you company."

Lisa paused to scrutinize Elsie, her brow wrinkled. "What for?"

"For fun," Elsie said. With a grimace, she wiped a streak of icing that was close to dripping on Lisa's arm. "I'm not the enemy, Lisa, really. To know me is to love me."

Lisa shrugged, heading through the doorway and into the hall. Walking behind, Elsie asked, "How's your buddy doing?"

Lisa stiffened. "I suppose you mean Tanner Monroe."

"Well, yeah," Elsie said, following Lisa as she made her way through the labyrinth of converted offices and down the stairs to the detention quarters. "I'm not picking a fight, honest to God. He's taken a shine to you, that's all."

Without turning to look back at her, Lisa said, "You should know that I'm opposing the certification."

Elsie's brow wrinkled with disbelief. "Even after the trip to Oklahoma? We found the murder weapon. And the blood on the knife is the victim's, Glenda Fielder; and the fingerprint expert at the PD says there's a print on the knife that matches Tanner Monroe. And there's no mystery man; didn't you hear that?"

Lisa paused at the first door in the residence hall. "Maybe you all just heard what you wanted to hear. There could be an explanation; we don't know everything that went on. That's what I keep telling Hank, every time we have a consultation here at juvenile." She rapped on the door and opened it a crack. "Madison? I've got something for you and Janelle." Turning back to Elsie, Lisa said, "You have no authority to talk to these kids."

"Wouldn't dream of it," Elsie said, taking a step back. "I'm just here for the obligatory holiday check-in. Here to help out." *Here to help straighten you out about Tanner Monroe*, she added to herself.

Lisa ignored her, opening the door just wide enough to slip through. No cool air wafted from inside the room; the temperature had to be as high inside as out. Elsie felt sorry for the kids in detention, in spite of herself; they were doing some miserable time today.

She heard Lisa's voice, murmuring something about a treat from the judge, and a clear response from the recipient.

"Shit! Gross!" one of the inmates cried.

Lisa reappeared and pulled the door shut.

"Don't tell me. They loved it," Elsie said, and was rewarded by a flash of mirth in the juvenile officer's eyes.

"Wouldn't you," Lisa responded, lifting the oozing cupcakes up to Elsie's face.

Afterward, they walked more companionably down the hallway, though Elsie took care to stand back when Lisa entered the detention cells. As they reached the last doorway, Lisa pulled a key from her pocket.

"These guys are in lockup," she explained. With a warning look, she said to Elsie, "No snooping."

With a look of innocence, Elsie held up both hands. Lisa balanced the cupcake box in her left hand, turning the key with her right. After a quick rap at the door, Lisa opened it a crack, saying, "Tanner? Barry?"

Tanner Monroe's voice came through the door. "Wassup, Lisa?"

"I've got cupcakes for you."

Elsie leaned against the plaster wall of the hallway, as Lisa slipped through the door into the room, shutting it behind her.

Her nose wrinkled. A terrible smell had wafted through the door when Lisa had opened it. *Like someone crapped his pants*, she thought.

When Elsie heard Lisa's screams, she flung herself on the door, but it was locked. Elsie fumbled with the knob, pounding on the door with her other hand.

"Open up, for God's sake," she cried.

Lisa's screams evolved into a keening sound, and Elsie saw that someone was rattling with the doorknob on the other side of the door. When the door flung open, Lisa stood before her, her face a frozen mask of shock. An overwhelming stench hit Elsie, as the stink of defecation came from inside the room.

Elsie stuck her head in the door. A body hung by a bedsheet from the support beams overhead. The box fan in the barred window ruffled the dead boy's hair, blowing it around his gray face. Under his dangling feet, the cupcakes were scattered on the dirty tile floor.

Elsie tore her gaze from the body, turning to stare at Tanner Monroe. Tanner reclined in the top bunk of a metal bunk bed, his head resting on two pillows. He held a ballpoint pen in his right hand, using it to draw on his left.

The boy looked up from his task. "Hey, man," he said. "Can I have his cupcake?"

Chapter 19

Despite the bright Monday sun shining outside, the interior of the third floor courtroom was dim. The venetian blinds at the windows were drawn and shut; the courtroom door was locked, and yellowed fabric blinds had been pulled down to cover the glass panels of the entry. One of the fluorescent bulbs in the overhead light fixture flickered, threatening to cast the room into darkness.

Judge Barnes, who handled the juvenile cases, sat at the bench, mulling over the paperwork in a file. At the counsel table before him, Tanner Monroe sat with his guardian ad litem, Maureen Mason, at his side. Hank Cox, the chief juvenile officer, stood near the bench, waiting for the judge to speak.

Judge Barnes looked up, his face grim. "Where are the boy's parents?"

"We gave Mr. Monroe's mother notice of the hear-

ing, your honor. Sent it to her address by registered mail;
she received it," Hank said. Hank Cox was in his late fifties, with graying hair and a goatee, but his face still bore
the marks of his good-looking youth. A thirty-year veteran of the juvenile office, he spoke with confidence. He
dredged through papers resting at his spot on the left end
of the counsel table; finding what he sought, he handed
it to the judge.

The judge examined it briefly. "Mrs. Mason, can you
tell me why the boy's mother isn't present?"

Maureen stood, rising nimbly for a woman of her
girth. "I attempted to contact her by phone, your honor.
Multiple times, and I left messages. She didn't respond."

The judge looked over his glasses, focusing on Tanner.
"What about your father, young man?"

Tanner Monroe shrugged, a slight movement of his
shoulders. His face was frozen, with the look of shell
shock.

"Speak up, please. Have you talked with your parents
since you've been in juvenile custody?"

"No." The word was uttered in a whisper; Tanner
cleared his throat and spoke again. "No, man."

Maureen Mason laid a hand on his arm. "Address him
as 'judge.' Or 'your honor.'"

Tanner jerked his arm away from her touch. "I want
to talk to Lisa."

Seated in the back row of the courtroom gallery, Lisa
Peters stood and took a hesitant step toward the counsel
table, but the judge waved her back. "Mr. Monroe, you
need to consult with your guardian, Mrs. Mason. Miss

Peters works for the juvenile office, and they have filed a petition to transfer you to Circuit Court, to be prosecuted for murder as an adult under the general law. Do you understand?"

"Not Lisa," Monroe said.

"Yes, Mr. Monroe; she is a part of that office, she works with Mr. Cox here. And they have presented me with a report, asking for your transfer, because of the seriousness of the crime that you are alleged to have committed; and because the alleged offense involved viciousness, and force, and violence."

"Vicious?" Tanner echoed. He twisted around, turning to face Lisa at the back of the room. "You called me vicious?"

Lisa slumped in her seat on the wooden bench. Her face crumpled.

Hank Cox spoke up. "Your honor, the juvenile office had no choice in the matter. We have included copies of the police reports, with the evidence obtained from the school bus, tying Tanner Monroe to the murder of Glenda Fielder. It is imperative that he be transferred out of juvenile, to the custody of the Circuit Court and the care of the county jail. Especially now, after the death of Barry Bacon."

Judge Barnes cut him off, his voice sharp. "Hold on, now. Are you trying to say that this young man is responsible for the death of the Bacon boy?"

Hank took a step back from the bench. "Well, no," he said, as Tanner shook his head and whispered, "Shit."

"Because your report doesn't contain either evidence or allegations that Mr. Monroe had a hand in that death."

Tanner spoke from his seat. "What are they trying to say? Like I could tie a sheet around the dude's neck and make him jump off the chair?"

Maureen Mason moved in close to Monroe and hissed in his ear, but he shook her off.

Hank said, "Your honor, I apologize; I don't mean to bring up matters outside of the scope of this hearing. We are not alleging that the death of Barry Bacon is a murder committed by the juvenile, Tanner Monroe; we are only addressing the crime of murder perpetrated against Glenda Fielder."

"All right, then; so long as we're clear. Present your argument, Mr. Cox."

As the chief juvenile officer launched into his rhetoric, Tanner turned again in his seat, locking eyes with Lisa Peters at the other end of the room.

THAT MORNING, ELSIE was assigned to Associate Circuit Court, on the same floor as Tanner Monroe's hearing to stand trial as an adult. Seated at the counsel table, she craned her neck and peered through the window of the courtroom door, looking for signs of activity. Monroe's certification hearing would be concluding soon, and there was certain to be a buzz when it was over.

Veteran traffic attorney Roger Carr sat across from her, whispering intently in his client's ear. Elsie watched the exchange with impatience; she wanted to wrap this up, so she could head into the hallway and check on the status of the certification.

The door to the courtroom opened and she glanced over, hoping that it was a citizen scheduled for a small claims matter, or a child support complaint; something that would not require her attention.

The bailiff ambled to the door, where a young woman stood, holding a pink subpoena. He looked at the slip of paper through his bifocals, then intoned, "Elsie?"

Ah, shit, she thought, rising from her chair. She walked over to the woman with an autopilot smile. "What do we have here?"

The woman held out the subpoena, her eyes flashing. "I'm a victim."

Elsie took her in with a glance: a pretty woman, full-figured in the Ozarks corn-fed way, with curly brown hair pulled into a high ponytail. The subpoena was directed to Thelma James, a witness in the misdemeanor assault case of *State v. Bud Douglas*.

"You see, Ms. James, the time on this subpoena says 9:00 A.M. It's past ten now," Elsie said in a low voice. "You weren't here when the judge called the case. He dismissed it."

"What? Are you kidding me?"

Elsie edged away from the door, so the woman could make her exit. "You were the complaining witness. I couldn't proceed without you." She could see the indignation building in Ms. James's face. Elsie repeated, matter-of-factly, "You weren't here."

"My fiancé's shift isn't over till nine. He has the truck. What was I supposed to do? Hitchhike?"

Elsie glanced at the subpoena again, to get the name right. "Thelma," she began, but the woman cut her off.

"He grabbed my tit. Do you understand?"

Despite herself, Elsie glanced down. They were substantial.

"I was at the Blue Top, having a beer after Dad's chemo. Bud came up, all concerned, and asked after Dad. Then he stuck his hand in my blouse and grabbed my tit."

The defense attorney jumped up from the counsel table and pointed a finger at Thelma. "He apologized," Roger Carr cried.

The woman wheeled on Carr. "Not to me! He apologized to my boyfriend." Looking back at Elsie, she said, "Motherfucker drove to our house the next day, had the nerve to come knocking on the door. He wanted to apologize—to my boyfriend." Pointing at her chest, she said, "These are mine. I'm not anybody's property."

"You're right. Of course." She took Thelma's arm and steered her to the door. "Listen, I can fix this. The judge dismissed without prejudice. I can refile the charge."

Still standing, Roger wailed, "What do you want from Bud? He's sorry."

"Oh, he'll be sorry. That's for sure." Thelma looked back at Elsie, a challenge in the line of her jaw. "So you'll fix it?"

"I can refile. But next time, Thelma, you have to be at court on time."

The woman turned to go, but before she walked out, she called to the counsel table where Roger Carr sat. "You tell him he's a piece of shit. Tell him I said so."

Carr caught Elsie's eye and shrugged, then turned back to his client and resumed their whispered conversation. Elsie stared at the door for a moment, longing to make an escape and check out the progress next door. She walked back to the counsel table and leaned over the back of her chair. "Roger."

He glanced at her, but continued talking in his client's ear.

"Roger. Is he going to plead? To the hit and run?"

The defense attorney smacked the counsel table with an open hand; the sound made Elsie jerk away.

"Could you give us a minute? Would you mind? We're conferring."

"Absolutely. You bet." She stepped away from her chair so swiftly that it teetered. "I'll step out in the hall, give you guys some privacy."

As she pushed open the door, the bailiff called to her from his seat near the judge's chambers. "Where are you off to? Judge will be out here in just a minute."

She paused in the open doorway, her hand on the knob. "I'll be right outside here. Just on the other side of the door."

Roger Carr rose from his seat. "You can't run off. I've got another case set downstairs. I need to wrap this up."

He was still protesting as she shut the door behind her. Scanning the hallway, she saw that the blinds were drawn in the juvenile courtroom. That was the sign that Juvenile Court was still in session. The proceedings were closed.

Chuck Harris was pacing back and forth in the hallway. Elsie hurried over to him.

"What's up, Chuck?" she said.

He paused, then slumped onto a wooden bench set against the wall. "Fuck if I know. What's taking so long?" he asked.

She shook her head. "I've never been involved in the certification process. Makes sense it would take a while."

He shot a glance at her. "Why aren't you in court?"

"I am. I'm doing some traffic stuff, but it's about all pled out. I thought I'd come over here and see what's cooking."

He nodded. Elsie joined him on the bench and they sat quietly for a moment, Harris drumming his fingers on the wooden seat. When the courtroom door opened, she felt him jerk.

Lisa Peters burst through the door and sped past them, eyes downcast. Chuck jumped up and grabbed her arm.

"Well?"

"It's done."

"And?"

"They're transferring him to the county jail. He'll be tried as an adult."

Her face was tearstained. Elsie leaned forward on her seat and said, "You doing all right, Lisa?"

Hesitantly, Lisa nodded, then hung her head. In a low voice, she said, "Hank made the case for it for our office. But I didn't fight it, after everything that's happened. But I just don't know. He swears he didn't kill her. I don't know if I've done the right thing."

Elsie and Chuck exchanged glances. Rising from her seat, Elsie put an arm around the juvenile officer's shoulders. "This day was bound to come. You gave him the benefit of the doubt as long as you could, Lisa."

Lisa exhaled, still looking down. "I shouldn't blame him for what happened to Barry; there's no evidence that he had anything to do with it."

"No," Elsie agreed, adding dryly, "But he sure didn't seem too torn up about it." She nudged Lisa. "Sure wanted that cupcake."

An image of the hanging body of Barry Bacon flashed before Elsie, and she flinched. It would be a long time before that memory faded.

The trio turned as the courtroom door opened again. An ancient bailiff led Tanner Monroe into the hallway. The boy's face was stony, his hands shackled behind his back. Elsie and Chuck stepped back to let them pass, but Lisa Peters approached him, laying a hand upon his shoulder.

"You'll get a fair trial, Tanner. An attorney's going to come see you real soon."

In a flash, Monroe shoved Lisa with his torso, backing her against the iron banister built beside a steep stairwell.

"Stop him," Elsie cried over Lisa's shrieks, as Chuck ran into the nearby courtroom.

The old bailiff moved in slow motion, struggling to pull the boy back, but Monroe resisted; shaking the bailiff off with ease, he pressed his groin against Lisa and bent her backward over the banister. With his face thrust against hers, he said, "You said you were looking out for me. You said you were my friend."

A deputy ran from the courtroom, waving a Taser,

shouting at the juvenile to back away. Tanner ignored the order. He stuck out his tongue and licked Lisa's face, from the point of her chin to the top of her forehead. She twisted her head away, backing over the banister at a dangerous angle.

"You sold me out," he said, his last words before the electric volt was placed against his neck.

As he lay on his stomach on the hallway floor, twitching, Elsie could see markings on two of his fingers. *Like jailhouse tattoos*, she thought.

It looked like they spelled: "LP."

Chapter 20

ELSIE PUT AN arm around Lisa Peters's shoulders. "Come on, hon," she said, propelling Peters down the tiled hallway, toward the Division 2 courtroom. "I'm going to take up a quick plea. Then we'll head downstairs to get you a cup of coffee."

She could feel the woman's shoulders shaking under her cotton blouse. Elsie felt an empathetic tug; she had also been the victim of an angry defendant. It was no picnic, Elsie knew.

After Elsie finished up the traffic business, she steered Lisa to the basement, where the courthouse coffee shop was located. Looking around as they entered, Elsie didn't spy a vacant table. As she surveyed the shop, Bob Ashlock stood. Their eyes met, and Elsie registered a pang; she had not seen him since the terrible spat after returning from Oklahoma.

She and Ashlock locked eyes for a long moment. Just

as she lifted her hand with a tentative wave, he looked away. He studied the round table, picking up a report that lay upon it. Elsie flushed, as if she'd been rejected at the school dance.

But he lifted his eyes and shot Elsie an inquiring glance. "You all want this table? I'm heading out."

Elsie nodded, keeping her expression impassive. She and Lisa scooted through occupied seats and staked their claim to the table. When she walked by Ashlock, she said in a low voice, "Tanner Monroe attacked Lisa in the hall, after he was certified."

"I hate to hear that, Ms. Peters. I expect it shook you up."

Lisa didn't reply, and Ashlock made a move to leave, without further comment. Elsie, adopting a nonchalant tone to compensate for her wounded feelings, asked him, "What's in that report?"

He considered briefly before responding, "Better show it to Madeleine first."

Elsie's jaw sagged. Whatever their personal animosity, she never dreamed he'd cut her off professionally. "You're kidding me. What is it you don't trust me to know?"

Ashlock had the grace to look abashed. "It's not that. It's just that we've got a big break. She wouldn't like it, not being the first to know." When Elsie cut him a reproachful look, he added, "You know how she is."

When she continued to glare, he relented. "You'll keep it to yourself till after I talk to her?" he asked.

Elsie nodded, increasingly intrigued. Even Lisa, who had been sitting withdrawn and silent at the table, looked up with a flicker of interest.

Speaking a notch above a whisper, Ashlock said, "The coroner's report shows that the deceased woman had sexual intercourse shortly before her death. And the crime lab just confirmed—" He broke off to glance around, making certain he was not overheard. "The semen from the vaginal swab is a DNA match with the juvenile."

Elsie dropped into a chair. "Well, shit." She reached over and gave Lisa Peters's shoulder a gentle shove. "What do you think about that? He never 'fessed up to nailing her, that's for sure. Nothing about that came out during interrogation or in his written statement."

Turning to face Ashlock, she looked up at him with an eager expression. "This is great. I've got an idea. That cocktail waitress, that one at the casino. You remember she said he hit on her?" She scooted her chair close to Ashlock. "That is consistent with his sex act with the bus driver. He must have had a thing about doing it with old gals, must've given him a thrill somehow." Turning back to Lisa, she said, "When I said he likes old women, I didn't mean you, Lisa. Obviously."

"He did like me," Lisa said. "He trusted me."

"Don't tell me you're feeling bad for Tanner Monroe? After what just happened in the hallway?" Elsie asked, with disbelief etched in her face.

"I don't know. I don't know what I think. It just seems like, after Barry hung himself, the people in my office wanted to wash their hands of him. Get Tanner out of juvenile as soon as possible."

"Well, hell yeah, they did," Elsie said. Then she let out

a theatrical sigh. "This is huge. Last week we got the fin-gerprint results back, with Tanner Monroe's print right in the victim's blood on that knife. And now this. DNA doesn't lie. I'm officially done with any 'poor innocent kid' concerns. My shadow of doubt is put to bed. Finis."

With fresh energy, Elsie continued to Ashlock, "You think we should talk to the Oklahoma waitress again? Nail down some details about the juvenile's come-on? I could call her. Or we could go back on Saturday."

She paused when she saw the stillness in his face.

"It will be Madeleine's call," he said, rolling up the report into a scroll. "I better get this upstairs."

Slumping back into her chair, Elsie watched him walk out of the coffee shop. Lisa turned and looked at Elsie with a confused expression. "He's your boyfriend, isn't he?"

"Nah," Elsie said. "Not anymore."

"What happened?"

Pride made Elsie sit up straight in the plastic chair. Wrinkling her nose, she said, "We were never all that se-rious. Sheesh. Cops." Pulling a face, she muttered to Lisa, "Great lovers in the sack, lousy lovers out of it."

Chapter 21

WITH A SHOVE, Elsie pushed the door of the Baldknobbers bar open wide. When she stepped in from the blazing summer sun, the darkened room blinded her for a moment. She paused, blinking, as her eyes adjusted.

A poke at her back got her moving.

"What the hell are you blocking the door for?" Breeon groused. "Quit standing like a statue; I want out of this heat."

As the women slid into an empty booth, the cool air rattling out of the air-conditioning unit ruffled the damp hair at Elsie's neck. She slid her finger behind the thick vinyl window shade and peeked outside.

"I don't see anyone coming," she said in a small voice.

Breeon gave her with a skeptical look. "You're expecting a crowd? For your thirty-second birthday?" When Elsie shrugged in response, Breeon said, "But hon, you didn't get the word out. This won't be some kind of big celebration."

Elsie dropped the window blind, extinguishing the ribbon of light and restoring the cavelike atmosphere.

"I didn't expect anything big," she replied, a shade defensive. "I just thought word might get around. People might want to drop by."

"I told you: you should've gone over to your parents' house for supper."

"Nah. Don't feel like it. Seems kind of pitiful."

In fact, Elsie had agreed only a couple of days prior to eat dinner with her parents on her birthday. But when Marge called to ask Elsie's preference as to icing on the cake—buttercream or seven-minute frosting—the conversation turned to Tanner Monroe.

"How is the case going against that poor boy?" Marge had asked.

"You mean Monroe? He cut a woman's throat, Mother. How about the poor victim? Glenda Fielder is dead, thanks to Tanner Monroe."

"I have my reservations. I saw him on TV, on the Joplin news channel. He looks like a boy I had in class last year."

Elsie started to get riled. "Don't blur the lines, Mom. He's not anyone you had in class in Barton. He's a product of the St. Louis public schools. So it's not your fault."

"I didn't suppose it was my fault," Marge had said, tartly. "Lord. It's not a matter of looking for fault."

"As a matter of fact, it is. That's what criminal law is about: figuring out who's at fault, who committed the crime. And making them pay the penalty."

"Are you lecturing me? I don't like your tone. It sounds

like you're trying to pick a fight. Honestly, Elsie, you are cross as two sticks these days."

Elsie's face flushed with a combination of heat and hurt feelings as she said, in a snippy voice, "Then maybe I shouldn't force my company on you and Dad this week."

"Now honey, you're being ridiculous."

"I'm going to go out with the courthouse people. With Bree. I'll check in with you guys sometime this weekend. 'Bye." She hung up without letting her mother respond and proceeded directly to Bree's office to beg for a birthday date.

So they sat at the Baldknobbers, two women in a battered booth.

After they waved a signal to Dixie, two mugs of Bud Light appeared, droplets of moisture coursing down the sides of the chipped glass. "Happy birthday, Elsie," Dixie said, displaying a gap-toothed grin.

"See," Breeon said as the old barmaid sprinted away, "Dixie showed up for your birthday bash."

After swallowing a healthy measure of the mug's contents, Elsie idly sorted through the packets in the sugar dispenser, putting them in order: blue, pink, white.

Breeon sipped at her beer. "Who are you wanting to see? Someone in particular?"

Shrugging, Elsie plucked a stray NutraSweet and jammed it into place with its mates. "Didn't really think about it."

Surveying her with a skeptical look, Breeon shook her head. "Liar. You're ruminating. Over Ashlock."

Elsie's chin jerked up. Cutting her eyes away from Breeon, she gave her head a resolute shake. "Nope."

"Don't bullshit me."

"I'm not ruminating. I don't ruminate."

"You're doing it right this minute."

"Goddamn," Elsie said in a huff, "don't tell me how I feel."

The front entrance opened, and the silhouette of a man appeared in the light. Elsie froze, straining to identify him; but after a glance, she knew it wasn't Ashlock.

Chuck Harris strolled in and crossed over to their table, loosening his tie.

"I can't see a damned thing in here," he said.

Glad for the interruption, Elsie shot him a wry grin. "It's a beautiful day; let's go someplace dark."

Pulling a chair up to the end of the booth, he asked, "What are you all up to?"

"I was about to leave," said Bree.

Elsie swung toward her with an injured look. "What?"

"Baby, I told you I could only stay for one."

With a dose of self-pity, Elsie said, "I knew I should've picked another place. You hate the Baldknobbers."

"Well, you're right about that. I expect a Klan meeting to convene any minute," Breeon said, grasping her bag and rifling the contents. "But the fact is, Taylor will be home at six, straight from soccer; she'll be wanting her supper." Setting a five-dollar bill on the table, she slid out of the booth. "Settle up with Dixie. I'll see you tomorrow."

Elsie started to rise from her seat, but Breeon pushed

her back down with a smile. "Let the chief assistant buy you another round. And happy birthday, hon. You're still just a baby."

After Breeon departed, Elsie caught Chuck regarding her with a quizzical look. "What?" she asked in a cross voice.

"How old are you?"

She bristled. "Why do you need to know?"

He laughed, tipping back in his chair. "Just an innocent question. You're the one announcing your birthday like it's a state holiday."

"I know. You're right." She tucked a stray lock of hair behind her ear, grateful that she'd stopped sweating. "I'm thirty-two. Does that sound old?"

"Nah." Dixie delivered a beer bottle, and he took a swallow. "Younger than me."

Still morose, she studied her beer mug, wiping the condensation with her fingertip. Her glum mood had actually taken her by surprise; she hadn't expected to be troubled by the arrival of another birthday. She supposed her gloomy reaction stemmed from the recent breakup with Ashlock. But that notion was irritating, as well. She had never been the girl who defined herself by romantic relationships, unlike some of her friends, who scrambled from adolescence on to have a boyfriend perpetually in place.

It had never been Elsie's way. As she sat at the barroom table, she reflected. She knew that her life was full, that she was doing important work, that each day provided an opportunity to contribute something significant. But she missed Ashlock. His departure left a void that ached. She allowed herself a moment of longing before she shut the feeling down. Ashlock was gone: history. Out the door.

Maybe she should order another beer, she decided. Looking around the empty bar, she reasoned that there would be no crowd to witness her excess. That was a rare gift in a town the size of Barton.

"Dixie! How about a pitcher over here!"

Chuck switched seats, scooting onto the cracked cushion Bree had vacated. When the pitcher arrived, Elsie shared it, swilling with increasingly fuzzy good cheer as she and Chuck gossiped about the local defense bar in general, and Billy Yocum in particular.

An hour passed. Flushed and pleasantly numb, Elsie polished off another mug, and wiped the beer from her mouth with an incongruously dainty swipe. Lowering her voice to a stage whisper, she leaned across the table and asked, "So what does Madeleine think?"

Chuck's brow furrowed. She noted, with some annoyance, that he looked irritatingly sober. Draping his arm over the back of the booth, he responded in a cool tone. "About what?"

"About the report. The one Ashlock brought over yesterday."

He shrugged, poker-faced, noncommittal. "I don't know that I'm authorized to discuss it."

She flushed, stung. "I'm cocounsel, you idiot."

"You have a tendency to overestimate the importance of your role in this case."

Her eyes flashed. She felt aggrieved, like a boil was

rising deep inside her chest, aching to pop. "Fine. Don't say a thing about it. Hide that double-edged sword."

He shot her a look. "Why do you say that?"

Gotcha, she thought. Nonchalantly, she asked, "Say what?"

"That it's a double-edged sword. Madeleine was really excited about it. The DNA in the semen ties the juvenile to the victim, discounts his story."

Splashing another measure of beer into her mug, Elsie nodded sagely. "Yep. Sure does."

"So the kid is a liar, because his statement says nothing about having sex with the deceased. And when he claims he was just lying around in the back of the bus, saw nothing, knows nothing, did nothing—we attack his veracity. And," he finished triumphantly, "we spice up the facts, get the jury fired up about the rape."

Elsie stared at him over the rim of her mug. Gesturing with it, she inadvertently splashed beer on the table. "That's it. There's your problem."

When he didn't respond, she added, "Who raped who?"

"Whom. Who raped whom. But whatever. I don't get your point. The bus driver is dead; she's the victim, the violent one is the kid."

"Precisely." She slammed the mug on the table with a resounding clunk. "He's a kid. Fifteen. Below the age of consent. Any defense lawyer worth his salt will throw that back on the prosecution."

She watched dismay etch his features as he registered the import of Elsie's statement. She continued,

"The defense will maintain that the dead woman forced or coerced the juvenile to have sex with her. It's not an unbelievable claim; he's fifteen, she was a middle-aged woman. They'll say: Why would a young boy want to have sex with an old broad?"

As Chuck leaned away from her, she drove the point home, adding, "And if they play their cards right, they can make the jury believe that he killed her to defend himself from a rapist, a pedophile. Raise a reasonable doubt, anyway."

"Bullshit," he exploded, but Elsie cut him off with a laugh.

"Damn, Chuck, there's no point in getting mad at me. I'm trying to help you, by anticipating what the defense will do. Read the tea leaves, guess their hand. I always do that, when I'm going to trial."

He looked away, refusing to meet her eye. Why was he reacting so angrily? She was trying to help, to do her job and make a contribution as third chair. They sat in unhappy silence for a tense moment, before he bent sideways, pulling his wallet out with a jerk. "Time to go."

Oh hell, I've pissed him off, she thought.

"Okay," she said, pawing through her purse, "let me find my debit card."

She was still fumbling with her wallet when he slipped a bill under his half-full mug and stood to go. "Tell Dixie to keep the change." Then he made for the door.

She pulled a few cards from her wallet, but couldn't find the Visa. Had she left it somewhere? she wondered unhappily. She knew she had no cash; she had scraped bills and change together to buy a burger at the court-house coffee shop earlier that day. Rummaging through the contents of her bag a second time, she failed to notice a man approach the table.

Looking up, she beheld Noah Strong slipping into the seat Chuck had vacated. Despite the beer haze, an alarm went off in her head: Noah was a blast from the past, a boyfriend from the bad old days before Ashlock.

But he looked divine. A sunburned face with the fea-tures of a Nordic god, and hair bleached by the sun. His freckled shoulders were on display in a cotton tank shirt. Wearing a wife beater, she thought. Fitting.

"Hey there," he said, more loudly than necessary. He was grinning with a bluster she recognized as false con-fidence. She knew Noah well; too well, she thought rue-fully.

"Hey," she replied, refusing to meet his eye. Grabbing her bag with a sudden jerk, she added, "I'm heading out."

He looked away, toward the bar where Dixie was lean-ing on an elbow, smoking a cigarette. "Dixie," he called, holding up two fingers.

Elsie paused. "You meeting someone?"

"Nope."

"Drinking double fisted?"

His mouth crooked into a one-sided grin, an expres-sion she once adored. "Hope not."

Shrugging, she refused to take the bait. Even with her beer buzz, she had her guard up. Squinting up at the rotating ceiling fan, she commenced a calculation of his failings. His many, many shortcomings.

At length, he broke the silence. "Happy birthday, Elsie," he said, softly.

The tone, as much as the sentiment, initiated an unexpected and unwelcome reaction. Unaccountably, she teared up.

"Elsie? You okay?"

To her horror, a tear welled up and rolled down her face. She knocked it away, wiping furiously at her nose, which she feared would swell like a boxer's beak.

"Fuck," she breathed.

Dixie strolled up with two frosty cans of Budweiser and set them down. "You'uns want a glass?"

Noah shook his head, while Elsie turned toward the corner of the booth, to pull herself together. *Ridiculous*, she thought. *Idiotic.*

The Bud can popped with a hiss, and Noah pushed it in front of her. What the hell, she thought, picking up the can and taking a swig.

Setting the can down, she looked sharply at him. "How'd you hear?" She suspected that Noah had learned about her split with Ashlock; which meant Ashlock was talking shit about her at the PD. That would account for Noah's surprise birthday appearance. After all those months apart, he was sniffing around, to pick her up on the rebound.

"Hear what?" He was casual, innocent as a lamb, turning the can with his fingertips.

She made a scornful face. "Oh please," she said, tipping her beer for another swallow. "The talk."

Shaking his head, he said, "Only talk I've heard is about the kid."

A spark of interest flared, in spite of herself. "What's that?"

Shifting into the corner of the booth, Noah settled his broad back against the wall. He drank before he answered. "Everybody's pissed you're not in charge."

She sat up straighter; he had garnered her complete attention. "How's that?"

"Nobody thinks she'll keep after it." There was no need to ask who "she" was. "And nobody at the department thinks her little fag chief assistant has the balls to see it through."

She squinted; her contact lenses seemed fuzzy. Maybe the beer was drying her eyeballs. "He's not gay."

Noah's response was a cross between a snort and a cough. "Dixie!" he shouted, waving his empty can, but she ducked into the kitchen behind the bar.

A perverse impulse prompted Elsie to defend Chuck. "He isn't. He's just big city, that's all."

His teeth shone like a Cheshire cat. "Big city."

"You know, metrosexual. Fancy haircut, expensive clothes."

"Hair gel," he suggested.

"Yeah."

"My point exactly."

She flushed with resentment. Though she wanted to shut him down with a biting retort, she could only come up with: "You're stupid."

Dixie appeared at Elsie's shoulder with a plastic basket, lined with wax paper. She set the basket in front of Elsie with a flourish. It held a sizzling cheeseburger;

and in the top bun, which was shiny with grease, some-one had stuck a single birthday candle. Its short wick was lighted.

Dixie nudged Noah. "Are we singing?"

"No." He gave the basket a little push toward Elsie, his hand brushing hers. "Make a wish, baby."

Panic seized her; she thought, *Who is he calling baby?* "What is this?" she snapped.

"I saw your car, and I remembered. Wish I had a real present. But I know you love the cheeseburgers here at the Bald. You used to tell me you craved them, sometimes."

She scooted out of the booth. "That's nice of you; thanks. But I'm going now."

"Wait." He seized her arm. It wasn't a painful touch, but it held her in place. "You've got to eat something, or you're going to regret it. And honey, you're in no shape to drive."

Reflexively, she tried to jerk from his grasp, but he held on. Glancing back at the basket, she saw that the bun now had a quantity of melted pink wax on its surface. Still, it smelled delicious.

She relaxed and slid back into the seat. "I need the ketchup and mustard."

He reached behind him, swiping condiments from the next booth. With a smile, he said, "Eat. I'll give you a ride home."

Chapter 22

ELSIE AWOKE FROM a sodden sleep. Lying under a wrinkled sheet, she fought through the fog of the night with her eyes squeezed shut. *Please*, she thought, *please let me be in my own bed.*

And let me be alone. All alone.

Peeking through her eyelashes, she was comforted by the familiar sight of the dusty light fixture hanging over her bed. Sitting up with a sigh, she threw off the sheet and assessed the magnitude of her hangover. She shook her head, hoping to clear it, but without success.

It was going to be a rocky day, she thought, as she grappled for her eyeglasses on the bedside table..

Shuffling toward the kitchen, she shrieked at the sight of Noah Strong with his feet on the kitchen table, nursing a cup of coffee.

He laughed at her reaction. Aping her expression, he squealed in falsetto, "Help! Police!"

"Shit," she said, pushing her glasses higher up the bridge of her nose.

"There's a man in my apartment! Call the cops!"

She trudged into the kitchen and picked up a cup from the dish drainer. Pouring coffee from the pot he'd brewed, she said, "What are you doing here, Noah?"

"That's a nice way to greet your hero. The guy who drove your drunk ass home last night."

"Oh fuck," she muttered.

"And put you to bed. Got you out of your work clothes and shoes." He reached for her as she walked past, catching her hand and pulling her onto his lap.

Elsie set the coffee cup on the table and squirmed away from him and into the other chair. Wishing most desperately that she didn't have to ask, she said, "Did we do anything?"

"Like what?"

She turned on him with a flash of temper. "Don't mess with me."

"Did we watch TV? No ma'am we did not."

She picked up the coffee with a shaking hand as her anxiety spiked. She would not repeat the question. She would retain a shred of dignity.

With a sigh, she shifted in the kitchen chair, observing that there was no telltale twinge of tenderness; and after a dry spell, Noah's attentions would have left a morning-after reminder. She relaxed a trifle.

He nudged her. "Since you're having some recall problems, you might not realize that you don't have a car outside in the parking lot."

Elsie breathed in and out, carefully. He had the whip hand this morning, and was clearly enjoying it. In a polite voice, she said, "Would you mind if I take a quick shower before we go pick it up?"

WHEN ELSIE SAW the elevator door closing she made a run for it, dashing down the courthouse hallway. The doors shut just as she reached it. Panting, she headed for the marble stairway. As she trudged the two flights, she left damp fingerprints on the brass handrail.

Stacie looked up when Elsie pushed through the door of the Prosecutor's Office. "You're late."

A glance at the clock behind Stacie's head confirmed it. Elsie considered crafting a clever excuse, but she couldn't muster the wit.

"It's just one of those days, Stacie. One of those old days, as my mom says."

Stacie leaned over the desk, and in a stage whisper, she said, "Someone's waiting for you. She's been sitting outside in the rotunda since the courthouse opened."

Elsie felt the cloud over her head expand. "I don't have any appointments this morning."

"Well, you've got one now. I checked the calendar. You're not in court till one. I said you'd see her at nine."

Oh Lord, Elsie thought. It was only minutes before her surprise appointment. "Well, okay. I guess."

Elsie sank into her chair, surveying the paperwork on her desk. New police reports had been stacked on top of a

stack of Missouri cases she'd printed out. "I need a vacation. A summer vacation."

"Ms. Arnold?"

A woman appeared in her doorway. Elsie rose, startled;
she thought Stacie planned to announce the stranger first.
"Yes?"

"I been waiting for you."

The woman walked into the office, pulling a black
roller bag behind her. Not a briefcase, Elsie noted. When
citizens came into the office armed with a briefcase, she
could expect a long harangue.

The woman settled into the chair across from Elsie's
desk. As she pulled the black bag to her side, Elsie studied her. She wore a battered hat adorned with a cluster of
orange flowers; it sat askew on thinning black hair sprinkled with gray. Despite the morning heat, a pilled pink
scarf was knotted around her neck.

Elsie managed a smile. "What can I do for you?"

The woman turned piercing blue eyes on Elsie.
"There's something I can do for you."

Unsettled, Elsie fumbled as she turned to a blank page
on a legal pad. Uncapping a pen, she said, "Your name?"

"I been to the desert on a horse with no name."

Oh shit. Crazy. Elsie glanced at the bag resting at the
woman's side. She had been through security. If the bag
contained a weapon or an explosive, they would have detected it.

"That's interesting. Now what's your name, ma'am?"

The woman just smiled in reply, revealing a set of

teeth with several molars missing. She bent over the black bag and wrestled with a broken zipper.

Here we go, Elsie thought. The bag would surely contain a collection of paperwork compiled to convince the Prosecutor's Office to file a frivolous charge.

When the bag opened, Elsie leaned across her desk to confirm that her guess was correct. But the bag contained a wad of wrinkled clothing; mismatched shoes; a yellow wrapper around a portion of a McDonald's cheeseburger; and a folded newspaper. The *McCown County Record*, Elsie suspected. She wondered whether she was looking at the sum total of the woman's worldly goods.

The woman bent over the suitcase, pawing through the clothes. When she straightened in her seat, she held a deck of cards in her hand.

"I'm Cleo. I've been sent to help you."

Cleo set the deck of cards on Elsie's desk with a flourish. They were tarot cards.

Elsie pushed her chair away from the desk, waving a hand in dismissal. "I don't need my fortune told, thanks. Don't have a penny on me. Can't pay you."

Cleo ignored her. She shuffled the deck and placed the cards in a rectangular pattern on the desk.

In a sharp voice, Elsie said, "I'm serious. This is a workplace. I've got stuff I need to do."

Cleo studied the cards, nodding. She pointed at one of the cards, which depicted a young man on a horse. Tapping it with a grimy fingernail, she said, "There he is."

Elsie rose from her chair, determined to remove the intruder. "You have to leave."

Cleo tapped the card again. "Don't you want to hear? About the boy?"

Elsie froze. "The boy?"

Cleo picked up the card. "The Knight of Swords. It's the boy."

She reached into the black suitcase and retrieved the newspaper. As Cleo smoothed the front page on the desk, Elsie saw that it was the issue reporting Tanner Monroe's certification hearing, with a photo of the boy in handcuffs, lying on the floor of the courthouse hallway.

Cleo set the tarot card beside the newspaper photo. There was no resemblance; still, seeing the pictures side by side was eerie, Elsie thought.

With a knowing look, Cleo repeated, "The boy."

Elsie swallowed, wishing she'd stopped at Sonic for a Diet Coke. "Do you have some information about the Monroe case?"

Bending over the cards, Cleo studied them without answering. Elsie watched the woman, her impatience increasing and nerves jangling.

"If you have any pertinent information, I'd like to hear it. But if this is some kind of joke, you need to move on out of here and let me get to work."

Cleo shoved the undealt cards in the battered deck toward Elsie and said, "Draw."

Irritation shot through her; Elsie wanted to knock the cards off the desk and watch them fly through the air.

"This is ridiculous."

Cleo tapped the deck with her index finger. Elsie

looked away; the sight of the woman's dirty hand was unsettling.

"Draw."

Blowing out a frustrated breath, Elsie picked the top card from the deck, hoping she wouldn't catch a nasty bug from the cardboard rectangle. She examined the card briefly, then held it up so Cleo could see it.

Cleo nodded. "The Fool."

"Are we done here?"

"The Fool stands on the precipice. He doesn't look to see the dangers ahead." Cleo took the card from Elsie's hand. "This is you."

"Okay, that's it. Out."

Cleo settled back in her chair. "I've done it over and over again. It comes out the same every time." She picked up another card. "You're trying to imprison the Knight, but you can't. See? The Hanged Man." She waved the card close to Elsie's face.

Elsie jerked away. Rising, she walked to her office door and swung it open. "You need to leave."

Taking no notice of the dismissal, Cleo went on. "You want to be his destruction." She sighed, looking at the card with an expression of regret. "It's not your place. He'll do it to himself, if it's meant to be. He's been at the mercy of the dark forces."

Elsie leaned against the doorframe, crossing her arms. "Appreciate the advice. We're all done here."

"You'll leave the boy alone. The Knight."

"Cleo? Ma'am? Appointment is over. I'm serious. I'll call security."

Cleo chuckled, picking up the tarot cards in an unhurried fashion and returning them to the black suitcase. "It's okay. I'm used to it. No one wants to hear the truth."

Get her out, get her out, pounded in Elsie's head. When Cleo rose from her chair with a grunt, Elsie crossed her arms, willing the woman to hurry through the door and out of Elsie's sight. "Have a nice day," she said, hoping it would conclude the interview.

"No one wants to hear. No one really wants to know. Gypsies, tramps, and thieves, that's what the people of the town call us."

Is that a song? Elsie wondered, watching the woman make her way down the hall. She shut her door with a bang and turned the lock. Crossing to the small refrigerator sitting near her closet, she prayed that it would hold a silver can of medicine. Squatting down, she opened the door and shoved a bag of withering apples to the side. There it was: a single can of Diet Coke.

Elsie sighed with pleasure as she popped the tab, closing her eyes to savor the first cold swallow.

The crazy woman's voice lingered in her head. *The Fool*, she thought.

It was true enough. Waking up with Noah Strong in her apartment, for heaven's sake. The Fool, indeed.

Chapter 23

THE BATTERED METAL door of the solitary confinement cell at the McCown County jail swung open with a squeal. The head jailer, Vernon Wantuck, loomed in the doorway, his girth filling the frame.

"How you doing, boy?" he asked.

At the sound of the booming voice, Tanner winced and shrugged in reply. He slipped the ballpoint pen he held into the pocket of his orange jailhouse scrubs.

"Look at you, working on your jailhouse tats like a big man. You're a big shot now, aren't you, you little fucker?"

Tanner looked at the jailer with hooded eyes. "Am I going to court today? I thought it was tomorrow."

"Nah, you're moving. Come along with me."

A look of fear shot across Tanner's face before he could hide it. "I can't be in the population. It's dangerous, the judge said so. They'll attack me. The judge said it. In court."

The jailer shifted to his side, feeling for the handcuffs dangling from his rear pocket. One of his suspenders had come loose in the back, making his Sansabelt pants droop and exposing the elastic band of his underwear. "Let's cuff you up for your stroll to see your new friends." When Tanner didn't move from the bunk, the jailer's eyes narrowed to slits. "Now! Move, you little fuck."

Slowly, Tanner slid off the bed. When he reached the jailer, Wantuck stopped him with a beefy hand. "First thing, you're gonna give me that pen."

Tanner pulled it from his pocket with a jerk. As he set it in the jailer's hand, he said, "The lawyer says I'm supposed to help with my defense. I got to be able to write."

Wantuck grabbed Tanner's hand and looked at the ink marks. "You been doing some writing. Just like the big boys. What's that say?"

When Tanner didn't answer, Wantuck released his hand with a snort. "Tell your lawyer to get you another pen. Bet they got a whole box of them in his office on the square."

"He ain't got shit," Tanner said under his breath, so softly that Wantuck didn't hear.

The walk from solitary to the general population cells was short. Wantuck and Tanner Monroe turned a corner and the catcalls began, whistles and jeers sounding around them as the jailer led the juvenile to his new quarters.

The facility had not been updated in decades, because the McCown County voters responded to tax increases with a resounding "No." All inmates were grouped into the overflowing cells in twos or threes, exposed to full view of one another through the metal bars. Only Tanner would have a cell to himself.

The boy's demeanor remained stoic, but telltale beads of sweat formed on his upper lip. He reached out with his cuffed hands and tugged at the jailer's sleeve. In a low voice, he said, "The judge is going to be pissed. I want to talk to the judge."

Wantuck wheeled on him with a confused look. "Judge? What judge?"

Tanner almost collided with the man's belly; he backed up a step. "The juvenile judge."

"The juvenile judge?" In the voice of a whiny child, he repeated, "The juvenile judge?" Then the jailer threw his head back and laughed with such delight, his belly shook like Santa Claus.

Wiping moisture from his eye, Wantuck said, "You ain't no juvenile, son. Not no more. You're an adult." Turning to the men locked into the metal cells, Vernon said, "Ain't that right, boys?"

The inmates roared their approval. The cinder-block walls rang with the rebel yell.

Chuckling, Wantuck pulled a ring of keys from his pocket and shuffled up to an empty cell. A prisoner leaned his skeletal face, pocked with scabs, through the bars of the adjoining enclosure. "He's no juvenile, Vernon. He's a big man."

With speed that belied his girth. Wantuck slammed the heel of his hand into the inmate's nose, sending him back into the cell.

"Get your fucking head back inside your cage, you no-account freak show."

The inmate nodded, bobbing his bloody nose up and down. "Yes, sir."

"I am *Mr.* Wantuck to you, you piece of shit. Now what's my name?" he asked, punctuating each word with a bang of his fist on the metal bars of the cell.

"Mr. Wantuck," the inmate said, wiping the blood from his nose onto his sleeve. "It's Mr. Wantuck."

"You goddamned right."

Wantuck unlocked an empty cell and sent Tanner inside with a shove at his back. After Wantuck slammed the door shut, Tanner sat gingerly on the edge of a metal bunk. He picked at peeling black paint on the bed frame with a nervous hand.

The overhead light cast a garish glow on the scab-encrusted face of the man with the bloody nose. He grasped the bars with mottled hands bearing blood blisters at the fingertips. His fingers bore tattoos, also uneven marks depicting spiderwebs.

The man's eyes followed Wantuck as the jailer strode away with a heavy gait. When Wantuck disappeared, the inmate turned to Tanner with a smile.

"They won't let you smoke in here."

Tanner inclined his head in acknowledgment.

"Not even in the exercise yard, man. Don't let you smoke for nothing. Fucking douche bags want to stomp out smoking. Like they stomp out crime."

Tanner nodded, moving his head a fraction.

"They let you go to church, though. Send a preacher

in every week to save us on Sunday. We don't have to go. But I do."

The inmate pressed his face against the bars of the cell. The metal pressed into his cheek. He said, in a hushed voice, "I go. To get away from the rats."

At the mention of rats, Tanner's eye twitched. He looked around the cell and spoke to the inmate for the first time. "I don't see no rats."

"Oh, there's rats in here, big as a groundhog. You can hear them scuffling at night. Rustling around."

The boy leaned back on his bunk and didn't speak.

The other inmate opened his mouth in a wide smile, revealing bloody gums and decayed teeth. "And spiders. Shit, them spiders climb out of the toilet and into your ass."

"If you say so, man."

"They lay them eggs. Lay them spider eggs right in your insides. They'll do it."

Tanner narrowed his eyes, appraising the scabbed man. Slowly, he nodded in agreement. At the acknowledgment, the inmate giggled and said, "Then you got a mess. You'll be all fucked up, shitting spiderwebs out your ass. That's bad, man."

Softly, the juvenile said, "I hear you, man." After a beat, his mouth twitched with a smile. He said. "You're like Spider-Man."

An inmate with a lank mullet ponytail occupied the cell with Spider-Man; the man groaned and said, "Shut up, you crazy fuck." He pulled a rubber flip-flop off his foot and threw it at his cellmate. The shoe bounced off Spider-Man's head.

"Sorry, dude. Can't help it, man," Spider-Man said in a whispered entreaty to his cellmate. "It's them spider-webs."

"Talk about rats or spiders one more time and I'm gonna ream your ass." The ponytailed inmate sat up on his bunk to address Tanner. "Wonder how come Wantuck didn't double you up in here. Not like he gives a shit whether you's a bitch or you ain't."

Tanner gave the man a rocky stare.

"Who's your lawyer?"

Tanner shrugged.

"Don't you know? You so dumb you don't know your lawyer's name? You got the public defender?"

"I got some old man," Tanner said.

"Ain't no such thing as an old public defender. We all got the public defender in here, and they don't hardly look old enough to get they dick hard," the inmate said. "My name's Darren. You that Monroe kid, right?"

He nodded.

Darren leaned back in his cot, sucking his teeth as he contemplated. "Wantuck's doing you a favor, shutting you up by yourself. Only time I saw Wantuck give a fuck about an inmate's security was one time when a guy had hired old man Yocum. Is that who you got? Yocum?"

"Dunno," Tanner said with disinterest. "He's an old fuck. Smells like Ben-Gay."

"I don't care if he smells like a shit sandwich—I'd get Yocum if I had the green. Ain't got it. But Yocum's the ticket."

Pulling down his scrubs, Spider-Man crouched on the

stained toilet in the cell he shared with Darren. He commenced scratching wildly at his backside, making high-pitched noises. "Spiders, spiders hatching. Them eggs is hatching."

In a low voice, Tanner asked Darren, "Is the spider guy crazy?"

"Crazy motherfucker. Just waiting for his court date. Even the goddamned prosecutor's shrink says he's batshit crazy. They're letting him go NGI."

"So he walks? Because the doctor says he's insane?"

"Nah. He'll go to the state mental hospital in St. Joe."

"Is that better? Than prison?"

The man shook his head. "Dunno, kid. Ain't never been. Psycho time may be easier. Just about have to be. But it ain't gonna be no shorter. Callaway don't let a crazy walk out of the hospital till he's been there awhile."

Tanner stretched out on his cot and surveyed Spider-Man in the next cell. The inmate stopped scratching his butt and gave the juvenile a smile, revealing again the bloody gums and blackened teeth.

"Are you my friend," asked Spider-Man with a child-like longing in his voice.

"Yeah, man," Tanner answered. "You bet."

Chapter 24

Pushing open the door to Associate Division 3, Elsie spotted Chuck Harris at the counsel table in Judge Carter's courtroom. Chuck reclined in his chair, with his feet stretched out before him.

"You're the picture of relaxation," Elsie said.

"The product of a clear conscience," he replied.

She handed the *State v. Tanner Monroe* file to him. "Thought you might want this."

Chuck took the file and tossed it on the table. "Don't get all wrought up. The public defender is waiving preliminary."

"You mean the conflicts public defender," said Elsie.

The local public defender's office had declined to represent Tanner Monroe. They claimed they had a conflict, as they'd been appointed previously to defend Barry Bacon's drug case, and until investigation of his hanging was completed, they would not undertake Tanner Monroe's murder defense.

"Have you talked to the conflict attorney today?"

"Nope. Been busy." Chuck pulled out the *McCown County Record* and turned to the entertainment section. "Do you think I could get on *The Bachelor*? They're holding auditions in Oklahoma City."

Elsie managed to look away before he could see her expression. "Chuck, I think you match the profile perfectly. Go for it."

Eldon, Carter's bailiff, was sitting at his desk beside the judge's chambers door. Hanging up the phone, he said, "I'm going to the jail to get that boy. It's dang near time."

As he left, Elsie pulled up a chair beside Chuck and sat. "Conflict PD is late," she observed.

"Always," Harris agreed.

The door to the courtroom opened with a creak. Looking over her shoulder, Elsie saw Bob Ashlock.

She looked away with a jerk of her chin, turning in her seat so she faced the empty jury box. She and Ashlock had not spoken since their run-in in the coffee shop.

Chuck waved, calling, "What brings you here, bro?"

Elsie hid a smirk. She didn't expect Bob considered Chuck a brother.

Ashlock said, "I thought I'd make sure you don't need me today, Harris."

Chuck tipped back in the chair, crossing his feet on the table. "Wasted a trip, dude. Monroe's waiving."

Ashlock nodded. "I think I'll stay and watch. Make sure he doesn't do anything stupid." He took a seat in the back row of the gallery.

Elsie kept her back to him, her posture rigidly erect. Despite the frosty air-conditioning in the courtroom, she felt her face grow warm. She couldn't help but remember the words spoken in the car after the trip from Tulsa. The words still rang in her ears: Stupid. Irresponsible. Unprofessional. Immature. *Motherfucker*, she thought, her heart rate increasing.

Hanging over the back of his chair, Chuck asked Ashlock about the progress of the forensic testing on evidence seized from the bus. Ashlock answered in the baritone voice Elsie loved so well. *Used to love*, she corrected herself.

When Harris cracked a joke, Ashlock laughed, and Elsie's body reacted involuntarily to the sound.

What the fuck is the matter with me, she mused, running her fingers through her long hair and pulling it away from her face. She stood abruptly. "I better get downstairs," she said, and turned to go.

Harris stared at her, uncomprehending. "But it's just about to start. Stick around."

As he spoke, the courtroom door opened, and Eldon ushered in Tanner Monroe.

The juvenile crept in, his feet shackled so close together that he was forced to take baby steps. With his arms cuffed behind his back, his chest was thrust forward. But his head hung down, whether in despondency, or to watch his feet to avoid falling, Elsie couldn't tell.

Eldon escorted Monroe to the defense counsel table, where the boy sat alone.

The door to Carter's chambers opened, and the judge stuck out his head. "Ready?" he asked.

"Defense attorney's not here," Chuck replied.

The judge slammed his door shut. The noise made the juvenile jump in his seat, as he sat in his shackles, his head still hanging down.

Elsie, looking at him sidelong, watched a smile begin to play on the boy's mouth. He turned his face slightly toward her, shot her a wink, and returned to his woebegone position.

That boy is from crazy town, she thought, as she craned her neck to look at his hands. They were hidden in the chair, so she couldn't check out the letters she'd seen before on his fingers.

The courtroom door behind her opened with a mighty creak, and as she swung round in her chair, Billy Yocum made his entrance.

"Counsel for defendant appears," he boomed.

Elsie and Chuck looked at each other. Chuck piped up: "What you here on, Billy?"

"*State v. Tanner Monroe*," the attorney replied, walking up to the defense table and laying a kindly hand on the boy's shoulder.

Elsie said, "Billy, Mr. Monroe is represented by the conflicts attorney."

Opening his worn leather brief case, Billy pulled out a legal pad. "Conflicts attorney had a conflict."

Eldon rapped on Judge Carter's chambers door, and the judge emerged. Attired in his black robe, the judge took the bench. He was a slim man in his forties, with a head of prematurely silver hair.

"Appreciate you taking this on, Billy," the judge said, with a friendly nod in Yocum's direction.

"Glad to oblige, your honor," Yocum said, before he sat next to the juvenile and huddled in consultation with the boy.

Elsie jerked on Chuck's jacket, pulling him around to face her. "What's going on?" she hissed.

"How should I know?"

"Is he going to waive or not?" Clearly, the state was not ready for preliminary, and Elsie knew from past experience that Judge Carter would not be happy to hear that the state was not prepared to proceed with evidence. Elsie had been down that road before in Judge Carter's courtroom.

Chuck rose from his seat. Approaching Yocum, he tapped the lawyer's shoulder with a tentative hand. Yocum looked up with a scowl. He said, "Mr. Harris, I'm speaking to my client in confidence."

"Sorry, Yocum. You're going to waive preliminary hearing, right?"

The irritation disappeared from the old attorney's face, replaced by a toothy grin. Yocum guffawed as he slapped Chuck Harris on the shoulder.

"That's a good 'un, young man. I'll tell you something: in forty years of practicing law, I have never once waived preliminary. Not once. I regard it as malpractice." He slapped his pad on the table and clicked his pen. "Get your first witness ready."

Chuck looked at Elsie, bug-eyed. He whispered in her ear. "I'll ask for a continuance."

"You won't get it," she hissed, but Judge Carter was settling in his chair, and Chuck was already approaching the bench.

"Judge Carter," Harris said, apologetically, "we got a situation."

The judge peered down at Harris from the bench.

Harris continued, "We thought the defendant was waiving preliminary hearing. I had it on good authority, from the conflicts attorney."

"Conflicts attorney doesn't represent defendant," the judge snapped.

"Yeah, I know, I can see that. But that's why the state is not ready to go."

Judge Carter slammed his hand on the bench.

Yocum rose, shaking his head. "Your honor, these young attorneys know that my client—a mere boy—is being held at the county jail. Being exposed to hardened criminals in an open cell, with the risk every blessed day of their criminal influence. He's in danger"—and his voice dropped to a grave whisper—"of assault from perverse infidels."

Elsie turned to see how the juvenile would react to the exchange. She saw him shut his eyes during the attorney's speech. Tanner Monroe's chest convulsed; his lips twitched. *Is he laughing or crying?* she wondered incredulously.

The judge inclined his head to Yocum. "When did you enter your appearance?"

"Yesterday. Yesterday afternoon."

"The Prosecutor's Office should know that. They should be up to speed." As Harris opened his mouth to protest, the judge cut him off. "I don't even want to hear it. Proceed," he said, with a shake of the gavel.

"The state respectfully requests a continuance."

"Denied. Proceed."

"Give us a minute, Judge," Harris said. He hustled over to Elsie; bending his head to hers, he whispered, "What the hell are we going to do?"

"Just put Ashlock on," she whispered back. "He's holding his file; you know he's got the juvenile's statement in there. Ashlock can testify about the bus and the body and the statement and the knife. That's enough for probable cause."

Chuck's eyes were wild; she could see the whites all around the iris. "I don't have an exam prepared."

"Just wing it."

"I can't. I can't put him on cold."

Harris looked over his shoulder at Ashlock, then back at Elsie. "You do it."

"What?"

"You put him on. You can put him on cold; you're used to warming him up."

Elsie's eyes flashed. As she opened her mouth to snap a fitting retort, the judge intoned, "Call your first witness, Mr. Harris."

Elsie turned in her seat, facing Ashlock at the back of the courtroom. "The state calls Detective Bob Ashlock."

Ashlock's brow lifted slightly in surprise. He met

Elsie's eye squarely and walked up to be sworn. As he passed Elsie on his way to the witness box, their shoulders brushed, and she could smell the scent of the deodorant soap he used.

After taking the oath, Ashlock settled in the witness chair, file in hand. Elsie stood before him, unsmiling. "State your name," she said.

"Detective Bob Ashlock."

"What is your occupation?"

"Chief of detectives for the City of Barton Police Department."

"How long have you been employed in that capacity?"

"Ten years in the Detective Division, eight years on patrol before that."

"I direct your attention to the twelfth day of June of this year: did you have occasion to be called to a crime scene?"

"I did."

"Where?"

"I was called to the Muddy Creek bridge on Farm Road 233."

"Is that location in McCown County, Missouri?"

"It is."

"For what reason did you go to that location on that date?"

"I was called in to investigate a body found in the riverbed, under the bridge."

"Upon arriving, what did you observe?"

"A white female, aged forty to forty-five, was lying on her back in the bed of Muddy Creek. Her throat was cut."

So far, the exam was an easy give and take, a routine that both Elsie and Ashlock had danced many times before. She relaxed, leaning against the counsel table, and asked, "Was the woman alive?"

"She was not."

"Objection!" Yocum jumped to his feet, pointing a gnarled finger at Ashlock. "The witness has not indicated any medical training, he's not qualified to make that judgment."

Elsie looked at the old attorney in disbelief. "Is this going to be the basis of the defense? That the victim wasn't dead? Lord, Yocum, is that the best you can do?"

The defense attorney's angry reply was cut off as the judge ordered, "Qualify your witness, Ms. Arnold."

Cocking an eyebrow at Ashlock, Elsie said, "Describe the woman you found in the creek bed, Detective."

Ashlock's graphic description of the condition of the body, the location of the wound, the bloating from decomposition and the attention of the flies and the resulting maggots made the judge wince, but Elsie kept an expressionless demeanor. Ashlock concluded, "The victim was not breathing. Had no pulse."

"Detective Ashlock, in the course of your eighteen years of police work, have you had occasion to see a dead body?"

"Many times."

"In your opinion, what was the condition of the woman you observed in the Muddy Creek?"

"Ma'am," he intoned, "she was dead."

Yocum jumped up, waving a gnarled hand. "Your honor," he began, but the judge stopped him.

"Overruled. Whatever objection you were about to make is overruled. Let's move on."

Ashlock testified regarding the discovery of the woman's identification. On a hunch, Elsie asked, "Do you have the ID with you in court today?"

"I have a copy."

He opened his file and produced a copy of the license. Elsie had the court reporter mark it as an exhibit, and handed it back to Ashlock.

"I'd like to show you what's been marked for identification as state's Exhibit #1," she said. "Will you tell the court what that is?"

When Ashlock opened his mouth to reply, Yocum spoke from his chair. "Objection, Judge. Best evidence rule. Where's the original?"

The judge sent an inquiring glance Elsie's way. Smoothly, she asked Ashlock, "Can you tell us where the original document can be found?"

"At the highway patrol crime lab over in Springfield, Greene County, Missouri. Undergoing testing."

"Is state's Exhibit #1 a fair and accurate representation of the chauffeur's license you found on the deceased's person on June 12?"

"It is."

"Your honor, the state offers state's Exhibit #1 into evidence."

Yocum rose, shaking his head. "Now, wait a minute, Judge. The witness didn't say anything about the original being destroyed. They just didn't take the trouble to get the original to court today. I object to the admission of state's Exhibit #1."

"Your honor, we've demonstrated that it's unavailable."

Yocum scoffed. "You've demonstrated it's in Springfield, that's all. That's not 'unavailable.' You could get there in forty-five minutes. Thirty, if the detective turns his siren on."

Elsie was making moist palm prints on the counsel table, so she wiped her palms on her skirt. Her pulse raced; she had to get the license into evidence, for she must prove the identity of the murder victim named in the criminal complaint. Clearing her throat, she said, "Judge, the detective has testified under oath that the license is a fair and accurate representation. Mr. Yocum's objection to the exhibit is baseless."

Yocum slapped his hand on the table. "Bring in the ID! It's a piece of plastic. It's not like I'm asking to see the *Mona Lisa*," he cried.

"Now you're being ridiculous," Elsie snapped.

The judge intervened; with a weary look, he admitted the exhibit. "Let's get on with it," he ordered.

Elsie faced Ashlock again. "After finding the body, did you have occasion to take a statement at McCown County Juvenile Hall?"

"I did," he said. He opened his file and pulled out a document; it was the Tanner Monroe statement, the original, encased in plastic sheet protectors. Inwardly, when Elsie saw the light reflect off the plastic sheets, she breathed a sigh of relief.

She said to Ashlock, "When you arrived at Juvenile Hall, what did you do?"

"I met with Deputy Juvenile Officer Lisa Peters and members of the prosecutor's staff. After the guardian ad litem arrived, I conducted an interrogation of Tanner Monroe."

"Is the individual you questioned on that date present in the courtroom today?"

"He is."

"Would you point him out, please?"

Ashlock pointed at the juvenile, stating, "He's the man at the defense table, wearing orange county inmate garb, seated next to attorney Billy Yocum."

Turning to the judge, Elsie said, "Your honor, may the record reflect that the witness has identified the defendant?"

"It shall," the judge said.

"Did you apprise defendant of his rights prior to questioning?" Elsie asked.

Ashlock answered that he had, and handed Elsie the rights form. Elsie had the form marked and offered it as an exhibit.

"What, if anything, did the defendant say during questioning?"

"Defendant said that he was hitchhiking from St. Louis, and got a ride on a bus, driven by the deceased. He said a second passenger joined them down the road. Monroe said the second rider cut the deceased's throat, dumped the body, and took defendant prisoner."

Ashlock paused. Elsie prompted him: "Did he make a written statement?"

"He did," Ashlock said, handing Elsie the plastic-clad handwritten sheets.

Elsie had the statement marked as an exhibit, and offered it into evidence. She handed the statement to Yocum, who studied it intently, but didn't object.

Elsie continued, unable to contain a blush, "That week, did you have occasion to travel to Tulsa, Oklahoma?"

He avoided eye contact with her. "I did."

"For what purpose?"

"To examine the school bus which was found with defendant."

"What did you do on that occasion?" Elsie's cheeks were scarlet, and not from the heat.

Ashlock, without missing a beat, described the collection of evidence from the bus, detailing his collection of blood, hair, fiber, and fingerprint samples. "The evidence was bagged and tagged, and transported to the highway patrol crime lab for forensic testing," he concluded.

"Did you find anything else on the bus?"

"A knife."

Yocum looked up, squinting through his glasses. He craned his neck to see whether Ashlock had brought anything to court with him, other than the manila file in his hands on the witness stand.

"Please describe the knife."

"It was a hunting knife with a wooden handle and a four-inch serrated blade."

"What was the condition of the knife?"

"It was covered in a dried reddish-brown substance that appeared to be blood."

"Where did you find the knife?"

"Under the floor mat of the driver's seat of the bus."

"What did you do with the knife?"

"Bagged it, tagged it, took it back to the crime lab by way of the Barton Police Department."

"What was done with it at the Barton Police Department?"

"Preliminary tests were done to determine that the substance on the knife was in fact blood."

"Anything else?"

He lifted a brow just a fraction. Her eyes bored into his. He nodded.

"We tested for prints."

"And?"

"A print on the handle matched the defendant, Tanner Monroe."

Yocum reared up. "Whoa! Hold on! We're missing some steps here."

He marched up to the bench, protesting, "Who's doing these tests? Where's the expert? I object to the question!"

"Too late to object; he already answered," Elsie murmured, deadpan.

Yocum gasped, laid a hand on his heart. "Then I demand that his answer be struck. Struck from the record."

"On what grounds?" Elsie asked.

"Not qualified to make the statement."

Elsie clutched her heart, in parody of Yocum. "Object! I object to his attack on this fine, upstanding expert!"

Yocum swung on her, enraged. "The prosecutor is mocking me, your honor."

"Ms. Arnold," the judge said in a warning tone.

"Hey, Judge, I'm just serving up to him the same thing he's giving me."

"Well, stop it. Now." The judge took off his glasses and rubbed his eyes.

The juvenile tugged at his attorney's sleeve and murmured a question. Yocum whispered in response, and the two huddled at the table for a hushed consultation. Elsie drummed her fingers on the bench, waiting. At length, she turned to the judge and said, "Does he want a recess? To consult?"

The judge leaned forward at the bench and called, "Billy?"

The lawyer sat up straight, saying, "Where are we? Is direct exam concluded?"

Elsie cut a glance at Ashlock. If she had a shot at squeaking by with their patchy admission of fingerprint evidence, she should quit while she was ahead. "Yes, your honor."

"Mr. Yocum, your turn."

As Elsie sat down, Yocum descended on Ashlock. But while the defense attorney made considerable noise, he made no headway; Ashlock was unshakable.

Watching Ashlock deflect Yocum's questions gave Elsie more pleasure than she liked to admit; and when Ashlock scored a point by correcting Yocum on proper police procedure, she looked down to hide a triumphant smile.

When she looked back up at the witness stand, Ashlock's eyes were upon her, with a shade of the old warmth in his expression. She was starting to feel a little fluttery—in a good way—when Yocum asked, "Who all was present at the interrogation of my client?"

Ashlock looked away from Elsie and back at Yocum. "The juvenile officer, Lisa Peters; the guardian ad litem, Maureen Mason; myself; and Elsie Arnold and Chuck Harris from the Prosecutor's Office."

He said my name first, before Chuck's, Elsie thought with satisfaction, before the defense attorney interrupted her thoughts by shouting, "The Prosecutor's Office? What on earth was the Prosecutor's Office doing there?"

Ashlock gave him a level look. "Observing."

Yocum scratched his thinning hairline. "Well, that's a little out of the ordinary, wouldn't you say?"

Ashlock was silent.

"I'll repeat the question. Wouldn't you say—"

Ashlock interrupted Yocum. "I'd say it was an unusual interrogation in a couple of respects. Because it was an unusual situation, the suspect being a juvenile of fifteen."

"Indeed," the lawyer drawled. "Yes, indeed." He looked over his glasses at Ashlock, who suffered the glare with equanimity. "No more questions. For now."

Ashlock stepped down. As he passed by Elsie, their shoulders brushed. Ignoring the tingle the contact engendered, she whispered to him, "Get your print man here."

He bent down, his lips barely touching her ear, and whispered back, "He's in Jeff City."

The judge tilted his chair back and instructed Elsie to call her next witness. She and Chuck Harris exchanged glances. Harris still looked shell-shocked. To the judge, Elsie said calmly, "No further witnesses."

Yocum, moving in slow motion, started to rise from his chair, his face a study in apoplexy. The judge spoke up before the defense attorney could frame his address.

"Where's your fingerprint witness?" the judge demanded.

"We're saving the additional expert testimony for trial," Elsie said, sanguine.

Yocum blustered, "My client has not been tied to the offense."

Elsie replied, "Detective Ashlock tied the defendant to the offense; he testified that he observed defendant's prints on a bloody knife found on the bus."

Harris echoed from the prosecution table, "His prints are on the knife."

Yocum wheeled on Harris with a snarl. "Are you going to double-team me? That's two on one, Judge."

The judge waved a hand in Harris's direction. "One attorney at a time. Don't turn this into a circus."

Elsie approached the bench. "Judge, if you'd like to continue the hearing until a later time, we can call Officer Gates for additional testimony regarding the weapon."

"Get him over here now," the judge snapped.

"He's at the State Capitol," she said. "Important police business," she added. It damned well better be important.

The judge turned to Yocum. "Billy, do you want to come back later this week and hear from the print guy?"

"No, I do not," Yocum bellowed. "I want the charges dismissed and my client released from custody."

The judge sighed. With a glance at the prosecution team, he asked, "Why isn't the state presenting further evidence?"

Harris began, "The conflicts attorney told me—" but Elsie cut him off.

She said stoutly, "This is a probable cause hearing, your honor. We're not required to put forth our full case." She held up the criminal complaint, signed by Madeleine Thompson. "All we need is to demonstrate to the court that there is probable cause to believe that the defendant committed the offense with which he is charged. We are not obligated to prove him guilty beyond a reasonable doubt this morning."

The judge nodded. "That's true."

Encouraged, Elsie held up one finger. "Detective Ashlock's testimony established that the deceased was found in McCown County, Missouri."

Holding up two fingers, she continued, "We provided evidence that defendant, Tanner Monroe, was a passenger on the bus the vehicle was transporting. By his own admission, he was present at the time of the murder."

She was pacing before the bench. Holding up three fingers, she said, "Detective Ashlock testified that defendant's prints were on the knife."

"That's hearsay," Yocum cried.

Elsie whirled to face him. "You didn't make a hearsay objection when the testimony was offered."

"I objected."

"You objected to his qualifications as an expert—which had been already established. You didn't object on the basis of hearsay."

"I was consulting with my client." Turning to the bench, Yocum appealed to the judge. "I'm objecting now."

"It's too late," Elsie said. "Hearing's over. Can't unring a bell."

"Billy," the judge said, shaking his head, "pretty late to object to testimony. Witness has stepped down." With a skeptical glance at Elsie, the judge said, "This is awful slim evidence for a murder prelim. One witness."

"Barton PD's finest, Judge," Elsie said forthrightly.

"Still," the judge countered.

Elsie edged up to the bench. "Well, Judge, it's your call. Because you are the one who will bear the responsibility if a murderer is cut loose."

"Stop that right there," the judge said testily. "You're always feeding me that same line. I don't appreciate it." He fiddled with his file for a moment, then flipped it open and reached for his pen. "I'm going to bind him over to Circuit Court." To Yocum, he said, "You should've made that hearsay objection, Billy."

Yocum sprayed saliva as he cried, "I demand another hearing!"

"Simmer down, Billy." The judge pushed a button and his clerk appeared. As he dictated his finding of probable cause, Elsie turned to Chuck. She made a face, pretending to fan herself in relief. Chuck gestured to her, and she bent over to listen to him, when a voice behind her spoke from the defense table.

"I didn't do it."

Elsie whirled around, surprised to see the juvenile on

his feet, addressing the judge. Yocum put an arm around the boy's shoulders, and tugged him back into his seat.

"Of course you didn't do it, son. Best hush up now; I'm your mouthpiece."

"I'm not your son. Don't call me that." The boy rose again, rage coloring his features. "I've done some shit, but I didn't do this. I'm not going down for some asshole."

"Who's the asshole?" Harris whispered to Elsie, but the defense attorney had jerked the boy back into his seat and was hissing in his ear.

Chapter 25

WHEN ELSIE RETURNED to her office, she encountered Ashlock, leaning against the locked door.

"How'd it pan out?" he asked.

She rolled her head back on her neck. "Bound him over. By the skin of our teeth." Turning the key in the lock, she opened the office door. "Want to come in?"

He paused, as if debating the invitation. Stepping inside, he said, "Just for a minute."

"Better shut the door," she said over her shoulder, as she pulled open her file cabinet and dropped the Monroe file inside. "Yocum's down the hall."

He pulled the door shut behind him. Then he turned the deadbolt.

She shot him a quizzical glance.

"Privacy," he said, indicating the lock. In a casual tone, he asked, "You did a good job in court. Hell of a good job."

"Thanks," she said shortly, avoiding his eye.

"How have you been?"

"Good. I've been good."

"You sure look good." Crossing to her, he grasped her arm. At the contact, she looked up, and their eyes locked. He pulled her closer, and without stopping to consider, she wrapped her arms around his neck and kissed him hungrily. His tongue played with hers, and she could feel through the fabric of his pants that he was hard as a rock.

Stumbling together toward her desk, he pressed her up against it, stopping to knock the papers to the floor with a sweep of his arm. Elsie pulled his shirt from his pants as he jerked her skirt up to her waist and tore her underwear away from her body, ripping the fabric off at the crotch.

"Oh God," she whispered as her rubbed her flesh. She reclined on the desktop as he fumbled with his zipper. Just as he freed his erection, a knock sounded at the door.

"Elsie? You in there?"

They both froze. Ashlock was panting. "Don't answer," he said in a harsh whisper, pressing himself against her opening.

The knock came again, a persistent rap. In a louder voice, they heard Stacie say: "Chuck needs you."

In the room, they remained silent, but for their ragged breathing.

Stacie's voice came through the door a third time, petulant now. "I saw you go in. I know you're in there. I can hear you."

Ashlock groaned, and backed away. Sitting up, Elsie said, "Hold on a minute. I'm looking for something."

They tugged their clothes into place, Elsie smoothing

her skirt with a shaking hand. Elsie stepped over to the door and unlocked it. Taking a deep breath, she swung the door open and greeted Stacie with a smile.

Stacie looked over Elsie's shoulder at Ashlock, and her eyes widened. He slipped past the women without a word. As he retreated down the hallway, Elsie saw that his shirttail was hanging out.

Stacie interrupted her thoughts: "Chuck and Madeleine need to see you."

"Huh?" Elsie said, still a little breathless.

"Chuck and Madeleine," Stacie said, with impatience. "They're in Madeleine's office."

Elsie nodded, stepping in the hall and pulling her door closed. As she walked down the hallway to Madeleine's office, she was aware of a disconcerting throb between her legs. Reaching the closed door, she tried the doorknob. It was open, for once. Taking a second to tuck her hair behind her ears, she pushed the door open, and popping in head first, Elsie said with a jaunty air, "What's cooking?"

Chuck glanced at her wrinkled skirt. Elsie slipped onto the couch, keeping her knees tightly clenched together.

Madeleine was focused on the computer screen at her desk. Clicking the computer mouse, she said, "Chuck says you handled the preliminary hearing this morning."

Elsie nodded. "Yes indeed. Got that boy bound over."

"Barely," Madeleine murmured, her eyes still glued to the computer screen.

Elsie's temper flared, but she didn't rise to the bait. "We had a little surprise. PD's out, Yocum's in."

"That's what I heard." Madeleine turned away from the computer, pulled a leather handbag from a desk drawer, and peered inside the purse. "I have a connection of sorts to the Yocums. A personal connection." She fished in the handbag and pulled out a lipstick, examined the color in the tube, and dropped it back in the bag.

Elsie squinted at her, and when Madeleine didn't continue, Elsie offered, "PEO?"

Madeleine looked at her in surprise. "What?"

"Your connection. Is it PEO?"

Madeleine's brows knit together. "Yes, in fact, it is. How did you know?"

"Just a hunch."

"Well, it makes it a little ticklish for me. Peggy is my PEO sister. And that makes Billy my brother, after a fashion. How are you in tune with PEO, Elsie?" In a doubtful voice, she asked, "Is your mother a member?"

"No." Elsie replied, thinking, *My mother isn't into closed societies.* Marge Arnold had been encouraged to join the local chapter of the DAR, but had scoffed at the notion, saying, "Imagine what they would make of my Cherokee bloodline."

Madeleine nodded, satisfied. "Then that settles it. You can see how uncomfortable it would be for me and Billy to be adversaries in this case. Chuck, it's on you. Your first murder case in McCown County." Brightly, she added, "A real chance to distinguish yourself."

Chuck looked sick to his stomach. "Great."

"You'll need cocounsel, clearly. I expect you'll want to assign the job of second chair to Elsie."

Elsie turned to Chuck with an expectant air, excitement building in her chest. With a sidelong glance in her direction, Chuck said, "Elsie has been helping out with the case from the start."

"Fine. And she doesn't have any connection with Billy that creates a complication. So."

I'm in, Elsie thought. *Second chair in a murder case. And Madeleine's out.* The change of plan suited her very well indeed; she liked to keep her distance from Madeleine. Whatever Chuck's deficiencies, he would be easier to work with than the boss.

Chuck stood. "Is that all, Madeleine?"

"Not quite. You need to look at this. It came to the office today. Addressed to me."

Elsie and Chuck approached Madeleine's desk as she pushed a stack of files to the side and set a single sheet of paper where they could see it. It was a piece of ruled notebook paper, upon which three words were written in pencil:

STOP WRONG DUDE

Elsie stared soberly at the block letters, before looking up to meet Madeleine's gaze. "Where's the envelope?" she asked.

Madeleine pushed it toward her with the tip of a manicured fingernail. A plain white envelope bore the address of Madeleine Thompson, in the same penciled capital letters.

Chuck tsked. "Looks like Tanner Monroe wants to be your pen pal, Madeleine."

Elsie shook her head, an uneasy feeling replacing

the triumph she'd enjoyed moments before. "This didn't come from the jail."

"Why would you say that?" Chuck demanded.

"The envelope. No return address. All correspondence originating from the jail has 'McCown County Jail' stamped in the left corner."

Chuck took a step back, his hands raised. "We can have it checked for prints. That will solve the mystery. No problem."

But Elsie didn't share Chuck's confidence. "If there's a print—and if the print is on record, and they get a hit—we can identify the sender." She stared at the words again. STOP WRONG DUDE.

"The postmark is here in Barton, two days ago. Who does Monroe have on the outside?" she asked.

No one replied. Chuck pulled a tissue from a box on Madeleine's desk, and used it to pick up the envelope.

Elsie continued, "The kid is from St. Louis, doesn't have any local connections."

"You can check the visitors' log at the jail," Madeleine said. "Why don't you go on and do that now."

"Who would visit him? He's a stranger in town."

Chuck said, "Maybe Yocum sent it."

"Don't be ridiculous," Madeleine snapped. "Yocum is a consummate professional."

"Maybe that bleeding heart at the juvenile office is sending fan mail. Monroe's good buddy. What's her name? Peters?" Chuck looked to Elsie for confirmation.

"Lisa Peters doesn't seem like the anonymous letter type," Elsie said.

Madeleine broke in. "Excuse me. I don't know about you all, but I have things to do today."

Elsie and Chuck took the cue, and headed for the door. Once in the hallway, Chuck snapped his fingers. "It's Mom."

"What?"

"The author of the letter. It could be his mother. God, I hope she's not a violent freak, like her kid."

"It could be," Elsie nodded. "It's from someone who's rooting for him, and he's not a guy with a lot of close connections. It could totally be his mother."

Dodging into his office, Chuck said, "Let's look up her rap sheet. If she's a killer, I'd like to be forewarned."

Elsie stood behind Chuck's chair while he accessed the information from their Tanner Monroe file and ran Monroe's mother through the law enforcement database. With triumph, he pointed at the screen. "There she is. I knew it; a drug whore like her had to have a rap sheet."

Elsie bent over his shoulder, studying the woman's picture on the computer screen. "Jesus. She looks a lot like her kid. Doesn't she?"

"Well, she's his mother. What do you expect?" He pulled his keyboard to the edge of his desk. "I'll e-mail this over to the county jail. If they've seen her, I'll let you know."

"Okay," Elsie said, and left the office. As she walked down the hall, she wondered how Tanner's mother could have let him sit in jail for so long without getting in touch. But you never knew about the complexities of a mother and child relationship. Maybe she should give her own mom a call.

Chapter 26

THE MONTH OF July dragged along, sucking Elsie's energy like a massive tick. On a busy morning in Associate Circuit 3, she was pining for a cold drink; Judge Carter had given her a rough time on a DWI trial, sustaining so many defense objections to her direct exam of the arresting officer that she suspected the defendant must be a lodge buddy of the judge's.

When at last he declared a recess, she slogged down the stairs to the Prosecutor's Office. A can of Diet Coke was chilling in her miniature refrigerator; she fancied she could almost taste it.

But as she stepped into the reception area, Stacie gestured to her from the computer. "I've got something for you."

Reluctantly, Elsie paused, with a put-upon look. She had only ten minutes to relax and recuperate; and she did not relish sacrificing any of those minutes on a new wrinkle in some case.

"What?"

"It's a motion. Billy Yocum dropped it off about an hour ago."

"Has Billy ever heard of e-filing?" McCown County, along with the rest of the state, had finally adopted electronic filing of court documents; however, some of the older attorneys were slow to embrace the new technology.

"He said he was bringing it by so you wouldn't overlook it. If you were working on something else."

Waving a hand in dismissal, Elsie said, "Give it to Chuck. He's not assigned to court this morning. I'm up to my eyeballs in shit." She headed to her office, key in hand, but Stacie's voice stopped her.

"He said to give it to you," Stacie said, raising her voice to a higher pitch. "He said you needed to see it."

Turning back to the entryway, Elsie tried to keep her temper in check. The only advantage to being second chair, she thought, was that she should shoulder less responsibility for the case, rather than more. But everything about the case of *State v. Tanner Monroe* seemed out of balance. As Stacie tossed the hard copy of the motion onto the counter, Elsie snatched it up, flipping through the pages as she made her way to her own office.

A speedy review of the second page stopped her cold. "Oh Lord," she whispered, as anxiety formed a knot in her chest. "Oh Jesus."

She bypassed her office door, fairly running down the hall to find Chuck. Without knocking, she flung his door open.

Chuck was turned to face his computer screen, but

when Elsie appeared, he looked over his shoulder, affronted. "Ever hear of knocking?"

She tossed the motion onto his desk. "You're not going to believe this. Jesus."

Chuck picked the motion up with a long-suffering sigh. Examining the first page, he observed, "Motion to suppress. No big surprise. Yocum's just doing his job. He wants to shut down the kid's statement at Juvenile Hall; maybe it doesn't mesh with his defense theory."

"Turn the page," Elsie said tersely. The knot of panic had expanded, and felt like an elephant was sitting on her chest. Her head started sweating at the hairline; when she felt it trickle down her neck, she grabbed a Kleenex from a box on Chuck's desk.

With a countenance of exaggerated patience, Chuck turned to the second page; but his expression changed as he read. Dropping the paper as if it had burned his fingers, he whispered, "Shit."

Elsie nodded. "Yeah." She reached back to rub her neck, where the muscles were stiff. Her collar was wet.

Spinning in his chair, Chuck started to rise. "I've got to show this to Madeleine."

Elsie groaned, her feeling of dread increasing as she watched him scan a copy of the document on the printer beside his desk. When he handed her the copy, the pages felt hot in her cold hands.

Hesitantly, she rose. "I'm on recess in Carter's court. I only have a minute."

Laughing without amusement, he replied, "I wasn't going to invite you along. This won't be happy time."

Stepping into the hallway, she watched him enter Madeleine's office. Behind the closed door, she could make out the murmurs of their exchange. Then silence, followed by a shriek.

Leaning against the wall, Elsie sent up a petition for strength. "Here we go again," she whispered.

By the time she reached the third floor courtroom, the bailiff was trolling the hallway, looking for her.

"Where'd you run off to?" Eldon barked.

Mute, Elsie shook her head.

"Well, you better hustle into court, and fast. Judge Carter don't like to be kept waiting."

Slipping inside the courtroom door, she observed that the judge hadn't waited on her after all. A young woman was on the witness stand, complaining about an infestation of brown recluse spiders; it appeared to be a landlord-tenant matter.

Elsie took a seat in the back row. With trepidation, she unfolded Yocum's defense motion and smoothed it on her lap. Under the case title, it said: "Motion to Suppress." She read:

Comes now Defendant, by and through his undersigned counsel of record, and hereby prays the court for its order, pursuant to Supreme Court Rule 24.05, suppressing the following evidence from the state's case in chief in the above-captioned matter: any and all statements elicited from Defendant arising out of his detention by police, and including, but not limited to, the interrogation of Defendant at Juvenile Hall.

The printed words blurred before her eyes. Blindly, she turned the page, and with a shaking hand, ran her finger down the list of allegations. The early paragraphs contained standard language: that Tanner Monroe was the named Defendant in the case of *State of Missouri v. Tanner Monroe*; that in June, he had been detained in Oklahoma and placed under full-custodial arrest, and transferred to Juvenile Hall in McCown County.

Those recitations were typical; they were not the cause of her anxiety. She read on.

Defendant hereby challenges the legality of the custodial interrogation on the following grounds: Defendant did not knowingly and intelligently waive his Miranda rights prior to being interrogated by Chief Detective Robert Ashlock of the Barton, Missouri, police department.

Pinching her lips together, she tried to think: did he have a valid basis for that argument? She had reviewed the Missouri cases the night before they interrogated Monroe at Juvenile Hall. She could not recall a direct prohibition against their actions; still, the circumstances of the statement had made her uncomfortable at the time. Had they violated the appearance of propriety? That was the cardinal rule for attorneys in Missouri.

Her eyes dropped down to paragraph ten. A flush crept up her chest, reddening her neck as she read Yocum's claims.

And petitioner further alleges that the interrogator and the assistant prosecutor in charge of the case, to wit: Detective Bob Ashlock and Elsie Arnold, were engaging in a sexual relationship when the defendant's statement was taken, which affected the impartiality of the investigation; and that said sexual and romantic relationship has and will continue to influence the investigation and prosecution of this case.

The motion to suppress was a public record. Anyone could access it: other attorneys, law enforcement, the press, the public. Even Elsie's mother and father.

I feel sick, she thought. *I want to throw up.*

A voice broke her concentration. "Ms. Arnold."

She folded the pages before she looked up.

"Ms. Arnold," the judge repeated, with a waspish look.

Lifting her chin, she focused on the judge. "Your honor?"

"Do you have a recommendation?"

She gazed up at the people standing before the bench. The tenant and her lawyer were gone, replaced by a tattooed man in the orange scrubs of the McCown County jail. All eyes were on Elsie: she was the focus of the judge, the defendant, the bailiff.

It's an arraignment, she thought, scrambling to assess the situation. Rising from her seat, she said, "Beg pardon, your honor; can you repeat the charge?"

"Robbery in the first degree. Bond recommendation?"

"Fifty thousand dollars," she replied automatically. As she took her place at the counsel table, Elsie crumpled the motion in her hand, clutching the pages so tightly that they cut the flesh of her palm.

Chapter 27

IT WAS PAST five when Elsie received the summons: Madeleine wanted to see her in her office. Immediately.

She approached the closed door of Madeleine's office with leaden feet, knowing that an ugly scene would soon ensue. Leaning her forehead against the wooden door for support, Elsie gave a tentative rap with her knuckles.

"Get in here." The voice shot through the wooden barrier.

Elsie fixed a rueful grin on her face before she turned the knob. Entering with a diffident air, she saw that Chuck had already arrived and was seated in a chair at Madeleine's side. Sheets of paper bearing yellow stripes of highlighter were scattered on Madeleine's desk; the motion, Elsie supposed.

She took a seat on the sofa facing Madeleine's desk. The hot seat, she thought. She'd occupied that spot many times.

No one spoke. Chuck looked at Madeleine, awaiting her lead. Elsie tried to wait them out, shifting on the sofa cushion and pulling the hem of her skirt to the tops of her knees.

Madeleine continued to stare, pursing her lips and peering over her reading glasses. The beaded chain that hung from the frames glinted in the light from the window behind Madeleine's head. Elsie focused on the chain, thinking, *Don't speak, mustn't say anything, gotta keep my mouth shut.* She knew it would be foolhardy to break the silence. She knew it.

After thirty seconds, she broke. Pointing at the desk, Elsie said, "Have you ever seen anything so terrible in your life?"

Madeleine picked up a page of the motion and let it dangle from her fingers as she leaned back in her chair. "This?" she said in a blank tone. "You mean this?"

"Yeah." Elsie's voice cracked a little, and she coughed to clear it. "That motion is nuts. I've never seen anything so unprofessional in my whole career. In my life."

At that, Madeleine brayed with laughter, in a cackle that was so unexpected, it made Elsie jerk in her seat. Chuck also seemed taken aback, but he broke into a half-hearted chuckle in concert with the boss.

Madeleine tossed the paper in Elsie's direction. "You're a riot. You've never seen anything so unprofessional? That's hilarious."

Unaccountably, Elsie wondered whether Madeleine could see up her dress. She clutched her knees together at the thought.

"Because I don't think it would be perceived as an unprofessional motion," Madeleine drawled. "I think what's unprofessional is the conduct described in the motion."

Stay cool, Elsie counseled herself. This moment couldn't last forever; it would pass. Folding her hands together in her lap, Elsie affected an aggrieved look.

Madeleine said, "You can guess the conduct I'm talking about."

Elsie waited for her to continue, but Madeleine paused. She and Chuck focused on Elsie, two sets of eyes boring into her.

"Can't you guess?"

Elsie figured playing dumb would be a bad idea. "I assume you're talking about the romantic allegations."

"Allegations of a romantic and sexual nature. Sexual."

At that, Chuck's eyes darted away, scouring the ground. He's embarrassed, Elsie thought; embarrassed because she referred to sex. *What a hoot. If anyone has the right to be embarrassed, it's me.*

Elsie rubbed her nose, buying a moment to compose her thoughts. "Madeleine, it's not a secret that Ash and I were seeing each other for a while."

"Certainly not a secret now. It's a matter of public record."

Righteous indignation shot some blood into Elsie's system. "Come on, Madeleine; let's get a grip. We're not teenagers doing it in the gravel at Peckers' Beach. I think Bob Ashlock and I are entitled to pursue adult relationships."

"Not when it interferes with your professional responsibilities. You have tainted a murder case. Do you realize that?"

"No. I don't agree." Elsie looked to Chuck for support, but it was not forthcoming. His eyes were still glued to the rug. She pushed on. "All that's happened is Billy Yocum has found a way to stir up some trouble. He's pulling a rabbit out of his hat. If it wasn't this, he'd use something else."

Madeleine pulled her reading glasses off her nose and toyed with the beaded chain. "You make it so easy."

"What? How do you mean?" Elsie braced herself; the answer would not be flattering.

"You make it so easy for the defense to find an Achilles' heel. What on earth were you doing in that interview with the defendant?"

Elsie turned to Chuck, waiting for him to speak up and take responsibility. He was toying with a loose thread on his jacket, wrapping it around his finger. She watched him give it a tug and flip the thread onto the carpet.

He's not going to say anything, she thought, dumbfounded.

A spark of anger kindled in her chest. "Chuck?"

He inclined his head in her direction, but didn't meet her eye. "What?"

"Chuck, we were both there. At the interrogation."

He sighed and waved his hand in a placating gesture. "True. I was there, Madeleine."

Madeleine held up the motion. "Chuck's name appears once in this document. Exactly one time. Whereas your name, Elsie," and she commenced flipping the pages, "pops up on every page."

Story of my life, Elsie thought, slumping in the chair. *Story of my fucking life.* She took a deep breath and blew it out before asking, "So what are we going to do?"

Madeleine tossed the motion across her desk. "What you always do."

"What do you mean?"

Madeleine's face twitched, then she laughed without mirth. "What you always do. Storm in like a bull in a china shop and hope for the best."

Chuck reached over and picked the crumpled motion off the varnished top of Madeleine's desk. "Do you want me to handle this, Madeleine?"

"No." Madeleine's cell phone buzzed and she picked it up, a clear sign that the meeting was at an end. Before she answered the call, she said, "Elsie made the bed. Let her lie in it."

Chapter 28

ELSIE SHIFTED IN her seat at the front desk of the battered women's center, wishing that someone would see fit to donate a decent office chair. Her job, one Sunday morning each month, involved manning the phone at the front desk, which she was glad enough to do. But the rickety chair, which might have been part of the old building's original furnishings, was well beyond its golden years, and had been designed for a smaller posterior than Elsie's.

She'd begun volunteering regularly at the Battered Women's Center of the Ozarks since the close of the *State v. Taney* case, a hard-fought trial where Elsie secured a life sentence for a man charged with sexual abuse of his daughters. Her work at the desk was not difficult. She was essentially a doorman. While sometimes the hours dragged, she found insight and inspiration when she talked to the residents about their problems and met their children.

Gazing idly about the lobby of the old hotel, she was struck again by the beauty that remained in the crumbling building. The walnut stairway leading to the second floor still gave an air of grandeur, and the porcelain tile, though cracked and missing in places, showed the painstaking workmanship of the century before.

The lobby was empty that Sunday, because the director had loaded most of the women onto a van to attend a nearby church service. Those who remained were either sleeping or caring for their children. At 9:00 A.M. it was unusually quiet. Elsie wished she had thought to bring a Sunday newspaper. Or a magazine. Or maybe a paperback romance novel with a lurid cover.

Rattling the remaining ice cubes in her McDonald's cup, she stretched her legs and propped them up on the desk. Elsie had just found a comfortable position when the front door opened, and a woman in sunglasses, her brown hair cut in a shiny bob, strode up to the desk.

"You're Elsie Arnold," the woman said with surprise.

"Yes," Elsie said, a little guardedly; the woman seemed familiar, but with her Jackie O sunglasses blocking much of her face, it was hard to tell. "What can I do for you today?" After a beat, Elsie added, though it seemed unlikely, "Are you checking in with us this morning?"

The woman laughed. Pushing her glasses atop her head, she said, "Heavens no, Elsie; I'm Caroline Applegate. Bob Ashlock's friend."

Elsie didn't need further introduction. She remembered Caroline Applegate, a family law attorney from a nearby county, who had dated Ashlock before he and Elsie got together. Covertly checking her out, Elsie was discouraged by what she observed. The woman was dressed in a crisp sleeveless blouse, and shorts that displayed a good pair of legs. *Bet she works out*, Elsie thought, grudgingly. *Shit*.

Conjuring a polite voice, Elsie said, "Nice to see you again, Caroline."

"I'm here to see a client," Caroline said confidingly, with a regretful expression. "So sad."

"Yeah," Elsie said dryly, "everybody here is pretty sad."

The woman plucked a tiny speck from her immaculate blouse. "I know I'm not properly dressed. But I'm going to Branson with Bob today, so I thought I'd swing by here and get my client's signature on her divorce petition. It just worked out," she said, in a manner that was decidedly perky.

"Client's name?" Elsie said, deadpan, phone in hand. She did not want to hear about Caroline Applegate's jaunt through the hills with Ashlock. The wound was too fresh.

"Sammie Phillips," Caroline whispered. As Elsie spoke into the second floor intercom, Caroline looked around, relaxed, adjusting her handbag on her shoulder.

Elsie hung up the phone. "She'll be right down. In a minute," Elsie added; Sammie Phillips had sounded like she was brushing her teeth when she acknowledged Elsie's call.

"Good," Caroline said, "I need to wrap this up and hit the road. Bob and I are taking the kids to Branson."

Elsie looked up, shocked and hurt, despite herself. "You're going to Branson? With the kids?"

"To the *Titanic* exhibit. They are so excited." Making a wry face, she added, "Bob suggested that we take them to Silver Dollar City. But I talked him out of it. I think the *Titanic* is much more educational." Leaning into Elsie, she added, in a confiding stage whisper, "And much cooler."

Tears pricked in Elsie's eyes; she bit down on the inside of her cheek to dispel them. For a terrible moment, she feared that Caroline Applegate would see the tears shining in her eyes, so she tried to devise a fitting retort, but nothing came to mind. All she could think of was that Ashlock had offered Caroline Applegate the Silver Dollar City trip with his kids that Elsie had wanted; Elsie should be in the car, driving through the green hills en route to southwest Missouri's hokey tourist wonderland, not Caroline Applegate. Caroline didn't even want to go to Silver Dollar City. She thought it was too hot.

Elsie rubbed her nose, hard, thinking: *Fucking Ashlock, stupid fucking Ashlock, fuck you.*

Looking back at Caroline Applegate, the woman appeared to be awaiting a response. Elsie bared her teeth in an artificial smile. "So, how's Ash doing these days?"

Caroline rolled her eyes. "Oh, that poor man. I ran into him at the farmers' market on a Saturday. He wanted to pick up some tomatoes, but didn't seem like he knew what on earth to do: red or pink or yellow or green. I gave him a hand."

I bet you did, Elsie thought.

"And then I came onto the most beautiful white peaches, just luscious. So I made a pie, and I ran it by the house."

Yellow peaches make a better pie. My mother says so. But Elsie pinched her lips together.

Caroline set her handbag on the desk and unzipped it, rooting inside. "Those poor babies. You'd think those kids had never seen a homemade pie. Bob was so grateful." She smiled at Elsie, with triumph reflecting off each shiny tooth in her head. "He was so sweet. So sweet! And the kids begged me to stay for supper. You know."

You're gloating, Elsie thought. *Rubbing salt in the wound and having fun doing it.* "Wow, what a great story," Elsie said, shaking her head. "But I have a ton of stuff to get back to here. So, you have a great time in Branson."

"Oh, I will. Can't have a bad time in Branson. It's got everything."

Elsie nodded her head sagely. "Branson can be very educational."

"Want me to tell Bob hi for you?"

Bitch, Elsie thought. "Sure. Whatever." In a light tone, she added, "Eat a funnel cake for me."

Caroline Applegate laughed in response as her client appeared on the stairs. Watching as the women crossed the room to a furnished corner of the lobby, Elsie decided: If Ashlock could move on, so could she. It was over. Completely over.

Except for the aftermath. The motion to suppress hearing was set for next week.

Chapter 29

ELSIE'S GUT TWISTED into a knot. Her legs were shaking; with a false show of poise, she crossed them tightly at the knee to still the quivering.

Judge Callaway cleared his throat. "Mr. Yocum, you may proceed."

Yocum rose, standing tall, the overhead light glinting on his spectacles and his gray hair. "Your honor, now this may seem unorthodox. But in support of defendant's motion to suppress, defendant calls Elsie Arnold to the witness stand."

No no no no no, Elsie thought. Jumping to her feet, she spat: "Objection!" before the judge cut her off.

"Where is Mrs. Thompson?"

Elsie and Chuck exchanged a look. Chuck was seated beside Elsie at the counsel table, due to a last-minute change of heart by Madeleine. "Someone has to be a witness to this train wreck," Madeleine had said as she buttonholed him outside Elsie's office. "And it won't be me."

Chuck stood at the prosecutor's counsel table. "In her office, your honor."

"Why isn't she in court?"

Chuck replied, "We're here on behalf of the state. Me and Ms. Arnold."

The judge waved a paper copy of the motion with an impatient gesture. "Your names are included in the allegations. Repeatedly. Is this her case or isn't it? Does she only make her appearances before a camera?"

Elsie felt an unanticipated surge of appreciation toward the judge, glad to learn that they were of a mind about Madeleine's work ethic. Hiding a smile, she looked out the open window near the counsel table and watched a line of pickup trucks pass as Chuck defended Madeleine.

"Your honor, due to scheduling conflicts and conflicts of a personal nature, Prosecutor Thompson thinks it's best to hand the case over to me. I'll be representing the state." After a pause, he added, "Assisted by Ms. Arnold."

"That puts us in a pickle this morning, Judge Callaway," said Yocum, drawing out the words in a drawl. "Because I'm here to tell you: both Mr. Harris and Miss Arnold are witnesses for the defense."

Callaway closed his eyes. "Are they under subpoena?"

"Why no, your honor. Didn't think it was necessary to ensure their appearance by subpoena. I assumed they would be here. And as you can see"—extending his arm with a flourish—"here they be."

Judge Callaway sat with his eyes closed for some minutes while the attorneys stood before him. Elsie's knee began to jiggle again. She pressed her leg against the counsel table to stop it.

At length, the judge opened his eyes. "Billy, how about you call a witness who's under subpoena?"

"But your honor, the purpose of subpoena—"

"Billy. Call your witness." And the judge leaned back in his massive chair, breathing in a deep breath of the fresh, hot air blowing through the open windows.

Billy Yocum turned to the juvenile and bent to whisper in his ear. Tanner Monroe didn't show any reaction. Picking up his notepad, Yocum announced in a stentorian voice, "The defense calls Lisa Peters to the witness stand."

The door opened and Lisa Peters entered. She walked into court with the determined step of one who was facing an unpleasant duty. After being sworn, she scooted into the witness chair, glancing at Elsie sidelong and looking quickly away.

"State your name," said Yocum.

"Lisa Peters."

"What's your occupation?"

"Deputy juvenile officer of McCown County."

Yocum sat and draped his arm over the back of his client's chair. "Let's go back to the fourteenth day of June of this year. Were you a participant in an interrogation on that date?"

The young woman frowned, her brow puckering. "No," she said after a moment.

Yocum sat up straight. "Beg pardon?"

"No—I wasn't a participant. That's not accurate, because I didn't interrogate Tanner myself. But I was present, if that's what you're asking."

Yocum laughed. "I'll have to be careful, won't I, Miss Peters? Or we'll be splitting hairs in here."

The Peters girl is smart, Elsie thought. *She won't let him push her into a corner.*

"Who all was present—as you put it—at this interrogation on June 14?"

"Detective Ashlock. He asked the questions, took the statement. And Chuck Harris and Elsie Arnold from the Prosecutor's Office. And Tanner Monroe; he was in juvenile custody, at that time. And Tanner's guardian ad litem, Maureen Mason. And me."

Yocum whistled. Shaking his head, he said, "That's a houseful, isn't it, Miss Peters. Were Mr. Monroe's parents there?"

"No."

"Why not?"

"They hadn't been contacted."

"And why is that?"

"Tanner didn't provide the contact information, at first. He did later, though—tell us how to reach his mother."

"So he was questioned, without a parent present. Tell me, Miss Peters: What was the purpose of having those two prosecutors sitting in?"

"I don't know."

"Were they there at your invitation? Did you request it?"

"No. No, I didn't."

"Isn't it true, Miss Peters," said Yocum, warming to the task and getting into his theatrical mode, "that you openly voiced objection to the presence of Miss Arnold and Mr. Harris?"

Lisa Peters nodded. "I did."

"In fact, Miss Peters, did you not say that the detective and the prosecutors were 'dog-piling the poor kid.'"

Elsie tried to keep from slumping in her seat. Those were the very words Lisa had used. And they sounded pretty bad for the prosecution, when repeated in a court of law. Why hadn't Elsie listened to her gut that day, and excused herself?

Lisa didn't answer right away. Yocum left the counsel table and approached her like an old mountain lion cornering his prey.

"Weren't those your very words, Miss Peters?"

Lisa sighed, but before she could speak, Yocum added, "Need I remind you that you're under oath?"

She shook her head. "I can't recall my exact words. But that sounds like something I'd say."

"Well, let's go about this another way. On that occasion, did it seem to you that they were 'dog-piling' my fifteen-year-old client? Ganging up on a young juvenile, a mere boy? And taking advantage of him on that occasion?"

Please don't please don't please don't say it, chorused through Elsie's head, but it did not prevent the inevitable.

Lisa Peters took a deep breath and said, "Yes. That's what I thought."

We're in trouble, Elsie told herself.

Billy Yocum actually bowed to the witness, as if they'd finished a square dance set. "No further questions."

Chuck stood. Elsie watched him, praying that he would undo the damage.

"Ms. Peters, how old are you?"

What a stupid bullshit question, Elsie thought.

Apparently, Lisa Peters thought so, too. She cocked her head, eyeing Harris with a look of disbelief. "Why?"

"Just answer the question," he said.

"Twenty-two."

"Twenty-two," Chuck repeated. "And how many years of experience do you have in juvenile work?"

"Objection," Billy said. "The prosecutor is acting like we've tried to qualify the witness for an expert opinion, a matter of expert testimony, your honor, which the defense did not do. This line of questioning is irrelevant."

"Overruled." Judge Callaway picked up the court file and waved it back and forth before his face, a makeshift fan.

"How many years, Ms. Peters?"

"This is my first year at the juvenile office. But I have a degree—"

"Just answer the questions I ask, Ms. Peters, thank you. Do you have a legal background?"

Lisa looked at Harris, her face tense. "No."

"Have you had any experience in police detective work? As a law enforcement professional?" Harris paced before the stand, chest thrust out like a rooster.

"No. Like I said, I'm a juvenile officer."

"A deputy juvenile officer, you said. So please tell the court, Ms. Peters," and he stopped pacing, pointed a finger at her, and raised the volume of his voice, "where you got the idea that you are qualified to sit in judgment on the McCown County Prosecutor's Office? And the Barton Police Department?"

"I'm just answering the questions—" Lisa said, as Yocum rose and shouted, "Objection! Badgering the witness!"

Ignoring Yocum, Chuck stepped closer to the stand. "What qualifies you to second-guess an attorney?"

Oh shit, Elsie thought.

Yocum cried out: "Objection! I have raised an objection, your honor. Does the prosecutor not understand that we are under a duty to hear the ruling of the court? Boy, what did they teach you about proper court procedure up in Kansas City?"

The judge rolled his head backward, cracking his neck. "Sustained."

Chuck turned on his heel. "No further questions."

Watching Lisa step down, Elsie saw her make eye contact with Chuck. When Elsie glanced Chuck's way, she caught him shooting a wink at the juvenile officer. Elsie almost choked. *What a dick*, she thought; was he trying to cut their throats at the prosecution table?

Yocum interrupted her thoughts; he announced, "The defense calls Detective Robert Ashlock."

Elsie's head jerked around to look through the courtroom door. Through the chicken wire embedded in the glass, she could see that his face was grim.

After Ashlock was sworn, he took his seat on the witness stand, his back stiff. His eyes were flinty as Yocum approached the stand.

"State your name for the record, Detective."

"Robert Dean Ashlock."

"Occupation?"

"Chief of detectives, Barton Police Department."

"How long have you held that position?"

"Nearly ten years."

"Ten years as chief of detectives," Yocum repeated, sounding impressed. "That's a long old time."

There was silence, not broken until Yocum added, "Wouldn't you say, Detective?"

"Yes."

"I expect you've conducted a lot of suspect interrogations in that time."

Ashlock nodded. "Yes, sir. I have."

"How many, you reckon?"

Ashlock paused, his brow wrinkling as he calculated. "Hundreds. Hard to give a precise number."

"Well then, let's say 'many.' Would that be accurate?"

"Yes."

"Among all those 'many' suspect interrogations, did you ever question a juvenile suspect?"

"Yes."

"How many?"

"From time to time. Less serious offenses, generally."

"Many juvenile interrogations. Less serious offenses. This the first time you've questioned a juvenile suspect in a murder case?"

"It was. Is."

Yocum made a show of walking back to the counsel table, digging through his worn briefcase for a pen, checking off an item on a legal pad. Then abruptly, he swung back to Ashlock; peering over his glasses, he asked, "Is this the first time you brought your girlfriend along for custodial interrogation?"

Sweat dampened Elsie's armpits as her heartbeat increased. To her surprise, Chuck jumped from his seat with heroic zeal.

"Objection!"

Judge Callaway had not given signs of his ordinary somnolence throughout the testimony. He turned his attention to Chuck. "What grounds?"

"Assumes facts not in evidence." In response to the judge's quizzical look, Chuck added, "She's not his girlfriend." Deflating under the judge's scrutiny, he added, "Anymore," and sat back down.

Billy Yocum smiled, his teeth shining like ivory keys on an old piano. "I appreciate Mr. Harris's candor, Judge, I surely do. But he is not under oath. I prefer to obtain the information from the witness on the stand."

"Objection overruled. Proceed, Billy," said the judge.

"Detective Ashlock, let me put the question another way." Billy offered Ashlock a cordial nod. "Do you customarily bring your girlfriends—your ladyloves—along when you interrogate suspects?"

"Ms. Arnold was a professional colleague," Ashlock said.

"Well now, Detective, that's not what I asked. I didn't

ask you whether Miss Arnold is a professional." Turning
to the bench, Yocum said, "Judge, could the court reporter read back the last question, so the detective can
answer?"

The court reporter pulled the strip of paper from the
machine. " 'Do you customarily bring your girlfriends—
your ladyloves—along when you interrogate suspects?' "

Elsie watched Ashlock as he focused on Yocum. She
tried to read his face, but it was a stoic mask.

"No," Ashlock said.

"Specifically—murder interrogations? Custodial interrogation of murder suspects?"

"No."

"How about interrogation of a juvenile suspect in a
murder case? Did you bring your girlfriend along on that
one?"

"I was accompanied by two members of the county
prosecutor's office, Chuck Harris and Elsie Arnold."

"And?"

"At the time, Ms. Arnold and I were socializing, if
that's what you're getting at."

"What exactly does that mean—'socializing'? Does
that refer to an exclusively social relationship?"

When Ashlock didn't respond, Yocum zeroed in.
"Romantic relationship? Sexual relationship? Come on,
Detective, you were dicking Miss Arnold, weren't you?"

Elsie's heart palpitated; *I'll never live this down, never.*

All the air seemed to be sucked out of the hotbox
of a room. Elsie looked around in slow motion; no one
moved. The judge wore a sour look. Ashlock's face had

turned a shade of red bordering on purple. Chuck sat with his mouth agape. Billy Yocum leaned against the jury box, waiting.

The juvenile caught her eye. He was watching her. He pursed his lips and sent her an air kiss.

The kiss jolted Elsie from her trance. She jumped from her seat, shouting, "Jesus Christ!"

The judge swung his gavel in Elsie's direction. "Is that an objection?"

"Yes, your honor; oh yes it is," she said, recovering her wits in a rush. "Mr. Yocum's tactics are underhanded and unethical. He is badgering the witness, intentionally inciting him with questions designed to inflame the witness and the court."

Yocum raised his hand, preparing to respond, but Judge Callaway cut him off.

"Sustained."

Billy looked like he'd been delivered an electric shock. "Your honor!"

"Now Billy, I gave you some leeway with this, let you make your point. But you're going into territory that's best left alone."

"Your honor, I can demonstrate bias—"

"Hold off, Billy. You're done here. And you won this round."

Elsie, who had half risen from her seat, sat down again. Chuck leaned in to whisper something to her, but she only listened with half an ear. She waited for the judge to continue, clutching her pen in a tight grip.

The judge said: "I'm not going to ask you all to pre-

pare written suggestions, because my mind is made up.
I'm suppressing the statement. The state cannot submit it
at trial as part of the state's case in chief."

Billy straightened his tie before he spoke. "Judge, I respectfully request that the state also be barred from using
the statement for purposes of cross-examination in the
event the defendant testifies."

Elsie was busy calculating the damage that the judge's
decision would do to the state's case when she heard
Ashlock speak up.

He was still in his seat on the witness stand. "Judge,
we got all the forms signed, read him his rights—did it
by the book, from A to Z. And you're throwing it out? I
don't understand."

"And I'm not obligated to defend my ruling to you,
Detective. But this once, I will." The judge cut his eyes at
Elsie, then turned his chair toward Ashlock. He spoke so
softly that Elsie could barely make out the words: "I don't
much care who you're fooling around with. But I don't
like you interrogating a boy that age without a parent
present. Doesn't sit right with me." He tossed the file
folder to his clerk. "Court is adjourned."

Chapter 30

AFTER JUDGE CALLAWAY left the bench, Elsie followed Chuck out of the courtroom, holding herself so tightly that her jaw hinge locked up. Rounding the rotunda on the second floor, Chuck pointed to the back entrance of the Prosecutor's Office and said: "First stop: Madeleine."

Elsie ignored him. She dodged into the stairway and tore down the steps, nearly tripping over her own feet. On the ground floor, she made for the exit, pushing the ancient oak door open wide and letting the sun blind her. For a moment she stood, sucking the hot air into her lungs, with her eyes squeezed shut and her face turned up to the sky.

Jeanette, the court reporter, brushed past her.

"That was some hearing, huh?" the woman asked with a laugh.

Elsie nodded, her head bobbing like a toy on a string.

"I've got to get back in a hurry and work up the transcript for the court file. Wouldn't want to be you today. You're going to be famous."

Elsie stared at the woman's back as she marched away, her heels clicking a beat on the hot concrete. She tried to summon a surge of anger toward the reporter, but it wouldn't come. The words she'd spoken were the Lord's own truth.

A weathered pair of park benches rested on the edge of the courthouse lawn where it met the street. *I've got to sit down*, Elsie thought, making her way toward them. *I need to sit and think.*

She lowered herself onto the planks, taking care to keep her bare skin from touching the peeling slats of wood. All she needed to make the day complete was a splinter in her ass.

A distinctive stink registered, and she looked around warily, to find the source. It was near at hand; a trash receptacle beside the bench was topped by a metal ashtray wriggling with maggots.

"Jesus." She groaned, scooting away from the odor; but as she thought the afternoon couldn't be more uncomfortable, she saw Lisa Peters coming toward her on the walk.

Lisa walked toward Elsie at a determined clip and planted herself in front of her, as if daring her to leave. Elsie looked up into her face, but the sun was so bright she had to squint.

"What?" Elsie said.

"It wasn't personal."

"Shit," Elsie said, her voice almost a sigh.

Lisa stood rooted to the spot, clutching a big white Sonic Drive-In cup to her chest. "Really, I want you to know: I think you do a good job. I understand the prosecutor's role, what you do. And Chuck. But I was under oath."

Elsie rubbed her eyes; the sun was too bright. "Yeah."

"I swear to God," Lisa said, dropping onto the bench beside her. "I wouldn't throw a rock at you. I've come to have a lot of respect for you."

"You didn't have a choice," Elsie said.

"I didn't have a choice," Lisa said, as if Elsie hadn't spoken.

They sat in unhappy silence until Elsie pointed at the storefront across the street.

"Do you remember the old Ben Franklin? Or are you too young?"

"Kinda. It was a craft store, right?"

"No, that was just at the end, before it closed down for good. It was a five-and-dime before that, the real thing. Great candy. And weird shit. Random stuff." The women gazed at the porcelain tiles that still covered the two-story structure. "Somebody should do something with that property."

"The square is dead."

"Don't tell the Chamber of Commerce."

"Chamber of Blow Jobs."

For the first time that day, Elsie laughed out loud. It felt like a tonic. She turned to Lisa and said, "Don't worry. I'm not going to stick pins in a voodoo doll because you did what you had to do."

"Really, I want you to know: I think you do a good job. But I was under oath."

"I know."

"I was; I had to tell the truth. I'm sorry you had such a terrible time in there. But I did the only thing I could do. You knew I didn't like the way that statement went down. I was straight with you about it."

Elsie started to speak, but thought better of it.

"I just told the truth. That's all." Making a face, Lisa said, "It smells like death," then took a long pull on a Sonic Drive-In cup.

Elsie settled back on the seat, scooting back far enough to feel the wood warm her thighs. She knew Lisa didn't have a choice. She'd been under subpoena; when questioned, she answered truthfully. "Apt description. It's maggots." She nodded toward the offending trash can.

Lisa leaned in the direction of the can, appearing to examine the vermin. Nodding, she said, "It's the heat. Flies love the month of July. Nothing you can do about it."

The women sat in silence, side by side, until Elsie roused herself from her inertia and said, "There's always something."

Lisa sucked on the red straw. "How's that?"

"About maggots. My mom told me. Her family didn't have a garbage disposal when she was a kid, so maggots were fierce in the summer. But my grandmother sprinkled 20 Mule Team Borax in the garbage cans. Flies don't like borax."

Lisa nodded, looking genuinely impressed. "That's good to know."

Elsie let out a short laugh. "Honest to God, my mother knows some crazy shit."

"Okay. Give me another one."

Elsie lifted her hand to shield her eyes from the sun. "Sunburn."

"What about it?"

"Apple cider vinegar for sunburn. She'd pour it on me in the tub. I bitched about the smell, but it works like magic."

Lisa nodded. "That's a good one. But I've heard it before."

Taking the challenge, Elsie inched closer to Lisa. "What about leg cramps? Charley horses? Mom puts a bar of soap under the fitted sheet. I never had trouble with muscle cramps in the night when I lived at home." To herself, she added, "I ought to do that now."

"That sounds like an old wives' tale. There could be a million other reasons to explain the phenomenon."

Elsie did not deign to reply.

Lisa went on, "I always heard gin and tonic is good for muscle cramps."

"Gin and tonic is good for what ails you," Elsie said, but remembering the cocktails that led to her casino war with Ashlock, she fell silent.

Lisa sighed. "I can't help it, I worry about him."

"Tanner Monroe?"

"Oh yeah. Tanner Monroe. My first assigned juvenile case. What a kickoff." She held out her Sonic cup. "Have a drink."

Elsie shook her head. "No, thanks."

Lisa ignored the refusal; she put the drink in Elsie's hand. "It's cherry."

Elsie stared at the cup. She had no desire to share the cherry slush; she was not a germophobe, but she wasn't ready to smoke the ceremonial peace pipe with Lisa, if that was what the cup represented.

"I'm not thirsty," she said, but Lisa snorted.

"If you don't suck on that straw right this second, you ain't got a hair on your ass."

That caused Elsie to crack a smile; she'd always liked that expression. Obligingly, she sucked on the straw.

Fire poured down her throat and made her eyes water. "Shit," she choked, "you should've warned me."

Lisa cut her eyes at Elsie with a conspiratorial look. "Vodka. I needed a big dose of something after that court hearing."

Elsie shuddered, the aftereffect of the unexpected shot. "Do you think you're okay?"

"I'll survive."

Narcissistic little shit, Elsie thought. *Maybe you should try to survive being the Hester Prynne of McCown County.*

"Lisa, what I meant was—are you okay to drive?"

"I've got a ride. I'm waiting."

Elsie rested against the back of the park bench. The vodka must have deadened her sense of smell; the maggots were more bearable. "Give me another bite of that snake."

Lisa offered the cup, saying, "You're sure you're not hating my fucking guts?"

"Just a little. Less than I was." At the sight of Lisa's

anxious face, Elsie laughed. "Aw, shit, hon; he had you in a spot. I can't hate a girl for telling the truth when she's under oath." Elsie hand back the cup. "Because I'm not like that."

"I finally figured that out." Lisa lifted the lid and showed Elsie the icy remains. "We're down to the slushy stuff." She tipped the cup and took a mouthful.

Looking away, Elsie said, "Sometimes I wish I'd never heard of Tanner Monroe."

Lisa choked and gagged. After spitting a chunk of ice on the sidewalk, she said. "Hey, sista. I'm thinking that every single day."

A voice cut across the courthouse lawn. "Peters! Petie!"

Both women looked around to see Chuck Harris standing under a shade tree near the side entrance of the courthouse, loosening his tie. He jerked his thumb toward the employee parking. "Ready?"

"Gotta go," Lisa said, tossing her Sonic cup into the maggoty waste can. She strutted up to Chuck, and as they walked off together, Lisa's hand slipped around Chuck's waist.

Elsie's jaw unlocked and she stared at the pair, open-mouthed. "Fuck me running," she whispered.

Chapter 31

WHEN ELSIE OPENED the door of Billy Yocum's store-front office on the town square, a chime jangled to herald her arrival. She looked up and saw a tarnished brass bell dangling overhead.

Elsie heard a toilet flush, and a moment later, an ancient secretary appeared. The woman shuffled toward Elsie, squinting through tortoiseshell glasses.

"It's Elsie, isn't it? Little Elsie Arnold."

"Hey, Veda." Elsie gave her a smile. Veda Wilson had served as Yocum's secretary for decades.

The woman shook a finger at her. "I used to babysit your mama."

Elsie nodded. "Yes, ma'am, I know. You've told me." Veda Wilson reminded Elsie of the babysitting connection each and every time Elsie encountered her.

"She was such a nice girl. And smart! Why, she could read the newspaper in first grade."

"She's still reading that paper, Veda. Every morning. Say, Veda, is Billy around?"

"Yes, indeed. Let me stick my head in his office." Veda stepped over to a closed door; without bothering to knock, she literally stuck her head inside. "Billy, she's here."

His voice boomed into the outer office. "And who's this 'she'?"

"Billy, it's Elsie. Elsie Arnold. Marge's girl."

"Have her take a seat. I'll be out in a minute."

Elsie dropped into a chair of mustard yellow vinyl, thinking that the delay was a power play on Billy's part. She stretched her legs in front of her, settling in for a long wait, and started to simmer. She did not intend to waste her afternoon in Yocum's office; he was at the very top of her shit list, even over Madeleine and Ashlock. Elsie hadn't deigned to look at Yocum since the motion to suppress hearing a fortnight ago, much less speak to him; but he'd surprised her with a phone call that morning, demanding in a curt voice that she come by his office after lunch. He said he had important news to share. And before she could protest, he hung up.

Elsie picked through the magazines on the table beside her chair. They were Mrs. Yocum's discarded issues of *Good Housekeeping* and *Southern Living*, with the address labels still intact. On a lower shelf of the side table, she saw a stack of old yearbooks: Barton High, Home of the Mountaineers! She picked up the one on top, bearing a worn green cover with the year set forth in faded gold: 1960.

"Jesus," she whispered, flipping through the black and white pages of Yocum's glory days. In the senior class photo, the caption revealed he was president; she spotted him on the basketball team; and the debate team ran a half-page photo of Billy, a staged pose, with his arms crossed as he scowled at his opponent. Two pages later, she found the prize: Billy sitting on a hay bale beside a girl wearing a gown of layers of tulle: Barnwarming King and Queen.

Elsie guffawed at the picture, drawing a curious stare from Veda. As she closed the yearbook and slipped it back in place with the others, she nearly upset a huge pottery ashtray. Elsie pushed it back to safety by the magazines. It was a vintage jewel of speckled aqua, with room for a dozen smokers to ash and rest their cigarettes and extinguish butts. It held a matching lighter. Elsie picked it up and flicked it, but it didn't work.

"You itching for a smoke, Miss Arnold?" Billy stood in the doorway of his office, regarding her with a raised brow.

She jammed the lighter back into its spot. "Lord, no, Billy. I've never smoked." The statement was not entirely true. "I was just wondering—why do you have that thing out here? They just passed that new smoking ordinance. You're violating city law."

"I don't plan on using it."

"Then what's it here for?" In a mocking tone, she said, "Sentimental reasons?"

"It was a gift. When I opened my law practice. A gift from my late father."

Aw, shit, Elsie thought. Billy Yocum always played the dead family card on her. She had no comeback; she followed Billy into his office and settled into a bloodred club chair that faced his desk. He sat across from her, staring, his right hand toying with a paperweight that sat atop a manila file folder.

"Billy. What did you call me over here for? I'm busy."

"I have a report to share with you." Billy set the paperweight aside and opened the folder, pulling a stapled sheaf of papers from the top of a pile. As Elsie watched, jiggling her foot with impatience, Yocum scanned the document through his bifocals.

At length, she interrupted his silent reading. "Billy, you could send that to me. E-mail me, and attach it. Or fax it. You could send it U.S. mail, if you're not in a hurry. Or, I don't know, maybe just drop it off with Stacie. That's how I got your last important motion."

Yocum continued to examine the papers. Elsie stood. Her voice was snappish when she spoke. "I'm heading out, Billy. I'll be damned if I'm going to sit here and watch you read. I'll tell you the truth: I'm not really in the mood to hang with you, after that hatchet job in Callaway's court."

She nearly reached the door when Yocum's voice stopped her. "My client suffers from mental illness. Mr. Monroe."

Elsie turned, scrutinizing him with a wary eye. "What's this? What happened to Other Dude Done It?"

Billy didn't answer. His eyes were trained on the document.

Elsie said, "If Tanner Monroe didn't cut the woman's

throat; if, as you and your client contend, another person did the deed, then what does it matter whether he's crazy or not?"

Billy Yocum replaced the document in the file folder and closed it, carefully setting the paperweight on top. "Then you have no interest in the content of my medical report."

Elsie edged back to her chair. "I'm interested, sure. What's the diagnosis?"

Billy sighed. Shaking his head, he said, "My client is a troubled young man."

She smiled in response, genuinely amused. "No shit."

"Miss Arnold, could you please refrain from using vulgar language in my office?"

Resentment washed over Elsie like the tide. "Oh please. Excuse the fuck out of me, Billy. I thought I was talking to the guy who accused Ashlock of 'dicking' me in open court."

Billy leaned back in his chair with a patient expression. "Miss Arnold, you fancy yourself a litigator. I'd expect you to understand trial tactics."

Behind Billy's head was a shelf containing two prizes: a plaque from the Missouri Trial Attorneys Association, naming him the Trial Lawyer of the Year in 1982; and the trophy for Division 1 High School basketball in 1960. She imagined the satisfaction she would derive from knocking the treasures to the floor.

"It was personal. You crossed the line, Billy."

"Miss Arnold, you have some hard lessons to learn. Not the least of which is how to stand clear of that line.

You walk right into the line of fire, you know that?" He tapped the file folder with his index finger. "Antisocial personality disorder."

Elsie made a hissing noise, waving her hand in dismissal. "Is that the best you can do? Every inmate in the Department of Corrections can claim that disorder; just means they commit crimes. You were better off with ODDI."

Yocum adjusted his glasses, smiling broadly. "I guess you'll find that out soon enough."

She didn't like his expression. "What do you mean?"

"At trial. You'll learn about our defense pretty soon now."

"What do you mean? We won't go to trial for months yet. We're way down on the docket."

"I'm filing a motion. Veda just typed it up. Maybe you should be there when the judge takes it up."

Her face flushed; he always kept her off-balance. "Billy, what's going on?"

"My wife and I are taking our fortieth wedding anniversary trip. She wants to see the castles of Europe."

"Judge Callaway isn't going to rush a murder case to trial so you can go on vacation."

"Oh goodness, no. He'll do it for the safety and security of a minor. My client is in the general population at the county jail; did you know that?"

Elsie felt a twinge of angst; she'd supposed they'd placed Monroe in some kind of protective custody, away from the other inmates. "I don't know the particulars."

"He's in grave danger, on a daily basis. I'd think such a wrinkle would occur to you. You purport to be greatly disturbed by sex crimes against young victims."

She almost winced. "If there's a problem, you should talk to Vernon Wantuck at the jail. He'd listen to you."

"Oh, I think I'll take it up with Judge Callaway. I believe I will."

Elsie's head started spinning; if they were looking at a trial date in the near future, she needed to start anticipating the defense's hand. "Hey, Billy, who's your doctor? Who did the mental eval on Monroe?"

"Dr. Boone. In Springfield."

"That quack?" Elsie recognized the name; Dr. Boone was a psychologist in private practice who was popular with the criminal defense bar, due to his propensity to declare criminal defendants unfit to stand trial and unable to comprehend that their behavior was wrong. "Boone thinks everyone is crazy. He'd diagnose me with antisocial personality disorder."

Yocum didn't reply; he just looked at Elsie with his brow lifted.

"Don't you dare," she said. "Don't say it. We're on thin ice as it is, you and me."

"Miss Elsie, you can't read my mind. And you mustn't be disposed to paranoia. Such an unattractive quality in a woman."

She stood in a huff. "Give me the goddamned report, and a copy of your new motion. And I'll get out of here before you make me lose my temper."

He patted the manila folder with a blue-veined hand;

on his fourth finger, he wore a Mason's ring sporting a large faceted ruby.

"I think I'll take your suggestion, Miss Arnold. I'll send this motion to you and Mr. Harris through the U.S. Postal Service. It should reach you next week. If Veda gets it in the mail in the next day or two."

Elsie didn't bother to reply. She walked away from Billy and made for the exit. Before she reached the door, Veda called to her.

"Elsie, honey, hold up. I've got something for you."

Elsie turned. "Is it the new motion in the Monroe case? I'd like to see that."

"No, I don't have that ready for Billy to see. This is something else." Veda lifted a stack of envelopes that appeared to hold the morning mail.

"Really, Veda, I'm in an awful hurry."

"Well now, I had it right here." She opened the top drawer of her desk and began to paw through it. "I had it just a minute ago."

"Mrs. Wilson, I'm sorry, but—"

"She was just here. Just right here with it."

As Elsie burned with impatience, Veda scoured the drawer a second time, breaking off the search with a laugh. Reaching for the blue Kleenex box on her desk, she said, "I put it right on top so I wouldn't lose it. Sometimes I think I must be getting the old-timers."

Veda extended an open hand; when Elsie saw what it held, she quailed. It was a tarot card. The Fool.

She didn't want to touch it, but Veda held it out with an expectant face.

"A woman was looking in here for you, but she wouldn't wait. She said to give this to you. Said you'd understand."

Elsie examined the worn card, its cardboard edges soft and frayed. The Fool was stepping off a cliff. Because the Fool didn't look to see where he was going.

These days, it felt like she was doing the same thing.

Chapter 32

"WE'RE GOING TO trial."

Chuck had been lounging in his office, his feet propped on his desk, but Elsie's announcement made him twist sideways in his chair.

"What? What are you talking about?"

"Yocum. I just came from his office. He dropped the bomb." She leaned against the door frame of Chuck's office, pressing her hot face against the wood. "You want to hear about it?"

When Chuck nodded, she walked to the air-conditioning unit under his window and sat on it, grateful for the cold air shooting up her back.

"It's too early," Chuck said. He picked up the receiver of his landline phone, and stared at it; then with a grimace, set the phone in its cradle.

"Too early for who? Yocum says the defense is ready to go."

"So what's the defense, then? ODDI? Yocum hasn't even taken depositions. He'd have to notify us."

"Maybe he's not taking depos. Too expensive, maybe; who knows if the state would pick up the tab on the court reporter? He could be taking statements over the phone; he has all the contact information on our Oklahoma witnesses from discovery. Or he might've sent an investigator to Oklahoma; who knows? But he's got a new angle now. MD or D."

Chuck gaped at her. "Insanity?" When she nodded, he asked, "Says who?"

"Billy."

"No, I mean—who's the expert?"

Elsie pulled a face. "That quack from Springfield: Dr. Boone. Have you heard of him?"

Chuck didn't answer the question, asking instead, "What's the mental disease or defect? Did Billy say?"

"Antisocial personality disorder."

Chuck spun his chair around and pulled a thick volume from the credenza behind his desk. "That sounds bad. Serious."

"Oh, Chuck. Please. Everybody in prison probably qualifies as antisocial personality disorder."

"Are you listening to yourself? I think you're missing a key point. It engenders sympathy for the defendant. People feel sorry for a person with a mental disorder."

"Where? In Kansas City?" Elsie scoffed in dismissal. "The people in this county won't buy into an insanity plea unless a guy actually thinks he's Napoleon. Or Elvis. We never see a 'Not Guilty' for insanity in McCown County.

They consider an NGI verdict to be an easy out for the criminal element. Like getting off on a technicality."

Chuck wheeled to the computer and clicked his mouse. "I'll Google it."

While he toyed with the computer, Elsie crossed over to the chair facing his desk. "Chuck, have you ever tried a case with an MD or D defense?"

He didn't answer, just continued scanning the computer screen.

"Chuck, I don't mean to dog you about this, but I need to know where we stand. Have you done it before?"

At length, without looking her way, he said shortly: "No."

She let out a long breath. "But you're from that huge Jackson County office. Seems like KC would have had insanity cases—"

"There was a woman on our staff: Mary Birmingham. She handled all the insanity trials." He scrabbled the computer mouse around the pad, as if it would help him uncover the answers he sought. "But it sounds like a major problem. Shit—we have to prove that he's sane."

"Well, not exactly. We have the burden of proving that he committed the crime—the murder. But if Yocum and Tanner Monroe claim insanity, they have the burden of proof on that defense. He has to prove to the jury that he was insane when he killed her."

Chuck's face took on a resentful look; Elsie knew he didn't like to be corrected by her. She was, after all, his assistant.

Stacie appeared in the doorway. "Chuck, got something for you."

He turned a baleful eye on the receptionist. "I'm busy," he said.

Stacie's mouth thinned to a lip-glossed line. "That's a nice way to thank me for my trouble. Next time, I'll just let you come to me. You can wear your shoes out walking down by the reception area." She slapped a manila envelope on his desk and turned on her heel.

With an impatient hand, Chuck tossed the envelope onto an in-box on his desk; but then he gave it a second glance. Picking the envelope back off the stack, Chuck examined it.

"This is from Billy Yocum," he said.

"What the fuck? I was just over at his office. What's in it?"

Elsie watched Chuck tear into the correspondence; he ripped the envelope with such ferocity, she worried that he might tear the document it contained. She stood and walked over to his side at the desk, so she could see what Yocum sent.

"The doctor's mental evaluation of Monroe. Dr. Boone," he said.

She let out her breath with a hiss. "That old shithead. He wouldn't give it to me. I was sitting right there in his office; I asked him for it."

"Maybe he wanted to deliver it to the attorney in charge of the case." Chuck flipped through the pages. "There's a second document. It's a motion. He wants the case set for trial. Jesus."

Elsie sat on the edge of the desk, facing Chuck. "Chuck, I think we'll be okay if he goes with the mental disease defense. I've only done it once, but I saved everything; I have the jury instructions and voir dire questions and the doctor's examination. And I just don't believe he'll get off, if his mental disease is antisocial personality disorder. It's too common. It's not the kind of defect that will convince a jury that he didn't know what he was doing, couldn't control his behavior, doesn't know right from wrong. I don't think the jury will believe he's incapable of obeying the law."

"Would you get your butt off my desk? If you don't mind?"

Elsie stood; disgruntled, she walked back to the chair, but she pressed on. "Really, Chuck. He may have a personality disorder, but he's not insane enough to be found NGI. Just not crazy enough."

Chuck didn't appear to be listening; he was studying the report. He threw his head back and groaned.

"What?" Elsie said.

"He's crazy. Batshit crazy."

"What? What is it?"

Chuck snatched up a highlighter and started marking on the page. "He thinks his body has been invaded at the jail."

"Oh Jesus," Elsie whispered, with a sinking feeling in her stomach. "Chuck, has he been raped?" The stomach knot gave way to a tide of panic. Surely, she thought— surely Vernon Wantuck wouldn't let that happen. Elsie could hear her mother's voice: *A boy of fifteen is not a man.*

"No, that's not it. He doesn't say anything about being assaulted. He says," and Chuck stopped to run a hand over his face, as if to wipe sweat away, though Elsie couldn't see a telltale sheen, "he told the shrink that spiders have invaded his body. They crawled up his anus and laid their eggs." He flipped to the next page. "When he defecates, he sees spiderwebs spinning out of his rectum."

Elsie looked away, stunned. "Oh my Lord."

Chuck tossed the report onto his desk. "How the fuck will we counter that?"

Elsie exhaled, her breath coming out in a long sigh. "Maybe he's faking?" she offered feebly.

"Spiderwebs out the ass? You can't make shit like that up."

Chapter 33

Elsie's office faced the west side of the town square. At five o'clock, the sun beat through the glass with a vengeance, setting her face on fire. She reached up to pull the string that closed the metal blinds, but they refused to close all the way; the blinds were half a century old, and though she fought with the string, stripes of white sunlight peeked through.

She settled in her chair and opened the *State v. Monroe* file. With the trial speedily approaching, Chuck had assigned their roles and divvied up tasks. He announced that he would do voir dire and jury selection, Opening Statement, Closing Argument, and examination of key witnesses: Ashlock, the coroner, and the crime lab witnesses who would testify about the forensic evidence. The autopsy, DNA, fingerprints, blood, and hair would be his territory. The glamour jobs, Elsie thought.

She was assigned the county deputies who assisted

Ashlock at the scene, and the Oklahoma witnesses. And Chuck had ordered Elsie to initiate contact with everyone on the witness list, to let them know that trial was approaching.

The grunt work.

She picked up the phone at her desk and dialed the first name on her to-do list: a McDonald's employee in Vinita, Oklahoma, named Camryn Hornbuckle. When the phone picked up on the other end, Elsie sat up straight in her chair, preparing to speak.

"'Hey, this is Cammie. I'm not here right now. Leave me a message, okay? I'll get back with you.'"

Elsie sighed. She hung up the phone without comment; she'd learned from hard experience that it was unlikely she'd get a callback if she left a message to call the Prosecutor's Office. Too scary, she supposed. She would try again later.

The second McDonald's witness was male: Jeff Bartlesby. When she dialed his number, an electronic robot voice informed her that it had been disconnected.

She slammed the receiver down. "Well, that's just great. Shit."

Her coworkers were leaving; Elsie heard their voices in the hallway. Stacie was bickering with the traffic clerk about their carpool.

Breeon appeared in the doorway of Elsie's office with her purse dangling from her shoulder. "Are you hanging around? You should know by now: they don't pay us any overtime."

Elsie pointed at the open file. "Monroe case. Trying to line up my out-of-state witnesses."

Breeon said, "Go on home. Give yourself a little downtime. You can make those calls later, after you've had something to eat."

Shaking her head, Elsie sad, "Chuck wants me to get right on it."

Breeon's face took on an expression of mock sobriety. "Then you get to work, girl. Chuck knows best."

Elsie and Breeon exchanged a look. They had privately exchanged notes on the new chief assistant's skill set.

"Hey," Elsie said, her voice dropping to a whisper, "I saw Chuck going off into the sunset with the new juvenile officer. Lisa Peters."

"The one who testified at the suppression hearing?"

"Yeah. Red hair."

Bree shrugged. Elsie said, "Well? Doesn't that seem strange?"

"Why? She had to testify."

"No, that's not what I mean."

"Then what? They're both single, both working for the county, new to town. Makes sense they'd hook up."

"But they couldn't stand each other. They acted like mortal enemies when they first met."

Breeon laughed. "Then it was bound to happen. Tale as old as time. I'll see you tomorrow, sis."

After Breeon left, the office felt empty as a tomb. The only sound was the white noise of the air-conditioning unit under Elsie's window, masking the traffic on the square.

She checked her next witness: Jewel Winston, the cocktail waitress at the Jackpot Casino. With a wry smile, Elsie remembered her coup when she discovered the woman's story; but the smile faded. "Fucking Ashlock," she whispered.

The witness's phone picked up on the first ring. "Who's this?" a voice demanded.

Elsie grabbed a pen. "Ms. Winston?"

"Who wants to know? What area code is this? Where's 417? I don't know a soul with a 417 number."

"This is Elsie—"

"If you're selling something, you can forget it."

"No no no—not selling a thing, honest. Ms. Winston, this is Elsie Arnold; we met at the Jackpot. I'm the prosecutor from Missouri who took your statement, remember? About Tanner Monroe, the young man in the bloody bus."

There was silence on the other end. Elsie said, "Ms. Winston? You remember?"

At length, the woman responded. In a reluctant voice, she said, "Yeah. Back in June, I think."

Smiling into the phone, Elsie said, "That's right. You gave me excellent information; and you identified the photo of Tanner Monroe. He's been charged with the murder of the bus driver."

"But he's a kid, isn't he? Is this a juvenile thing?"

"No, it's a criminal case in Circuit Court. Because of the serious nature of the crime, Mr. Monroe has been certified to stand trial as an adult." She started speaking in a rush, afraid she might be interrupted. "And the case is being set for trial—soon. So I'm touching base to let you know you'll be called to testify."

Silence again. While Elsie waited, she tapped her pen in a nervous rhythm.

"I don't know."

Elsie closed her eyes. Dragging reluctant witnesses to the stand was a common prosecutorial chore, but it never grew easier. "Ms. Winston, you'll be under subpoena. It's an important responsibility, a civic duty. This is a murder case. You know, the victim was a woman about your age." She paused for a moment, to let the last statement sink in. "It's crucial that the jury hear what you know."

"I don't think I can get off work."

Elsie's voice was brisk, her tone positive. "Not a problem. Your employer has to let you off; they don't have any choice. A subpoena is an order of the court."

Ms. Winston dropped her voice; Elsie had to strain to hear. "Okay, here's the thing. I don't trust that kid. You say he's a murderer. What if he gets out? He'll come after me, cut my throat next. I'm just not going to take that risk."

"He'll be in prison, Ms. Winston." *I hope*, she added to herself.

"He could escape."

"Well, that's unlikely." With her pen, Elsie made rapid notes by Jewel Winston's name: *RELUCTANT WITNESS—get her back in the fold.*

"Plus I can't afford it. The gas will break me. And I don't have anyplace to stay."

"Don't you worry about that. The county will pay for

your transportation"—and she added another note: *Get deputy to drag her ass down here*—"and we'll provide hotel accommodations. We have a real nice place on the highway: the Motel Rancho. It's like a Hampton Inn." *Liar*, her conscience whispered. The Rancho was an old mom-and-pop strip motel, a survivor of the Route 66 era. "It has a pool," she added cheerfully.

"If I want to swim, I can do it at my apartment. Right here in Oklahoma."

Elsie changed tactics. "Ms. Winston, I don't want to fuss with you. You'll be such a fantastic witness—the jury will love you. Because you're glamorous, and you communicate so well."

Flattery worked sometimes when reassurance failed.

Ms. Winston warmed up a shade. "I'd like to help out. Really. I'm just thinking it's not in my best interest."

"Ms. Winston, we're going to take good care of you. Are you still working at the Jackpot?"

"Yeah."

"And your contact info: I know I have the right phone number; how about your address? Still on Will Rogers Drive?"

Elsie heard the sigh: resignation. Acceptance. "Yeah. Still there."

"Excellent. I'll be back in touch when I have the firm date, so you can put it on your calendar."

Grudgingly, Jewel Winston said, "Okay, I guess."

As they rang off, Elsie made stars by Jewel Winston's name in purple ink, reflecting that she'd need to get the woman into the courtroom even if she had to hogtie her.

Because Jewel had a role even more important than establishing the juvenile's solo presence at the casino.

Jewel Winston would have to rehabilitate the victim.

Elsie knew Billy Yocum would zero in on the DNA evidence and use it against them. He would bludgeon the victim with the evidence, use it to portray her as a pedophile, a woman who preyed on boys.

She had to get Jewel up on the witness stand, because Jewel could help to minimize the fallout. "Jewel," Elsie said to the phone, "you'll need to paint a picture for the jury. That Tanner Monroe would fuck any old gal in granny panties."

She just hoped that the jury would buy it.

Chapter 34

A HORSEFLY INVADED Judge Callaway's courtroom through one of the screened windows. Elsie heard the buzz before she saw it; twisting around in her chair, she looked up and watched it zigzag around the room.

Judge Callaway was seated at the bench, flipping through the pages of Billy Yocum's motion. "Billy," he said, "what are you thinking about this?"

"Your honor," Billy said, rising to his feet, "my client is only fifteen years old. The county jail is a perilous environment for him. He is in danger of attack from all sides. I could elaborate, but"—with a courtly nod at the court reporter—"there is a lady present."

At the prosecution table, Chuck leaned close to Elsie and whispered, "He doesn't mean you."

"Shut up," she said.

The judge said, "Billy, this is a change of tune. The defense generally pleads for more time."

Billy nodded. "Your honor, that's true. But we have an uncommon case here. My first concern has to be the safety of this child." He pointed at Tanner Monroe, who sat cuffed at the counsel table.

Elsie glanced over at Monroe and heard him mutter: "I'm not a child. Jesus fucking Christ."

Billy put a hand on the young man's shoulder and gave it a squeeze; the gesture looked supportive, but Elsie guessed that Yocum's fingers were digging in hard enough to deliver a message. Yocum then walked around the table and blocked Monroe from the judge's view. Elsie smiled, in spite of herself; Yocum was a smart old dude.

"So we entreat the court, with all due respect, to try the case without delay. In the interest of my client's safety. And the interest of justice. And you know, Judge Callaway"—Billy grinned, baring his piano-key teeth— "I'm not getting any younger."

The horsefly had targeted Elsie. It buzzed in angry circles around her head. She ducked, an involuntary response, but it dive-bombed her. She waved a frantic arm to shoo it away.

"Ms. Arnold?" Judge Callaway said, as Chuck hissed, "What are you doing?"

She dropped her hand to the table. "There's a fly in here," she said.

The judge tuned back to Yocum. "So Billy, what are you asking for, time-wise?"

"Your honor, the court knows I'll be unavailable in the fall, due to Peggy and my anniversary celebration. But I think I can see my way to freeing up some time before then. In the summer, Peggy and I generally spend time at our place on Table Rock Lake. But she and I had a talk, and she is willing to make a sacrifice on behalf of my client. Peggy can't sleep at night for worrying about that boy."

The horsefly moved to the defense table. It circled before it landed on the file in front of Yocum's empty chair. Elsie watched in fascination as it walked along the varnished surface of the tabletop.

The juvenile's hand moved so swiftly that it made her blink. He caught the fly in his hand and looked over at Elsie. Cocking his brow, he lifted his fist in triumph.

Elsie watched his hand, curious to see what he would do next. Monroe squeezed his fist; she could see his fingers clench. Then he opened his hand and let the fly drop onto the tabletop.

It wasn't quite dead. It flopped around, its buzz muted to a death rattle. Monroe toyed with it, pushing it with his index finger.

He had new letters tattooed on his fingers, and she could almost make them out. She leaned toward the defense table, scooting her chair in his direction.

"Ms. Arnold?"

She jerked back, sitting up straight. Judge Callaway was looking at her with a disgruntled expression. "Ms. Arnold, could we have your attention? You're representing the state of Missouri here today, aren't you?"

"Yes, your honor." She offered the judge an apologetic smile, resisting the urge to glance back at Monroe's hand. At her side, Chuck looked at her with disbelief.

"Are you high? Pull your head out of your ass," he hissed.

"Okay," she whispered.

"Get your shit together."

"I'm fine. Hush."

Judge Callaway was leafing through his black leather-bound calendar. "Billy, if I move some things around, I can give you four days in August."

"I'll take it."

Chuck jumped up. "Judge, that's awful soon. We'll have to check and see whether the state's witnesses can be available on such short notice."

"Get them here. You're set for trial."

Chuck walked up to the bench, holding papers from the file. "Judge, the defense just sent me a mental evaluation of the defendant, claiming he has a personality disorder. We'll need to have a doctor examine him on behalf of the state."

"Then do it. I expect Mr. Monroe has plenty of free time for the appointment."

"Judge, it will take some time to arrange it."

"Mr. Harris, we have a fifteen-year-old in lockup at the McCown County jail, and the defense is ready to proceed. Get your case in order."

"Judge Callaway," Chuck said, his voice bordering on a whine, "We need to know whether the defendant is changing his plea from 'Not Guilty' to 'Not Guilty by Reason of Mental Disease or Defect.'"

Yocum ambled up to the bench, chuckling. "Thinking about it," he said.

Elsie glanced back at the defense table, anxious to see Monroe's reaction to the insanity discussion. He was holding the fly by a broken wing. When he saw her looking, he said, "I'm not crazy."

But she didn't respond. Because over Monroe's head, she saw a woman's face pressed against the glass panel of the courtroom door. Elsie recognized the hat with the crushed orange flowers: it was Cleo, the fortune-teller. She was staring at Elsie.

"Shit," Elsie whispered. Before she could look away, Cleo pointed a finger at her.

Chapter 35

When Judge Callaway left the bench, Elsie didn't hesitate. Without waiting for Chuck, she bolted for the door, nearly colliding with Emil as the bailiff fumbled with the keys to truss Monroe.

"Whoa," Emil cried, but Elsie didn't pause. She shot through the courtroom and ran to the Prosecutor's Office.

At the reception counter, she found Stacie, toying with a lip-gloss wand. Without looking Elsie's way, Stacie said, "I can't do anything for you. I'm going to lunch."

"Stacie. I cannot let that woman have an appointment. Did she come in here? To see me?"

"I'm not making appointments for anybody. I'm out of here. Madeleine said I could lock up the front office till one o'clock today."

Elsie glanced over at the door. Stacie had taped a CLOSED sign with bold numbers: 12:00–1:00.

Elsie let out a grateful sigh. "Okay, then. That's good. But did that woman with the crazy hat come by? The homeless woman? She's stalking me. Seriously."

"I don't know."

"What do you mean, you don't know? You're the receptionist."

"Hey. It's a public office. All kinds of nut jobs come in."

"But did the hat lady come in? Today?"

"I don't think so. Unless I was in the bathroom. I do have the right to go to the bathroom, don't I?"

Elsie searched the counter, lifting Neighborhood Watch Committee pamphlets and citizen complaint forms. No tarot cards had been hidden, nothing to jump out at her.

"Stop messing that stuff up," Stacie said. "I have to get over to the Wagon Wheel for the reunion planning committee. It's our five-year."

"Great." Since Elsie turned thirty, she tossed the annual Barton High School reunion notices. She was tired of looking at baby pictures and warding off old lady jokes. "See you at one."

She headed to the inside hallway with her keys in hand. A note was taped to her door, a piece of paper that looked like it had been pulled from a waste can. She ripped it down and carried it to her desk.

She stared at the wrinkled paper with trepidation. *Maybe it's from Bree*, she tried to convince herself; *maybe she was in a hurry and grabbed a piece of waste paper to write on.* But it wasn't likely. Elsie delayed confronting the note for another minute. Turning away from it, she stepped over to her miniature refrigerator. Once she had a Diet Coke in hand, she settled in her chair, picked up the note, and opened it.

I WARNED YOU,

QUEEN OF SWORDS

"Ohhh," she breathed out in a moan. The capital letters were written in a spidery hand, so faint that it looked like the pen had run out of ink. With a reflexive gesture, she dropped the paper, as if it had burned her fingers.

Her stomach twisted as she examined it, thinking it was a cowardly, chickenshit gesture to send anonymous messages. "Show your face, motherfucker." Then she paused, rethinking the challenge; Elsie didn't really want to see the person who left the note. She had just tried to dodge the obvious author, Cleo.

And why had Cleo promoted Elsie to queen? She was not a bit happy with the title of Queen of Swords. She had been more comfortable with the Fool. The mention of swords made her nervous.

It was necessary to notify someone higher up, she decided. This game should not escalate; she knew the danger from past experience. The Taney incest case, one of her toughest yet, had involved nasty backlash from a local religious group that took a violent turn.

She opened a desk drawer for a plastic bag, but the box was empty. She had forgotten to pick more up at the grocery store. She lifted the note by the corner, wishing she didn't have to touch it. It made her uneasy, sending a shiver down her back, like someone was walking on her grave.

Chuck was typing at his keyboard and didn't look up when she walked into his office. "What?" he said.

"Chuck, look at this."

"I'm trying to update Madeleine. Come back later."

A flash of irritation sent a buzz through her. "I'm serious. You have to help me." She dropped the note on his keyboard.

He recoiled. "Don't put trash on my keyboard. What's on this, mustard? Jesus."

"Read it, Chuck."

He glanced at the note, picked it up with two fingers, and dropped it in his waste basket. "It's a crank."

"It's a threat."

With an exasperated groan, he wheeled his chair to face her. "Don't make me babysit you. This kind of shit happens in an office like ours."

"Yeah, but it always seems to happen to me."

"Oh, come on. In Kansas City, people got this kind of thing all the time. You're not so special. Man up, Elsie."

Her face started to flush. That particular expression always incited her ire. "That's easy for you to say, since it wasn't taped to your door. What if you were the Queen of Swords?"

Chuck turned back to the keyboard and focused on the computer screen. "Well, I'm not. Because I'm not a queen."

"Ha. Funny." Elsie stepped behind his desk and dug the note out of the trash. She could run it by someone else. Ashlock, maybe.

"Nope," she said aloud. She walked back to the nearest chair and sat down. Elsie watched in silence as Chuck finished his e-mail and hit Send.

Turning to her, he said, "Are you going to stay here all day? Don't you have work to do?"

She gave him a look. "I always have work to do. It never ends."

Ignoring her response, he continued, "Because we're set for trial August 10. That gives us basically zero time to prepare. Quit fucking around."

The mention of the approaching trial date sent a wave of panic through her. Even after four years in the office, she always fought anxiety before a jury trial. Once it began, adrenaline kicked in and took over, making the job easier. But knowing that she would have her game face when the time came never helped to prevent the initial sensation of drowning.

I'm second chair, she told herself. *It's not all on me. I'm the assistant.*

Chuck broke into her reverie. "Here's the first thing I need you to do. Get the ball rolling on the state's mental exam of Monroe."

"You want me to do the paperwork?"

"What did I just say? You claim to be the insanity defense expert. Get moving on it." He opened his desk and pulled out a Clif Bar. As he unwrapped it, he said, "Get us a doctor who will say he's okay. Fit for trial and sound as a dollar."

Elsie's brow wrinkled. "Chuck, I can't control the evaluation. The doctor will reach his own conclusion." Sitting, she waited for him to agree.

He pulled an impatient face. "Why are you still here?"

She made for the door, thinking that he acted more like Madeleine every day.

"Hey, Elsie," Chuck said.

She paused in the doorway. "What?"

He was toying with a pink notepaper; a phone memo, she thought. "I've been meaning to tell you. You were right."

"What?" she said again, taken aback.

"About the interrogation. As I recall, seems like you wanted to bug out, leave the room. I guess that would've been a good idea. Looking back, in hindsight."

"Yeah. A real good idea," Elsie agreed, but she felt a glow of appreciation at his admission, and her opinion of Chuck rose several notches. "Thanks for saying so." *Took you long enough*, she added to herself.

He tossed the pink phone memo across his desk. "Return that call for me, okay? I need to get that woman off my back."

She picked it up and read the name. "Who's Phyllis Garrison?"

"Some friend of the murder victim. She keeps calling; like I've got all day to talk to the dead woman's friends." He snorted and turned back to his computer.

So I guess I'm the one who has all day to do your grunt work, Elsie thought. "Shit runs downhill," she said aloud, but Chuck didn't respond.

Back in her office, she first made a note to contact Dr. Salinas, to see if he was available. Salinas had an established psychiatric practice in Joplin, Missouri; he made a strong witness for the prosecution. If the juvenile was a faker, Salinas would pick up on it. He could bring the insanity defense down.

Elsie picked up the receiver of her office phone and dialed Phyllis Garrison's number, giving the line five rings before she hung up. She had no sooner set the receiver in the cradle before it rang with a vengeance.

She picked up. "This is Elsie Arnold."

"I want to talk to Chuck Harris," a female voice said. "This is the Prosecutor's Office in Missouri, isn't it?"

"It is, the McCown County Prosecutor's Office. But you dialed my line; this is Elsie Arnold. I think Chuck's tied up," she said, checking the caller ID; it was the number she had just dialed a moment before. "Can I help you?"

"I want information on the Glenda Fielder case."

"Right; that's *State v. Tanner Monroe*." She checked the pink message again. "Is this Phyllis Garrison?"

"Yeah. And who did you say you are?"

"Elsie Arnold; I'm cocounsel on the Monroe case."

She could hear the woman huff into the phone. "Finally. I've been chasing that Harris guy's tail for weeks. He won't talk to me."

"How can we help you?"

"I'll tell you what you can do to help me. You make sure the guy who killed Glenda gets the death penalty."

Elsie rubbed her forehead as she spoke into the receiver. "Well, there's a legal issue. You see—"

The woman cut her off. "I want you to promise me that."

Elsie raised her voice slightly and said, "The defendant—Mr. Monroe—is fifteen. There's no death penalty in Missouri for persons under the age of sixteen. It's the law. But we will do our best to see that justice is done. So, how do you know the deceased, Ms. Fielder?"

"She was my wife."

Elsie sat in silence for a moment, digesting the statement. "You and Glenda Fielder were married?" Elsie had no idea whether gay marriage was legal in Michigan; she knew that the state constitution of Missouri refused to permit or recognize same-sex unions.

Elsie heard a catch in Phyllis Garrison's voice as she said, "Not legally. We were partners, for over eleven years. Married in every way but the law. You know?"

"Yes. I understand."

"I wanted to do it; begged Glenda to go with me to Massachusetts and get married there, back when it was the only place that we could go. But she didn't want to fight the battle with her family."

Gently, Elsie said, "We've been in touch with Glenda's niece, and she never mentioned the relationship."

"Yeah, well. They never accepted it. Shit, there we were—in our forties, living together for over ten years, but had to play some lie for her family, like we were just friends. Roommates. Really good friends." She laughed into the phone with a hollow sound.

Elsie asked, "Did you own property together?"

"We didn't own much. I'm on the car title. And we both signed the apartment lease."

"Good. That's good." Elsie's heart rate increased as

the significance of Phyllis Garrison's revelation hit home. Glenda Fielder was looking better by the minute. Even Billy Yocum would have a hard time convincing a jury that a forty-year-old lesbian in a committed relationship was the seductress of a teenage boy.

"Phyllis, the case has been set for trial, and I'd really like for you to be here. Can you come to Missouri?"

"You're goddamned right I'll be there," Phyllis said.

Elsie secured the dates with her new witness and hung up the phone with a smile on her face.

Feeling thoroughly self-satisfied, Elsie tilted back in her chair and propped her feet on her desk; but her jubilant mood dissolved when she saw the soiled and wrinkled anonymous message under the heel of her left shoe. In the quiet of her office, she heard a voice whisper in her head: *Queen of Swords.*

Chapter 36

VERNON WANTUCK UNLOCKED the door to the interview room at the McCown County jail. His beefy hand gripped Tanner Monroe's shoulder. But as the jailer prepared to push the boy inside with a hard shove, he paused. The room was already occupied by a tall man with wire-rimmed spectacles. Wantuck dropped his hand from the boy's shoulder.

"Doctor," Vernon Wantuck said, in a hearty voice.

The man rose, setting a typewritten report aside. "Mr. Wantuck."

"Doc Salinas, I've got a live one for you. This is him, Tanner Monroe." To Monroe, Wantuck said, "Sit down."

Tanner shuffled in his cuffs and sat in a folding chair, facing the doctor across a metal table. "Do I get to lose the cuffs?" Monroe asked.

Wantuck laughed. "I think me and Doc Salinas would just as soon keep them cuffs on you, boy." He walked back through the door. "I'll post a jailer outside, Doc. Just knock when you're ready."

The doctor inclined his head in response. He didn't speak until Wantuck left the room and shut the door behind him.

"Tanner Monroe, I'm Dr. Salinas."

The juvenile pushed his chair back, making the metal legs screech against the concrete floor. "Okay."

"The state has asked me to conduct a mental evaluation of you. To determine whether you are fit to stand trial, whether you understand the nature of the charges against you and can assist in your defense."

"I know all that. I've been through this before."

The doctor raised a hand, a signal that he wanted to continue. "And to determine whether you have a mental disease or defect that prevents you from understanding the nature of your actions, or confining them to the requirements of law." The doctor paused. "I know that sounds technical, especially to someone so young. I can break it down for you, explain it in a different way."

"I'm not stupid."

The doctor reached for a pad of paper. "Did you think that I implied that? When I offered to explain?"

"I'm just saying let's cut through the bullshit. I know what the evaluation is all about. I did it before. With that other doctor, the one my old dickwad lawyer hired."

"Who is your lawyer?"

"Yocum."

"What's his first name?"

"Shit, man, I dunno. Old man Yocum. He's like a hundred years old."

"Do you understand that he has been appointed to represent you on a murder charge?"

"Yeah. I get that."

"Do you understand that the state is prosecuting you for the murder of a woman who was driving a bus, who picked you up and gave you a ride?"

The boy rolled his head back on his neck and gave a weary sigh. "How many times do I have to say it? I didn't kill her. I. Did. Not. Do. It."

The doctor studied Tanner, not evidencing any judgment in his expression. He bent his head and scrawled a note on his pad. Under his breath, Tanner whispered, "Stupid bitch."

Dr. Salinas looked up. "What's that?"

"Nothing."

"Did you just say 'stupid bitch'?"

Tanner shifted in his seat, slumping against the metal chair back. "Yeah. Forget it."

"Who were you referring to? The bus driver—the woman who gave you a ride?"

"Okay. Yeah."

"You just told me you didn't kill her. So, what are your feelings about her?"

"Feelings? I didn't even know her."

"But her untimely death. How do you feel about that?"

"She's not anybody to me. Just a bitch driving a bus."

Suddenly, Monroe laughed, his face transformed by mirth. When Dr. Salinas stared at him, Monroe covered his mouth.

"Can you tell me what struck you as funny?" When

Monroe shook his head, the doctor said, "Please. I'd like to hear it."

"I was just remembering something. From way back."

"Tell me."

Tanner sighed, a long-suffering sound. "Okay. I was a kid in foster care—for a pretty long stretch, that time. I had to take the school bus to school—big yellow one, just like the one I ended up in. But it was St. Louis."

"And?"

"And the bus driver was a stone bitch. Goddamn, I can still see her face."

"What was so bad about her? What did she do?"

"She hated me. I got no fucking idea why, she just did. She rode me every day, chewed me out for nothing."

The doctor nodded, and Tanner continued the story, anger kindling in his face. "She started skipping my bus stop on the way home, just to jack me around. Made me ride around an extra thirty minutes on that bus, just to fuck with me."

The doctor tapped his pad with his pen. "If the driver didn't like you, why would she want to extend your time on the bus?"

"Shit, man, don't ask me to explain it. I can't get inside that cunt's head. So one day, after school, I was kind of needing to piss the minute I got on the bus. I was just a kid, man—maybe third grade. Could've been second. And she drove and drove. I came up and asked her to let me off, take me to my street. She passed right by it. Told me to sit my butt down.

"I held it as long as I could, then finally let go. I

couldn't help it; I pissed my pants, right there in the seat."

"That must have been very embarrassing."

Monroe's chin jerked up. "She bitched me out—can you believe that? Made me the fool right there, in front of everybody."

Monroe fell silent, lost in reflection. Then his face lit up. "So I got home, and my foster mother wanted to know, what the fuck? So I told her. Damn, she went off."

"She was angry with you?"

"With me? Hell, no; she was pissed at the bus driver. So she got me and her out that night, and we walked the streets of our hood, and picked up every piece of dog shit in a six-block square. Put it in a plastic bucket."

With more animation in his face, he continued. "And she was standing there by me the next morning, when the bus pulled up, and the door opened, my foster mother swung that bucket, and dog shit went flying. Right inside the bus, all over that driver. In her face and on her hair and everything. You should've seen her face." Monroe laughed out loud.

With a shrug, he added, "They didn't let me ride the bus after that. But it was worth it, man."

"How did you feel about the woman? Your foster mother?"

"Her? Oh shit, man, she was kind of nuts. But she had my back. She was better than the ones who came later." Lost in the memory, he snorted.

The doctor leaned toward Tanner, resting his forearms

on the desk. "So what connection does that memory have with the deceased in this case? Glenda Fielder?"

"Huh? Nothing, I guess. No connection." When the doctor made a note on the pad, Tanner's voice took on a defensive note. "It's just a story, man. You asked me."

Dr. Salinas nodded and said, "Tell me about your family relationships."

Monroe snorted. "That won't take very long."

"I'd like to hear about your parents. Tell me how you get along with them."

"You tell me something first. We can trade some information, okay, man?" Tanner returned the legs of the chair to the floor. Leaning forward, he rested his hands on the scuffed table. "What's it like at the state hospital?"

In a quiet voice, the doctor persisted. "From the history provided to me, I see that you lived primarily with your mother in St. Louis, but you had moved out. Did something happen that made you decide to leave home? How would you describe your relationship with your mother?"

The boy rubbed the tattoos on his left hand before balling his fingers into a tight fist. "I want to hear what it's like. If a person ended up there, what kind of a vibe there is. You ever been there?"

Relenting, Dr. Salinas said, "I did an internship there. Years ago."

"What kind of hospital is it? Is it pretty nice, or is it a shithole?"

"It's a prison. Just like the Department of Corrections."

"Yeah, I get that. But is it easy time?"

"No, I wouldn't say so."

"Is it better to go there? Or to DOC? That's what I'm asking. I need a straight answer. Solid."

The doctor watched him in silence before answering. "If an individual suffers a mental disease or defect that made him commit a crime, the state hospital is the proper place for him. Is it easy to be locked up at the mental hospital? No. Not at all. Now tell me about your mother."

Monroe cocked his head and squinted, scrutinizing the doctor's face. "Are you from Mexico? You look Mexican."

The doctor offered a slight smile. "South side of Chicago."

"Salinas sounds like a Mexican name."

"It is." He picked a typed document off the table and placed it next to his notepad. "Have you been having any more intestinal issues?"

"Huh?"

"Stomach trouble, bathroom trouble. Spiderwebs. You reported that spiderwebs appeared when you went to the bathroom, when you had bowel movements."

"Where'd you get that? Have you got that other guy's report, the one Yocum set me up with?"

Dr. Salinas sat quietly, watching.

Monroe ducked his head, thinking, toying with the fabric of his county jail scrubs. At length, he looked up at Salinas. "Yeah, I probably need to clear that up. I was fucking with that guy." Tanner Monroe smiled broadly, exposing his protruding eyetooth. "Just messing with him."

"Why would you do that?"

"He was a dumbshit."

"He was hired to help you. Why would you want to mess with him?"

"For fun."

The doctor scratched on the notepad with his pen. Looking up, he said, "You had a roommate at Juvenile Hall." He checked his notes. "Barry Bacon."

"Oh man—not that douche bag."

"Why do you call him a douche bag?"

"Okay, he was a loser—do you like that better? I'm sick of people pinning that on me. Back at juvie, they all acted like it was my fault. That kid was depressed. Seriously mental. It's not my fault if he wanted to tie a sheet around his neck and jump."

"How did it make you feel? When he committed suicide in front of you?"

When Monroe didn't respond, the doctor went on. "Did you want to stop him? Looking back, do you regret that you didn't intervene?"

"I regretted it the minute he shit his pants. I was locked in there with that for hours, man. Disgusting."

Monroe leaned back again, tipping the chair and balancing it on two legs.

"Be careful. Don't tip over," warned the doctor.

"I'm good," the boy said. "I'm good. Ain't gonna fall."

Chapter 37

EARLY IN THE morning on August 10, Elsie stood in the bathroom of her apartment, studying her appearance in the mirror. Though she masked the dark smudges under her eyes with concealer, they still showed through. She pulled out the wand again, applying a thicker coat.

"Now I look like a raccoon," she said aloud. She rubbed the cosmetic cream smeared under her eyes with her fingertips, reflecting that the jury might be sympathetic toward a prosecutor who looked sleep deprived.

Because, in fact, she was. Though Elsie had fallen into her bed at three o'clock that morning, sleep eluded her, a typical pretrial occurrence. With her eyes trained on the ceiling, she ran through the testimony in her head, worried about the weak spots in the evidence, and fretted over the defendant's youth. When her alarm buzzed at six o'clock, she hadn't slept a wink.

Digging through her cosmetic bag in search of a lipstick that might counteract her pallor, she thought she heard her cell phone ring. Elsie paused, turning her head toward the living room of her apartment. Because the phone was at the bottom of her purse, the ring was muted, but it was calling her.

Groaning, she ran to grab the phone, unearthing it just as it fell silent. She checked the number of the caller: Chuck Harris. *What's gone wrong?* she wondered, a seed of worry germinating in her head. Then her landline started ringing. Snatching it up, she said, "Chuck?"

A bleak voice greeted her. "Elsie? That you?"

"Who else would it be?" she said. "What's up?"

"God, Elsie, I hate to do this to you, really. I'm not going to be able to make it today."

Her heart began to hammer in her chest. She pulled up a kitchen chair and dropped into it. "What do you mean, you can't make it? This is your case. We're picking the jury today."

His voice came through the receiver with a plaintive note. "God, I know. I can't believe it. But I'm sick. I didn't sleep all night."

Elsie's face hardened. No illness short of death could excuse a trial attorney from showing up for a jury trial. "What's the matter with you?" she demanded.

"You don't want me to go into it, I promise. It's diarrhea. The trots. And it's bad." When Elsie didn't respond, Chuck added, "I must've gotten a case of food poisoning."

You must've gotten a case of cold feet, Elsie thought. She sighed, and speaking in a calm, reasonable tone, said, "You've got to pull it together, Chuck. Run to CVS and get a bottle of Pepto-Bismol. That'll plug you up. You have to be in court today; you're doing voir dire and the Opening Statement. You've got direct examination for the first witness."

His voice growing stronger, Chuck snapped, "What is wrong with you? I can't go to trial with food poisoning. Do you want me to sit at the counsel table and shit my pants?"

The line fell silent. Elsie fumed on her end of the wire, cursing him in her head, with the full utilization of her extensive vocabulary. She tried to wait him out, but time was precious. Elsie spoke first, saying, "Please don't do this to me, Chuck."

"Elsie, you're just going to have to man up," he replied, and terminated the call without waiting for her response.

She sat frozen for a moment on the kitchen chair, absorbing the reality that she would have to go it alone. She felt light-headed; she put her head on her knees and tried to control her breathing and bring her heart rate under control.

She jerked up from her seat, eyes ablaze. "Man up? Man? Motherfucker. How dare you talk to me about manning up." The reaction got her back in fighting mode. She ran into the kitchen, grabbed a can of Diet Coke from the refrigerator and stuffed it into her overloaded bag, then headed for the door.

"Man it up your ass," she muttered as the door slammed shut.

ELSIE FORCED A smile as she walked through the door into Judge Callaway's chambers. Billy Yocum had already arrived, and reclined in one of the leather club chairs facing the judge's desk, his walnut brown wingtip oxford shoes stretched out before him. The shoes looked freshly spit-shined.

"You're running a little late this morning, Miss Elsie," Yocum drawled.

The judge checked the carriage clock on his desk. "Nope. She's right on time."

Affecting a breezy manner, Elsie dropped into the seat beside Yocum. "Wouldn't dare to be late. Don't want to give you a chance to woodshed the judge this morning, Billy," she said.

Billy's eyes flamed; he sat erect in his chair.

"Are you insinuating that the judge and I are colluding, engaging in unethical behavior?" he demanded, with his chin jutting out.

The judge sighed. "She's just joking around, Billy. Ms. Arnold didn't mean any such thing. Did you, Elsie?"

Elsie gave Yocum a cheeky wink. "Just teasing you, Billy."

The judge flipped his paper file open. "Ms. Arnold, where's Mr. Harris?"

"Judge, I can't understand these young lawyers; attorneys of my generation would never keep the judge waiting."

"He called me this morning," Elsie began, but Yocum interrupted, speaking over her.

"I have been late to court exactly one time in forty-two years, and it was because my car broke down between here and Mount Vernon, when I was headed over to court in Lawrence County. I hitched a ride from a farmer, and still made it to court before the docket call was over."

Ignoring him, Elsie said, "Chuck is sick."

The judge did a double-take, while Yocum barked a scornful laugh.

"Sick?" Yocum repeated. "Well, I'll be dog."

"Is he in the hospital?" the judge asked.

"No," Elsie said, her cheeks aflame. It was bad enough to be abandoned by Chuck; now she would have to defend his absence. "Sounds like maybe he's picked up a bug. Stomach stuff."

This time, the judge joined Yocum in his merriment. The men guffawed, exchanging a meaning look.

"Don't make them like they used to," Yocum opined.

"Billy, that's so," the judge agreed.

"How many lawyers have you ever had, Judge, who called in sick on the day of a jury trial?"

The judge thought for a moment. "Can't think of a one. There was the time Leon Farthing needed chemo. But he came to court in a wheelchair and asked for a continuance."

"How many prospective jurors do we hope to have today?" Elsie asked, hoping to move on. "I'm afraid we'll lose some on the age issue."

"We may. I told the clerk to round up one hundred and fifty, but we'll see who shows. Lots of folks on summer vacation."

The vision of vacations past loomed before Elsie. She thought longingly of lounging poolside with an icy drink, reading the supermarket tabloids. Pushing the vision forcibly from her head, she said, "What questions will the court ask before the prosecution begins with voir dire?"

The judge scratched notes on a piece of paper. "What do you say, Billy? I'll get their employment history. Do you want me to ask about family and marital status, kids?"

"Oh yes," Billy said.

"Ages of children?"

"Yes, sir."

Elsie nodded in agreement. Both sides needed to know which jurors had teenage children. A parent with a fifteen-year-old son would certainly be sympathetic to defendant, hesitant to convict a juvenile of murder.

"Anything else, before you two take over? Want me to talk about the mental disease or defect defense?"

Elsie looked at Yocum; the insanity issue was the defendant's problem. She believed that jurors were still suspicious of the insanity defense, so she planned to stay away from it. The fewer prejudices uncovered in jury selection, the better for the prosecution.

Billy made a face, wrinkling his nose as if he smelled something rotten. "Nothing jurors hate more than an insanity defense. They all think you're trying to get that Hinckley boy acquitted for shooting President Reagan. I haven't had an easy time with the insanity defense since 1981."

Elsie leaned on the arm of her chair. "Too bad you're hanging your hat on mental disease. You ought to get that boy on the stand. He could sway the jury with his natural charm."

For once, Yocum did not bristle. He locked eyes with Elsie, and gave her a conspiratorial nod. "Some kids don't appreciate good advice, you know that?"

"I'll bet your client falls in that category."

"But what am I to do? Miss Elsie, the prosecution's own expert, the good Dr. Salinas, determined that my client suffers from a mental disease. Both the doctors for the prosecution and defense agree that young Mr. Monroe is just not right."

"Antisocial personality disorder. That doesn't excuse him from criminal responsibility," Elsie insisted. She and Billy had gone around and around on this point since Dr. Salinas submitted his report.

"Well, I expect that will be for the jury to decide."

"It certainly will," said Elsie.

"Although it seems to me, Miss Arnold, that the responsible position for the prosecution to take would be to accept the insanity plea. Bearing in mind the tender age of the defendant."

"Billy, I can't. You know that."

Yocum sighed, and leaned over to pick his satchel. "Judge, do I need to file a motion in limine? May I remind the prosecutor that she is not to mention the suppressed statement of my client?"

The judge gave Elsie a warning look. "Ms. Arnold, don't say anything about the defendant's statement. I don't want any trouble on that score."

As Yocum stood, he added, "And I don't want to hear anything about the suicide of that unfortunate boy in Juvenile Hall."

Callaway nodded his assent. "That's right. Ms. Arnold, be sure you remain within the confines of admissible evidence. Don't stray into questionable areas."

Elsie pinched her lips together. *We'll just see about that*, she thought. *I'll be keeping my options open.*

Chapter 39

ELSIE PULLED OUT her standard jury selection presentation, writing madly in the margins as she added the particular questions Chuck had intended to ask the prospective jurors. She knew they had to cover the age question; it was crucial that they uncover and ferret out any jurors who would be reluctant to penalize the defendant on account of his youth. She needed to suck the poison on the DNA evidence as well; the jury shouldn't be surprised to learn that a forty-year-old woman had intercourse with the boy. Elsie needed to let them know that up front.

Pausing, she shook her head to clear it; what else had they decided to ask? Her pen was poised over the notes as the courtroom door opened and the jury panel filed in.

She heard a woman gasp as she entered, and saw her turn to the man behind her and ask, "Is the air-conditioning broken in here?" The man shook his head with an expression of disbelief. Elsie kept her face neutral. *If you think it's hot now, baby, just wait till the afternoon sun beats in*, she thought.

The men and women on the jury panel filed in behind Emil, filling all the seats in the jury box and the gallery. More jurors waited outside, because the room accommodated only sixty or so. Elsie scoured them with a keen eye; some jury panels were better for the prosecution than others. As a rule, she knew that her best jurors were blue-collar males, between thirty and sixty years old. In her experience, they were law and order types, not inclined to fall for defense attorney tricks and unlikely to vote based on sentiment. In her early trials, she had learned the hard way that she could not pack the jury with women and hope to win. Women jurors, as a rule, were more sympathetic to the defendant and more inclined to return a "Not Guilty" verdict.

The jurors were a mixed group, containing both elderly panelists and young people in their twenties, she noted with displeasure. She'd get rid of the young ones. They were always pro-defense, and with a defendant as young as Tanner Monroe, they would be much too likely to identify with his plight. And the old-timers could be problematic as well; they might tend to be too merciful in spirit, as they approached their own Judgment Day.

The judge entered. "All rise!" said the bailiff, and everyone stood. Settling into his seat, the judge greeted the jury with exaggerated cheer. Judge Callaway was up for reelection soon, and as the trial judges in McCown County, Missouri, were still picked by popular election, jury trials provided the candidate with excellent opportunities for face time with the public.

Elsie glanced over and surveyed Yocum and his client at the defense table. She had to hide a smirk; Tanner Monroe showed a marked change in his personal appearance. He had obtained a haircut at the county jail, but the look did not flatter him; Elsie suspected that the jailer who provided the trim had placed a mixing bowl on the boy's head. *Terrible*, she thought, *but that's Yocum's problem, not mine.*

But the look was so very dated and jarring, Elsie wondered whether it might lend an air of pathos to the defense, and touch the heart of someone on the jury. The boy was dressed in an old suit and tie, undoubtedly borrowed from Billy Yocum's closet, with pants and sleeves that were far too long. It added to the image of youth and immaturity.

Tanner pushed at his sleeves, revealing the jailhouse tattoos on his hand. Squinting at the marks, Elsie was determined to see whether the tattoos on his fingers spelled out a message or contained a code. She craned her neck for a closer look. She had suspected in the past that the tattoos on his hand had spelled "LP." If he was creating a grudge list, she needed to know. It could be a basis for a cross-examination question, if she played her cards right.

The juvenile turned his head toward her, and as if he could read her mind, he splayed both hands on the counsel table, so she could see them plainly at last.

Elsie stared at the fingers of his hands; each digit bore a letter. The left hand spelled out: "FREE" The right said: "METM."

What the hell, Elsie thought; is he advertising free

meth? She leaned in for a better look. The right hand was within her sight; his four fingers read: "METM."

Okay, Tanner, Elsie thought. *Got it.* A letter to the jury, signed by Tanner Monroe. "Free me, T. M."

She glanced sidelong at the boy, to gauge his mood. He was laughing at her. While she watched, he wiggled his middle finger on the table.

Right, she thought. *Well, fuck you, too.*

Judge Callaway commenced his general voir dire questions, and Elsie transferred her attention to the jury panel, jotting notes onto a chart she'd made on her legal pad. At length, the judge finished, and turned to Elsie.

"Ms. Arnold," Judge Callaway said with gravity, "you may proceed."

Elsie stood, her knees just a touch wobbly. "If it please the court."

The judge inclined his head and she walked to a wooden lectern, setting her jury selection file on it and sending a warm smile around the courtroom.

"Ladies and gentlemen, as Judge Callaway told you, I'm Elsie Arnold, assistant prosecutor of McCown County. The defendant in this case is Tanner Monroe, and he has been charged with the felony of murder in the first degree." She turned to the defense table and shot Monroe a long look. He met her eyes with an innocent expression, and lifted his shoulders in a shrug.

She returned her attention to the jury panel. "This part of the trial is called voir dire. The attorneys—-Mr. Yocum and I—will ask you questions. And I want you to know, it's not our intent to be nosy, or pry into your personal affairs. It's just that we have to conduct this kind of inquiry to obtain a fair and impartial jury, a jury that will be fair to both sides."

A man sitting in the back row of the jury box, sporting a striped tie, listened intently, nodding. Elsie made a mental note: she wanted the guy with the tie. He was tuned in, and taking the matter seriously.

"In our American system of justice, all defendants are innocent until proven guilty." Elsie wanted to cover the presumption of innocence so Billy Yocum couldn't pretend that he'd invented it. "It's the state's job—my job— to prove him guilty by calling witnesses and putting on evidence in this trial, which I will do. Does everyone understand that the fact that defendant has been charged with a crime is not evidence? Evidence will be provided by witnesses who sit on the stand and testify. Do you understand that all defendants are innocent until proven guilty? If not, please raise your hand."

Please don't please don't, Elsie begged silently. *Please don't raise your hand.*

Some of the jurors looked around, waiting to see how others would respond. She saw several men and women sit with their eyes downcast, and a few who looked bored or disgruntled. But not a single hand was raised.

She walked through standard questions on the burden of proof and the jury's obligation to follow the court's instructions of law. She covered the DNA bombshell, though when it didn't garner any major fireworks, she wondered whether she had soft-balled the issue. She was approaching the big question: the elephant in the living room. But she led up to it gradually.

"In this trial, it will be your job to find this defendant guilty or not guilty." She tried to convey sobriety and understanding in her voice. "There are some people who, because of personal sensitivity or religious or philosophical reasons, just aren't comfortable with the prospect of serving on a jury in a criminal case. Who just aren't certain they could find someone guilty of a crime even where the state proves its case beyond a reasonable doubt. Is there anyone in here who feels that way? That they just can't sit in judgment on their fellow man?"

She scanned the room expectantly, nodding, encouraging the faint of heart to speak up. Elsie had no use for anyone who would hesitate to convict because of feelings of personal delicacy. She needed to show them the door.

To her satisfaction, she inspired three women and one man to raise their hands. After consultation with the panelists at the bench, the judge excused them, over the loud objection of Billy Yocum.

Elsie grasped the sides of the wooden podium with both hands. In a clear voice, she said, "The defendant in this case is fifteen years old." The people in the room shifted: moving in their seats, shaking their heads, exchanging glances.

Elsie left the comfort of the lectern. "He is standing trial as an adult for the crime of murder in the first degree. Is there anyone on this panel—and I need you to give this question your most serious consideration—anyone who would hesitate finding him guilty because of his age?"

When there was no immediate reaction, she persisted. "Because he is so very young. Only fifteen."

A woman in her twenties was the first to break the ice. Elsie saw her glance around the room before raising her hand. Elsie took a step toward her. "Ma'am?" she said.

"Can I talk to the judge?" the woman asked. She was dressed in worn denim jeans and a T-shirt; working class, Elsie thought.

Elsie turned to Judge Callaway with an inquiring expression. He beckoned to the woman. "You may approach."

Elsie and Chuck joined her at the bench. In a low voice, the woman said, "I have a little brother; he doesn't live here anymore. But he got into trouble with the law, back in high school. Vandalism. Some shoplifting stuff."

You can't serve on this jury, Elsie thought. *You gotta go.*

But Yocum spoke up; with a coaxing tone, he said, "But it's your duty as a citizen to serve. You can put all that out of your mind, I'm sure, and base your decision on the evidence alone. Can't you? I'm sure you can. Clearly, you are an intelligent young woman."

The woman looked over her shoulder, focusing on Tanner, then shook her head. "He reminds me of Bobby. He kind of looks like him."

"But you can be fair," Yocum began, and Elsie interrupted. "Judge, she has made it clear—"

Judge Callaway cut them both off. "Ma'am, I appreciate your candor. Thanks for being so forthcoming with us. You're free to go."

She nodded; and with a last glance at Monroe, the woman headed for the door.

Nearly a dozen panelists followed, mostly mothers

of young sons. One man who smelled like stale booze pleaded to be excused because of sympathies stirred by the defendant's youth. Elsie suspected that he wanted to bail out of the courtroom so he could return to the party; it seemed Judge Callaway thought so, too, from the hairy eyeball he gave the man. But he excused him from the panel, punctuating his decision with a private look over his glasses to Yocum. Yocum smiled broadly in response.

Chapter 40

THE JURY WAS selected, at last. The afternoon sun shone through the windows with a vengeance as Judge Callaway instructed the jurors to raise their hands and administered the oath where they swore to do their jobs as jurors in the criminal case.

"Be seated," he said. He told the jurors they would hear preliminary instructions, and pulled out the page to read aloud.

An elderly woman raised her hand. Without calling on her, the judge asked, "Anyone need a restroom break before we begin?"

The woman broke into a grateful smile.

As the courtroom cleared out, Elsie relaxed a little. Pulling out her Opening Statement, scrawled in hasty moments before she left her apartment that morning, she gave it a quick run-through in her head. After a second quick review, she felt comfortable and was ready to go.

Elsie hated flying by the seat of her pants. She returned the handwritten pages to her folder and set it on the corner of the counsel table.

Stacie appeared at her shoulder. In a whisper, she said, "Chuck Harris called this morning and told me to pick these files up at his house. They are the direct exams for his witnesses."

Elsie nodded and flipped through them quickly.

In a harsh whisper, Elsie said, "What's going on? He had five witnesses to call; there are only four files here."

Stacie blew her breath out with a sympathetic face.

"Yeah, I know. He said he didn't get around to the last one, because he wasn't feeling good."

"Motherfucker," Elsie began, before she caught herself; the jurors were filing back in.

She composed herself and stood as the thirteen men and women filed by: a jury of twelve, plus an alternate, just in case. Elsie always rose for the jury; she did it to demonstrate respect, but also to put herself at eye level with them. Since no communication was permitted between the attorneys and the jurors, she needed to connect with them through eye contact. As they passed by, she tried to smile at each one in turn; most of them looked away. She wasn't worried. They weren't ready yet. By Closing Argument, she would be eye fucking half of the women and all of the men.

When the judge called her to present her Opening Statement, Elsie made a surreptitious swipe with a wad of Kleenex to collect the sweat beading on her face. Rising and pulling her shoulders back to appear confident, she approached the jury box. "Ladies and gentlemen of the jury," she began.

"Again: I'm Elsie Arnold, assistant McCown County prosecutor. And the defendant in this case . . ." And Elsie paused, to point an accusing finger at Tanner, as she would in any criminal case. She couldn't let the jury think that she was reluctant to point a finger of guilt at Monroe because he was so young. ". . . is Tanner Monroe, charged with murder in the first degree. This"—to vary the tone, she lowered her voice—"is what the evidence will show."

She ran through a summary of the witnesses and testimony they would provide, stressing the presence of Tanner Monroe's fingerprint on the murder weapon and the DNA match with the victim's vaginal swab. She knew juries liked scientific evidence, even expected it, due to their exposure to television. While *Perry Mason* had conditioned her parents' generation to expect an in-court confession in every trial, the *Law & Order* series taught modern jurors to anticipate sophisticated forensic evidence. Elsie was glad that, in this case, she could offer the hard evidence they wanted to see.

When it was Yocum's turn to proceed, he rose from his chair with an effort, sighing and shaking his head as he approached the jury box. He had no note cards in his hand, and bypassed the nearby lectern, choosing instead to lean on the wooden bar of the jury box with both hands.

"What a sorry state we have come to, ladies and gentlemen, a sorry state indeed—when the prosecuting attorney in McCown County wants to dispose of a murder case by pinning it on a mere boy. They want to blind themselves to the facts, and lock up an adolescent boy, still wet behind the ears."

Elsie jumped up. "Objection—your Honor, this isn't proper ground for Opening Statement; it sounds like Billy is giving his Closing Argument."

Yocum glared at her. "Miss Arnold, could you give me a chance to get started here, before you rudely interrupt with your objections?"

The judge nodded. "Let him have a chance to speak, Ms. Arnold."

Yocum continued, in an indignant tone: "Your Honor, I did not interrupt her once, not one single time when she was speaking to the jury. I have not completed my first blessed sentence, and she is already disrupting my address to these fine citizens. I ask that the prosecution be censured."

Oh Lord, so this is how it's going to go, Elsie thought, as she said, "Billy, I gave you no cause to object to my Opening Statement; I didn't say anything objectionable."

"She has interrupted me again, your honor," Yocum said in an aggrieved voice.

"Ms. Arnold, sit down. Mr. Yocum, continue."

Elsie sat, swallowing back a retort. *I hate them both*, she thought, smiling beatifically.

Yocum leaned in so close to the jurors that Elsie wondered whether they could smell his breath. He said, "Wait till you see the evidence, ladies and gentlemen. This crime was not perpetrated by a child. This is the act of a man, a grown man, a strong man who could overpower a woman and cut her throat."

Elsie had to hide her surprise. He was using the ODDI argument. What happened to the insanity defense?

As if Yocum could read her thoughts, he continued: "But this young man, this boy sitting in the courtroom today, could not be considered competent to commit any crime. Sad to say, ladies and gentlemen, a tragic thing, in fact—my client has a mental disease which prevents him from understanding the nature and quality of his actions or conforming them to law. The evidence will show that my client, this young boy, is, sadly, not sane."

"Bullshit," Tanner snapped.

A juror gasped. Elsie blinked, spinning to look at Monroe; then she swung her gaze back to the jury box, trying to assess the impact. A man on the back row—the juror in the striped tie— frowned, and let her catch his eye.

Yocum paused for only a beat; he continued with his opening, raising the volume of his voice. "He is not responsible, you see, because a person who has a mental disease or defect will not be held accountable for his crimes."

Elsie rose again, saying, "Judge, this is argument," but no one heard her, because Monroe stood at the same time.

Pointing at Yocum, Tanner Monroe called out, "You're fired, old man."

Yocum reeled away from the jury box, regarding the boy with a look of disbelief. "Sit down, Mr. Monroe," he barked.

Monroe snorted. "You sit down," he said. "I'm taking over, I'll do it myself. I told you, I don't want you to use that insanity shit; I ain't going to the nuthouse with the crazies. I'll do this myself, better than you." To the jury, he said, "I'm not fucking crazy, by the way. You can forget all about that."

The judge pounded his gavel.

Yocum stepped away from the jury box. "Judge, may we approach?"

"You may."

Elsie hustled up to meet Billy at the bench. Glancing at Tanner Monroe, she saw him step around the defense table, preparing to join the bench conference.

Judge Callaway pointed his gavel at the juvenile. "Stay right where you are, Mr. Monroe."

"I want to hear what's going on."

"Did you hear me? Sit down."

Tanner sat, dropping into his chair with a rebellious face. "I'm entitled. I should know waddup."

At the bench, the judge hissed at Yocum, "Billy, get your client under control."

Apparently the juvenile had sharp ears. "I'm not his client. He's fired. He won't listen to me, won't do what I tell him."

Billy bowed his head and gave it a shake. "Never dealt with a client quite like this one, not in my long career. We need to clear the courtroom, Judge, so we can do this out of the jury's hearing."

Emil Elmquist was rising from the bailiff's desk to stand by the defense table. Elsie saw him place a hand on the Taser he kept on his belt. *We're getting ready for a smackdown*, she thought.

The judge spoke again, this time in the barest whisper. "He's contaminating his own case. If you don't settle him down, Billy, I'll have to declare a mistrial."

"A person can represent himself in court if he wants," Monroe called from the defense table. The bailiff laid a hand on his shoulder, a silent warning.

Elsie whispered to Yocum, "Where did he pick up his legal acumen? Billy, have you been training him for an internship in your office?" Elsie knew the flippant comment was out of order, but she couldn't help herself. The fact that the trouble was in Yocum's lap, rather than her own, made her feel giddy.

"Don't treat this as a joke, young lady. You are out of line," Billy snapped. His face had turned purple. Elsie hoped he'd remembered his blood pressure meds that morning.

"I'm going to need to have a talk with him, I reckon," Judge Callaway said, clearly not relishing the prospect, "To disabuse him of the notion that he'll be representing himself pro se on a murder charge."

"It's been done," Elsie offered. "*State v. Zink*. We studied it in law school."

"You're not helping," Billy Yocum said.

"Zink fired the public defender at trial and represented himself. The jury found him guilty. He appealed on a Sixth Amendment 'right to counsel' argument. But the Missouri Supreme Court upheld his conviction," Elsie continued.

"Ms. Arnold, I am familiar with Missouri law, thank you," Judge Callaway said. "And you may recall that Zink was not fifteen years old."

A buzz from the courtroom increased in volume. The spectators and the jury were growing restless. Jurors were whispering among themselves, leaning forward in their seats to observe the activity. In the gallery, the spectators were conversing openly. A reporter from a Joplin TV station had her phone out and was texting madly. Elsie could imagine the message: "Get the camera crew over here."

A crack of the judge's gavel made her jump. "Ladies and gentlemen, we are in recess. Emil, escort the jury to the jury room." The judge pointed a finger at the television reporter in the front row of the gallery. "Ma'am, if I see that phone again, you'll be removed from court."

The reporter dropped it in her bag, with the guilty face of a kid busted for texting in class.

Emil strode to the jury box and shepherded the jurors through the courtroom. As they passed the defense table, the juvenile rose, holding out his hands so they could see his tattooed fingers.

"It wasn't my fault. I didn't do it, the other guy cut her throat. I just held her down."

The judge slammed the gavel, repeatedly beating it on the bench; but the boy raised his voice. It carried over the pounding of the gavel.

"I had to. He said he'd kill me if I didn't. He'd have done it, too, I'm not shitting you. The dude was a maniac."

The jurors stood in a single file line before the defense

table, gaping, some peering at Monroe's hands, others turning to the judge for direction. Judge Callaway rose, his robe billowing like a dark angel on a Judgment Day. "Emil!"

"He held her down," Elsie whispered. Her eyes sought out Billy's face; it registered frustration and anger, but not surprise. "Duress," she said.

Yocum shook his head, but with resignation rather than denial. Because Billy certainly knew, as Elsie did: a person who assisted in a crime because of the wrongful threat of another might use duress as a defense to some criminal charges. But not murder.

Duress was never a defense to murder.

Chapter 41

ELSIE GASPED AS realization hit home. "Oh my God." She turned to the judge. "It's a *Perry Mason* moment." The juvenile had just confessed in court. Never say never, she thought.

"Emil, keep the jury shut up in the jury room until I call you. And I want the courtroom cleared." The judge waved his arm like an orchestra conductor. "Wanda," he said to his clerk, who sat in a low chair on his right, "get those two deputies out in the hallway; they can escort the defendant back to jail. We are in recess. Billy, Ms. Arnold—I want to see you in chambers in ten minutes."

Seeking confirmation, Elsie tugged at Yocum's coat sleeve. "Billy, your client confessed. Duress isn't a defense."

Yocum turned on her with an inscrutable face. "Ms. Arnold, thank you for the insight. You may be surprised to hear this, but I've been up to snuff on the criminal law since before you were born."

He shuffled over and hefted his satchel, not glancing at his client, who was cursing the deputies who shackled him.

Elsie leaned against the bench, thinking. *That's why Yocum went with the insanity defense. He knew. Knew he couldn't put the kid on the stand and have him reveal his version of how the killing went down. Duress wouldn't work.*

Yocum was a smart old dog, she grudgingly admitted.

She grabbed her files and pushed through the door shortly after Tanner Monroe's departure. A throng awaited her.

The television reporter had succeeded in securing her camera crew. With the camera zooming into Elsie's face, she heard the woman ask, "Ms. Arnold, what will happen next?"

Elsie gave her head a weary shake. "Can't comment. Sorry."

There was a follow-up question, but Elsie didn't hear it; Stacie pulled her aside and whispered, "Madeleine's office, now."

Elsie suppressed an oath.

The state's witnesses who had been sitting on the benches outside the courtroom jumped up, surrounding her on all sides. Only Ashlock remained in his seat on the bench, but she sensed his presence, as if he emitted radar she couldn't avoid. Glancing in his direction, she could see, even with her view partially blocked by the bodies clustered around her, that he was wearing her favorite suit: a navy blue gabardine. She had unzipped those trousers on many occasions.

"Elsie." It was the crime lab expert, a man she had

worked with on a prior case. "What's going on in there? Is it a mistrial?"

"No mistrial. The rule is still in effect; you all need to be careful, don't discuss the case."

A stout woman in khaki pants shoved her way toward Elsie. "I just got here, just got in from Michigan. What the hell is going on?"

Phyllis Garrison, my ace in the hole, Elsie thought, as she extended a hand. "So nice to meet you, Ms. Garrison. I'm Elsie; we spoke over the phone." To the assembled group, Elsie said, "We've had some drama today, and the defense attorney and I will be meeting with Judge Callaway in a few minutes. Right now, nothing's changed. We'll cool our heels and be ready to go."

She smiled at the group. Seeing Jewel Winston at the fringes, Elsie offered a friendly nod. "Ms. Winston, I sure appreciate your attendance here today. I know it's inconvenient."

Jewel huffed a long-suffering breath. She wore a cocktail dress with sequins and gold beading at the neck. Elsie had instructed her to dress nicely, in clothing she would wear to church. Briefly, Elsie wondered how her guidance could have gone awry.

A young man stepped up. "I got to talk to you, ma'am."

Elsie longed to break away and lock herself in her office, but she stifled the urge. "Yes, sir. Have we talked on the phone?"

"Yeah. I'm Jeff Bartlesby; I work at the McDonald's in Vinita. I told you I seen that bus, and I did. In the parking lot. But there's something you got to know."

He was sweating, and his breath smelled like he had a bad case of nerves. The young man looked over Elsie's shoulder with a clear desire for privacy, but the crowded hallway couldn't provide it. Elsie peered around, to ensure they couldn't be overheard by other witnesses, or by the press.

"I seen the guy," he whispered. "The guy in court, who drove the bus. He waved a knife at me."

Now you tell me, asshole, Elsie thought, but she mustered a reassuring smile. "That's helpful, Jeff, really. Thanks for being so forthcoming."

"It's that, before, I didn't want to be involved. But I can't lie in the court. It would be a sin to swear on the Bible and lie."

No Bible swearing in court these days, Elsie thought, but felt no need to disabuse Mr. Bartlesby of the notion. "You're doing the right thing," she said, and stepped past him to confront the next person waiting on her: Cleo.

"Oh no," Elsie said, raising a hand to cut her off.

"Ms. Arnold," Cleo began, reaching out in supplication, but Elsie sidestepped her.

"No time, Cleo. Honestly. I don't have a second to spare."

Cleo's hand snaked out and she grabbed Elsie's arm. "Listen here," Cleo said.

Elsie stared down at the grimy hand grasping her forearm; she tried to shake it off, but Cleo held her in an iron grip.

"Ma'am," Elsie said in a firm voice, "you need to back off. Right now."

Cleo jerked Elsie close with a twist of the arm she held, squeezing so hard Elsie feared she'd cut off her circulation. "I warned you," Cleo whispered.

"What is wrong with you?"

"I warned you, clear as day, I told you he was the wrong one. The wrong one, the Knight, the wrong dude. Told you and told you."

In letter after letter, Elsie thought. Mystery solved. Anger coursed through her; the woman had caused Elsie a good deal of trouble and worry over the summer months.

"Don't be leaving me any more cryptic messages. You are no longer welcome in the Prosecutor's Office; you stay clear of me. I'm not interested in your psychic fortunes. And I'm not your 'Queen of Swords.'"

A momentary flash of confusion crossed the woman's face, followed by fury. "You're the Fool. Going after the Knight, when I warned you against it. I told you it wasn't him. And I should know. He's mine. He's my boy."

Elsie edged away, hoping the woman would release her. She's crazy, she thought, the real thing. The woman was delusional. Thinking she was Tanner Monroe's mother, when she wasn't, she couldn't be. Elsie had seen a photo of Tanner's mother, and it bore no resemblance to Cleo. "Okay, I'm the Fool. Or I can be both, if you want. The Fool and the Queen of Swords."

With surprising strength, Cleo pulled her back, so suddenly that Elsie stumbled. "Fool," the woman whispered, her face so close that Elsie could see the gaps made by her missing teeth. "I'm the Queen of Swords."

With her free hand, Cleo reached into her fabric hat band, under the crushed orange flowers, and pulled out a small metal object.

It was a double-edged razor blade.

Elsie tensed wildly but could not budge Cleo's viselike grip. In a move that seemed both slow and instantaneous, Cleo pinched the razor between her fingers and slashed at Elsie's throat. Elsie felt a sting; with a reflex gesture, as if in a dream, her hand reached for her neck. It was wet. When she took her hand away, it was red with blood.

A hubbub started around them, but the sound was dulled by roaring in her ears. As she sank to her knees, she saw Ashlock tearing down the hall toward them, but he seemed to be moving in slow motion, like a scene on a movie screen. Cleo loomed over Elsie, her arm raised, but Ashlock tackled her, knocking her back and pinning her to the floor.

Elsie saw the orange flowers as the hat fell from Cleo's head and rolled across the floor. Ashlock seized her wrist and the razor blade skittered away. Elsie's last thought, before she blacked out, was that they needed to find that blade. Bag it and tag it and preserve it as evidence.

Chapter 42

ELSIE LAY IN a narrow hospital bed, garbed in a backless cotton gown loosely tied at the back. Her throat was bandaged, with rings of gauze circling her neck.

She held her cell phone to her ear with her free hand; the other was still hooked to an IV.

Marge's voice was warm in Elsie's ear. "Honey, I've packed a bag, but I can't find any clean pj's in your apartment."

"There probably aren't any, Mom. I was buried before the trial, didn't ever get to the laundromat. Just throw in a T-shirt."

"Should I bring something of mine for you?"

Elsie cracked a smile. "That's nice, Mom, but I don't know—there's something a little weird about lounging around in one of your nylon nighties."

"I want you to be comfy. I'll run to the mall in Springfield."

"Mom, no! You don't need to do that. That's ridiculous."

"Lord, yes I do. You'll be receiving visitors, at the hospital and when we get you home. I'll be damned if I'll let my baby be seen in rags. I'll pick something up. Florals. Florals are nice for summer."

A vision of a pink flowered nightgown and robe set, suitable for menopause, appeared before Elsie; but she knew there was no stopping Marge. "That's sweet of you, Mom. Florals are nice." She couldn't stop from adding, "Not pink."

"It'll just take me a little while. Try to sleep. Do you think you can sleep?"

Elsie heard the note of worry in her mother's voice. She answered, "Sure thing. I'll sleep, Mom."

There was a pause; the silence lasted so long, Elsie wondered whether the call had been dropped. "Mom? You there?"

"I'm here." Marge's voice cracked as she said, "Baby, something I want to tell you—I should have said it earlier today. But I didn't. Because I don't want to make you think about this case anymore."

"Hard to avoid." Gingerly, Elsie touched the bandage swathing her neck. "What?"

"You were right. About that boy. I can't get over it—him holding that woman down while her throat was cut. And I let a difference of opinion come between us—between you and me. And I could have lost you--" Marge stopped, and Elsie could hear her make a shuddering breath into the phone.

"Mom, that's so funny," Elsie said softly. "Because you were right, your instincts were spot on. You never thought he held the knife."

In a firm voice, Marge said, "We mustn't fuss about your cases. Dad and I, we support you. We love you more than anything on earth."

It was the fifth time that day that Marge had expressed the same sentiment, but Elsie wasn't tired of hearing it. She swiped at her nose with the IV hand; the tape scratched her face. "I love you, Mom. You and Dad are the best. Don't know what I'd do without you."

Marge sniffled. "Well. I better get moving. I'll get your bag all set for you. Take a little nap, and I'll be back before you know it."

"Bye, Mom," Elsie said, setting the phone aside. With her other hand, she struggled to operate the remote control for the overhead television set, searching in vain for a local news channel. She doggedly punched the buttons, brows drawing together in growing frustration, until a knock sounded at the door.

"Come on in--I'm decent," she called, pushing the mute button.

When the door opened and she saw Ashlock standing in the doorway, holding a handful of pink lilies, Elsie tried to stifle the pleasure that welled up in her chest. She tossed the remote onto the bedside table, saying, "Lordlordlord. It's my damned hero."

Elsie shifted her legs in an effort to get off the bed, but Ashlock stepped quickly to her side to prevent it.

"You stay right there," he said. "You're the patient.

Have they got you all fixed up?" He quietly inspected her, looking at her bandaged neck with a sober face.

"Oh, I'm going to be all right. She slit a wide cut, but not deep; that was lucky, they said. I'm going to have a scar. My mom said she'd go stock up on scarves and turtle necks, but I said hell no. Battle scar. Mark of pride."

"That's the spirit." He smiled. "I brought some flowers for you." Looking around the room, he said, "I should've put them in a vase. Guess I wasn't thinking."

The stems were wrapped in a damp paper towel. She smiled; she knew Ashlock wasn't a hothouse bouquet kind of guy. "Did you get those from your yard?"

"My neighbor's yard, actually. I thought they smelled nice."

"They're naked ladies. My mom has them at her house, too; pretty, and such a sweet fragrance." A little too sweet, actually; a vase full of naked ladies could have her hospital room smelling like a French whorehouse. But she didn't really mind. "Hey, Ash, I've got to tell you," she said, her voice shaking a little, to her dismay, "you really did rescue me."

"Elsie, I don't want to hear it. It never should've happened. I was right there, in the damned hallway. If I hadn't had my head up my ass, you wouldn't be in the hospital right now." He eyed her bandaged neck again, and looked away.

"Oh, come on. I saw you. You came busting in there like," she gasped a little in agitation, searching for the right comparison. "Like Prince Valiant. Like fucking Prince Valiant in the funny papers."

Ashlock grimaced with mock dismay at the metaphor, and Elsie laughed, but tears jumped into her eyes.

Her voice dropped to a near whisper as she asked, "Has she been charged?"

Ashlock nodded. "First degree assault, but her background is a sight. In and out of mental facilities in the past five years; they'd boot her when the Medicaid money dried up. She should never have been in the foster parents program. Can't imagine that she passed muster. But maybe her mental history hadn't surfaced before she applied."

"Bree filled me in: Cleo was Monroe's foster mother. I guess that explains her obsession with the case."

"She had him in foster care when he was just a kid, for about six months, when his mother was in rehab. I guess she formed an attachment to him, back then." Ashlock paused, then said, "Madeleine told me she'll probably accept the NG—MD or D plea." He shook his head. "Crazy bitch."

"Which one do you mean? Madeleine or Cleo?"

He laughed, but it had a forced sound. Elsie picked at the bed sheet, trying keep her composure.

She said, "I heard the kid pled to manslaughter."

Ashlock looked up. "That's right. Madeleine and Billy knocked it out. You okay with that?"

"Well, it's not like anybody asked my opinion," she said, a shade miffed. But she relented. "It wasn't a bad resolution. The murder conviction was never a sure thing; the jury might have cut him loose. And if it went down like Monroe said, with the guy threatening him:

well, a jury would have been sympathetic to his situation, a young kid like that."

"I think you're right."

"I don't suppose the kid confessed to forcing intercourse on Glenda Fielder."

"Nope; just to manslaughter. Madeleine didn't press the sex issue. Seems like she just wanted to wrap it up."

"Are you opening up the case, to look for the other perpetrator? If Monroe's story is true, he's still out there."

"Already on it." Ashlock scrubbed at his face with his hand, a gesture she recalled; it meant he was wiped out. She took in his wrinkled suit coat and the shadows beneath his eyes.

"Ashlock? Have you been up all night?"

"Pretty much." He offered a rueful grin. "Probably look like hell."

"What are you up to?"

"Finding the other dude."

"How?"

"Well, I spent last night going up and down I-44. Hitting the gas stations, hunting video from June that showed the bus. In case we get a shot of another passenger."

"Oh, lord, Ash—that's like looking for a needle in a haystack."

"Not exactly. I know what I'm looking for. I got a hit on a print."

"How?"

"From the interior of the bus. When we ran the prints from the bus before, there wasn't a match in the system.

Something messed up; maybe we didn't run them all through, I don't know. But I did it again. Matches up with a guy in custody, picked up a couple weeks back, in Texas."

He paused and looked away, frowning. Elsie said, "And?"

He looked up. "And he's a big guy. Scar on his face. Tats on his hands. Priors."

"Then why are you looking blue about it? You may have found the other guy. The one who wielded the knife."

He expelled a sigh, and shook his head. "Because I should've uncovered it earlier. Seems like I was just seeing what I wanted to find. I'm feeling like a fool, I tell you."

"No more than anybody else on this damn case," Elsie said. "If it's any comfort to you. What was that old movie—'Ship of Fools'? Could've been sailing down Muddy Creek." She waited for him to comment; but he didn't respond.

After a moment's silence, she said, "I'm sure glad you've got a solid lead. It's creepy to think that the other dude could still be out there, on some road. A hitchhiker."

Ashlock glanced at the door; she interpreted it as a desire to make a quick getaway. The thought stung; tears pricked behind her eyelids, and she blinked.

"I don't want to wear you out," he began.

The tears rolled, and she turned her head away, mortified.

"Go ahead and go," she said, her voice breaking. "I know you're busy."

"Elsie," he said, his voice gentle. "That's not what I meant."

"Oh shit," she moaned, tears falling in tracks down her face. "You'll think I'm a nutcase, crying like a baby. Not even hurt that bad."

Ashlock reached for her hand, and held it in both of his for a quiet moment.

"Do you see any Kleenex?" she sniffled, looking around. He reached for the box and handed it to her. He watched while she self-consciously rubbed her nose with the tissue.

"Will your parents be taking you home later, Elsie? Because if they've gone on, I can stick around, go get you anything you need."

"Oh, yeah, they're taking me to their house, after I'm released. They're making me sleep in the old twin bed, under my Mary Kate and Ashley poster." She shuddered. "Scary."

"Huh," he said, clearly unacquainted with the Olsen twins. "Well, I guess you're all set, then." Before he turned to go, he said, "I came to ask you a favor. Not now, I mean; just whenever you're feeling better."

Curious, she swiped at her eyes and looked at him. "What?"

"I've got the kids for a couple more weeks. They've been at me to take them over to Silver Dollar City before they go back to their mom. I haven't done it yet; don't know why."

Because Caroline Applegate is a buzzkill, Elsie thought, but she held her tongue, waiting.

"I wondered, if you felt like you were up to it, if you'd come along. When I take them." He gazed at the bandages again. "I wouldn't want you to do anything to hurt yourself."

"No roller coasters," she said.

He said, "I'm not saying I expect you to go back to last June, to act like it never happened. Just wondered if you might join us." After a pause, he added, "No pressure."

She started to tip her head back to think about it, but the stitches gave a quick reprimand. She placed her hand at her neck, gingerly. "I sure do like a funnel cake," she said.

He smiled, like a light switch had been flipped on. "All right, then." Before he headed out, he said in a low voice, "Madeleine is out there. You've got a 'no visitors' status, so they didn't let her in. I slipped by on the pretext of police business. But she's hanging around. I'll let the desk know if you'd like to see her."

A flash of the old Elsie fired her expression. "Send her home. Please. I'd rather have a cob up my ass. Just like she does."

He winked. "Okay. I'll tell her to hit the road."

"You do that. A dose of Madeleine Thompson is the last thing I need right now."

Ashlock gave her a look. "Want me to pump some bullets in her?"

"Hell yeah," she declared. "'Code of the hills.'"

Acknowledgments

TAKING THIS NOVEL from the seed of an idea to publication has been a joy, and it's a pleasure to recognize some of the folks who assisted in the journey. I want to thank Trish Daly, the best editor in the whole damned world, for her vision as we crafted the story into its final form, and for liking Elsie's shortcomings as well as her strengths. My agent, Jill Marr of the Sandra Dijkstra Literary agency, is an angel with a halo; thanks go to her for taking on an Ozarks hillbilly. And I want to thank a trio of HarperCollins stars for their help: Andrea Hackett with publicity, Dana Trombley with marketing, and Eleanor Mikucki with copyediting.

Showers of thanks go to old friends and new who have supported the launch of Elsie and the Ozarks mystery series. At Missouri State University, special thanks go to Dr. Patti Salinas, Kim Callahan, President Clif Smart,

Dean Stephanie Bryant, Dr. Kent Ragan, and the wonderful students at Missouri State, especially my advisees in AKPsi (thank you Sarah D!).

My family has provided support in countless ways, from the legal expertise given by my brother John and sister Susie, to the editorial suggestions and encouragement from sisters Carol and Janice.

But above all, I must thank the three people who mean more to me than words can express: my beloved husband Randy, my precious Ben, my darling Martha. You are my rock and my salvation.

About the Author

_____

Nancy Allen practiced law for fifteen years, serving as Assistant Missouri Attorney General and as Assistant Prosecutor in her native Ozarks (the second woman in southwest Missouri to serve in that capacity). During her years in prosecution, she tried over thirty jury trials, including murder and sexual offenses, and is now a law professor at Missouri State University. *A Killing at the Creek* is her second novel.

@TheNancyAllen

www.nancyallenauthor.com

www.witnessimpulse.com

Discover great authors, exclusive offers, and more at hc.com.